THE
Evening News
COLLECTION

THE
Evening News
COLLECTION

With an Introduction by
Leslie Thomas

Conceived by Mark Williams

CHAPMANS
1991

Chapmans Publishers Ltd
141–143 Drury Lane
London WC2B 5TB

BRITISH LIBRARY CATALOGUING IN PUBLICATION DATA
The Evening News collection
I. Williams, Mark
823.0108 [FS]

ISBN 1-85592-003-4

First published by Chapmans 1991

Typeset by CentraCet, Cambridge
Printed and bound in Great Britain by
Cox & Wyman Ltd, Reading

The Evening News

Contrary to popular belief, the *Evening News* was not founded by Alfred Harmsworth (Viscount Northcliffe from 1906) but was an organ of the Conservative Party, into which the party had sunk £300,000 during the heyday of Liberalism in Britain.

By 1894 the *Evening News* was in severe financial straits. It appeared unlikely that the Conservatives would ever see a penny of their money back. There was severe competition, for, at that time, no less than six evening newspapers were published in the nation's capital.

There existed the *Star*; *Sun*; *Evening Standard*; *Evening News*; *Pall Mall Gazette* and *Westminster Gazette*. Each claimed to appeal to 'the upper classes' and all appeared with green- or rose-tinted newsprint. All embraced a literary style, to an extent at least. Only the *Star* featured horse-racing and made some appeal to those many Londoners who had learned to read and write at the new board schools.

The *Sun* had an assistant editor by the name of Kennedy Jones, who was by all accounts a brilliant journalist, and looking for a new job.

Jones had acquired, by a freakish wager, 12,000 seemingly useless shares in the *Evening News*. Jones, by way of this holding, obtained a fortnight's option to purchase the paper.

The option had almost expired when Jones thought of Alfred

Harmsworth, soon to found the *Daily Mail* (1896) and publisher of a number of weekly specialist periodicals aimed at various segments of society as exampled by the half-penny *Comic Cuts*, appealing to the nation's youth.

Through an intermediary, Jones made it known that Harmsworth could purchase the *Evening News*, lock, stock and barrel for £25,000, an amount calculated as being the annual profits of *Comic Cuts*.

Kennedy Jones explained to Harmsworth what he would do with the *Evening News* and Harmsworth closed the deal.

Under Kennedy Jones's inspired editorship, Harold Harmsworth's financial genius and Alfred Harmsworth's extraordinary popular copy foresight, the *Evening News* made a profit in its first year under the new regime, of £14,000 with an impressive circulation of 160,000.

From the first week, a fictional short story was frequently published. Weekly, three days each week and then daily, the short story proved to be a very popular item.

And a mix of known and unknown writers added to a growing cult of short story enthusiasts.

The *Evening News* flourished to the point of being the most popular of the capital's evening papers and at its zenith had a daily sale of over one million copies.

The *Evening News* short story always proved to be an item of demand with the paper's readers. Whenever, for reasons of production problems, the short story did not appear, indignant letters forced an early return.

The *Evening News* short story was traditionally a short, short. It averaged around 1500 words, and the editors looked for plots and variety, a selection where supply always exceeded available space by the hundreds each year.

Writers well known today cut their literary teeth in the *Evening News* short story pages. In their day H.E. Bates, Ray Bradbury, Leslie Thomas, Arthur C. Clarke, John Creasey, Monica Dickens, C.S. Forrester and many others have featured in the *Evening News*.

Many competitions were run over the near one hundred years of publication. In 1978 a first prize of £1000 was offered and brought manuscripts flooding in to the old Carmelite House offices. Postbags contained seven hundred, eight hundred and on one memorable day over one thousand stories in one post.

Judges for this competition included Leslie Thomas, Roald Dahl and Martyn Goff OBE, then Director of the National Book League. Ten of the finalists are spread over this anthology in various categories.

Edward Campbell was a much respected literary editor of the *Evening News* for more than a quarter of a century. It was somehow fitting that his retirement almost coincided with the 1980 closure of the *Evening News*. True, for a few short weeks in the middle eighties, as the London publishing war erupted with the ill-fated Maxwell publication of the *Daily News*, for a few weeks only the *Evening News* did appear on London streets again.

But to those of us who wrote for, subscribed to, and contributed occasionally to the paper, 1980 was the ending, leaving many happy and nostalgic memories.

Introduction

LESLIE THOMAS

The first short story I wrote for the *Evening News*, the first, in fact, I had ever had published anywhere, was based on a joke I overheard at a funeral. I was twenty-two and for several years I had been writing short stories and submitting them to magazines and newspapers, only to have them returned with such promptitude that I marvelled at the speed of the post.

Having heard the whispered joke I realized that all jokes are, in essence, short stories with the turn in the tail, and I set about fleshing it out, as they used to say, until it became 'A Good Boy, Griffith' and was accepted by the *Evening News*.

That was a happy day. (I was only disappointed that it appeared on a Saturday, when fewer people would read it and that it was, curiously, published in a single column.) But the fact that it was in the *Evening News* was all: I had become a new part of a long and great tradition.

This anthology provides an opportunity to return to those smoky days, London as it was: tramcars, real fogs, and street cries of *Star*, *News* and *Standard* – three evening newspapers for an outlay of three large, brown pennies, and the short story to read on the homeward train. Some of the stories are of later vintage, but the tradition was still strong until the *Evening News* finally died of modernization in 1980.

When I was in school just after the war I used to buy my *Evening*

News from a man with a huge bump on his forehead. The paper was thin, limited to four, occasionally six, broadsheet pages, for paper rationing was still stringent. But the bylines on its pages were magical names – E.M. Wellings on cricket, Jympson Harmen on films, Leslie Ayre writing about the radio programmes, Bill MacGowran's sports column, the marvellous J.A.J. and his 'Courts Day by Day' and, blessedly, the everyday short story.

My wildest ambition was that, one day, I would have my name in that newspaper. Some wild ambitions amazingly happen, and this one did.

It was through another famous *Evening News* series, 'The World's Strangest Stories', which was intended to run for a week, then a couple of weeks, then a month, and eventually went on for several years. It was a series about hauntings, earthquakes, revolutions, murders, legends and alleged miracles ('The Angels of Mons' etc). Anything difficult to believe; riveting reading for the Londoner on the train. Twenty guineas was the fee for those contributions (a short story was fifteen), and I wrote many of them. Then, with much trumpeting, it was announced that there was to be a competition for ten best stories of the year, first prize one thousand pounds. I did not come first, but I came fourth and won a hundred pounds and went to The Savoy to receive my cheque from the novelist H.E. Bates at a luncheon. It was the first time I had met a real novelist. Or been to The Savoy. As Reginald Willis, the florid and forthright editor of the *Evening News* shook my hand after the lunch, I whispered to him about a job and I got one.

The thrill of walking on my first morning into the old brick building of Carmelite House will never be repeated. I was a reporter on the biggest evening newspaper in the world, circulation more than a million. The dream had come true. What a place it was: corridors and twisting stairs, a swaying lift, little rooms with open coal fires and, as like as not, Bill MacGowran, with his north-country backside to the fire. It was smoky and littered; dusty papers and tea cups, *china* tea cups, piled together on heavy wooden desks. There were still gas mantles grinning on the walls. It seemed it had remained unchanged since Frank ('My Life and Loves') Harris had been editor in the nineteenth century. It was wonderful.

In the corridor one reporter was telling another that, after a night assignment which had necessitated a long period in a local public house, a man on a rival paper had thrown our chap's shoe from a tramcar and the following tramcar had cut it in half. I, who had avidly read Philip Gibbs's turn-of-the-century novel *The Street of Adventure* (still unrivalled as a Fleet Street Story) sighed happily.

I was given a place at the news desk. The news editor was called Sam Jackett, a tall, silvery man, a dandy dresser, who liked to say that if you walked any day along The Strand you would pass at least three unconvicted murderers. Murders were rarer but of better quality in those days, grisly and fascinating.

Sam Jackett soon gave me my first assignment. A bus had crashed into a small shop in Cannon Street, demolishing it. Demolished or not, the most sensible thing seemed to be to telephone the shop. I did. A man answered who confirmed the facts which he knew at first-hand since he was, at that moment, trapped *under* the bus. The undamaged telephone was at his elbow and when it rang, having nothing better to do, he picked it up. My story appeared on the front page in the afternoon edition.

John Millard was the fiction editor in those days, a gentle schoolmasterly man, peering out from his glasses. He had one of the little offices with a coal fire. At one time the features editor was Laurie Sharples who is still in harness, a career potently indicated by being torpedoed as a young wartime sailor and finding himself swimming among rolls of newsprint destined for the *Daily Mail* and the *Evening News*. Even though I was on the staff as a reporter I continued to contribute stories. One of these – 'The Birthday Book' – which is, like 'A Good Boy, Griffith', part of this anthology, had a sequel, almost a short story in itself.

Like so much fiction it had come from a fragment of life, an incident that had occurred in my childhood. In it I described a building, an orphanage at Kingston upon Thames, where I had spent some years after my parents' deaths during the war. When 'The Birthday Book' appeared, it was decorated with an illustration that was *exactly* like the building which anyone would think was only a figment of the author's imagination. I told John Millard this and, as it happened the artist was in the office at the time. 'Yes,' he agreed. 'I modelled it on an old orphanage building at Kingston upon Thames.'

The same illustrator later drew me as the character of one of my own stories which was about a reporter. Life and fiction can just as easily cross paths in a thousand-word short story, as in a two-hundred-thousand-word novel.

When I wrote my first novel *The Virgin Soldiers* I left the *Evening News* – and missed it greatly. John Millard even had a hand in the destiny of my book. I met him on the London Underground one day, and told him that I was writing a novel and had thought of calling it *The Virgin Soldiers*, but I feared it was a bit catchpenny for a title and had decided that *The Little Soldiers* was preferable. 'Call it *The Virgin Soldiers*,' he said firmly. 'The other title sounds like a children's book.' So I did and he was right.

John Millard was succeeded as fiction editor by Edward Campbell, a wry and wiry Scot, who sat at that desk for the final years of the *Evening News*. By the time the last story had been published in 1980, when the paper closed, contributions stretching over the years had included Edgar Wallace, P.G. Wodehouse, Dylan Thomas, W. W. Jacobs, H.E. Bates, Monica Dickens, C.S. Forrester, Ray Bradbury, James Clavell, Ken Follett and Arthur C. Clarke.

The *Evening News* was the last of the great commonplace newspapers. What happened in the streets was just as important, perhaps more so, than what was happening in the corridors of power. Whitechapel was often more newsworthy than Whitehall. 'We're producing a newspaper for London – not for Fleet Street!' the editor Reg Willis would bellow as he snapped his red braces. One day he was enthusing about a big fire in Finchley – 'Get it on the front page!' – when he realized that the blazing house was his.

It is all gone now; even 'Fleet Street' itself. The tradition will soon be softened to a legend, but part of that legend will be the *Evening News* and with it the short stories that were published in its pages for so many years.

The *Evening News* short story attracted its huge readership for a number of reasons, not least for the sheer scope of subject. Of course, variety was required by the story editor and if the subject matter was diverse so, too, was the authorship: established writers; writers soon to become household names; regular contributors (such as Herbert Harris, who notched up over a hundred stories); and the totally unknown and often just one-off storyteller, but whose writing was of a quality to match the high standard.

One of the pleasures in compiling this anthology was to enjoy again that variety of stories. A frustration was that not all of the authors could be traced. Thanks to the Society of Authors that number has been whittled down and current names and addresses provided. However, a few authors have not yet been traced. The compiler of this anthology would be delighted to be advised of such authors' current names and addresses, either by letter to the publishers or to the Society of Authors at 84 Drayton Gardens, London SW10 9SB.

Contents

A Good Boy, Griffith

LESLIE THOMAS

Griffith came over the hill behind the pit and turned the bend in the lane to the red brick cottage. It was too early for Morgan to be home from the garage yet, he knew that. Blodwen would be alone.

Walking up to the gate he noticed how the windows shone in the late afternoon sun, and how the lace curtains were each tied up with a little bow. Just like her, of course; always neat and decent. Never a speck of dust, never a thing out of place. She might have been his wife, but it was a good job she wasn't. He would never have been able to keep things the way she wanted them.

She came to the door almost immediately, prim in her starched apron and her blouse.

Griffith shyly reached for his cap. 'Hello Blod,' he said. 'Hope you don't mind me . . .'

'What d'you want, Griffith?' she asked suspiciously. 'It's not decent for you to be calling on me, you know. Not now I'm wed; an' people knowing how we were an' all. What d'you want?'

"Well, let me come in and I'll tell you, girl. Don't keep me out here.'

For a moment she was undecided. Then she opened the door wider and he ducked under the low beam and went into the living room. 'Just as I thought,' he mused. 'Not a plate out of place. Poor old Morgan. A good man, too.'

He looked at her, wondering if this could be the same girl he had asked to marry him on the night of the Institute dance. He realized now what a narrow escape he had had.

'Blod,' he said determinedly. 'I've come about the ring.'

A look of slow, smug triumph settled across her face. 'I thought you might,' she said. 'What about it? If you think you're getting it back, think again.'

He paled a little. 'Look, Blod,' he pleaded, 'it's important right now. Anyway, Morgan's given you a tidy little ring. Much better that one is.'

'Who do you want it for this time?' she said craftily. 'Seems that ring's been around a bit already.'

He told her that Gwen had come back.

'You know Gwen,' he said encouragingly. 'Little piece. You know – Davies Third Tenor. His girl.'

She laughed, a mean little laugh with no laughter in it. 'Oh, Griffith. You're going round in circles. She was the one before me.'

And the only one, thought Griffith. You caught me on the rebound. Now she has come back from Cardiff, and she is going to stay, and she says it was all her fault, and she wants to start again.

'But why do you want the ring, Griff? Jenkins High Street has plenty in the window.'

Griffith lost his temper. He went red about the roots of his black hair, and he banged his fist down so that the table shook and it scared her. 'Listen, Blod,' he said. 'I want that ring. I'll pay you. She doesn't know I gave it to you. She wants the same one.'

'Then it's fifty pounds, Griffith,' she said abruptly.

He gasped: 'Fifty! Don't be daft, Blod. It's not worth ten.'

'Fifty,' she repeated firmly.

'But I haven't got that much and I couldn't get it. Talk sense, girl.'

'There's some lovely dresses in Cardiff, Griff. Saw them in the paper. Morgan's taking me down in the car on Tuesday . . .'

He went out and slammed the door after him.

* * *

The next afternoon he went up the hill to the red brick cottage again. He saw the lace curtains move suddenly as he approached, and the door opened before he had even time to reach the knocker.

'Come back?' she asked tartly. 'If you've not got the money you might as well turn around and go.'

'Steady, steady, girl,' said Griffith, 'don't get so jumpy. I've got the money. Have you got the ring?'

He took the roll of white notes from his waistcoat pocket. 'Come on in then,' she said.

With a quick turn she walked from the room and he heard her going up the stairs. Then she came slowly down.

'There's your ring,' she said, half throwing it on the table. 'Keep it. I'd rather have the money.'

Griffith took the ring. 'One more thing,' he said. 'Nobody must know.'

'All right,' she said quietly. 'Morgan didn't even know I had the thing. I told him I had given it back to you.'

When Morgan came home he washed the grease from his hands under the tap then sat down to his meal. Blodwen poured the tea unsteadily.

'What's up, Blod?' he said. 'You don't look so good, girl.'

'I'm all right,' she said.

'Was Griffith here today?' he said casually, cutting a thick slice from the loaf.

She blanched but he did not look up. 'Yes,' she admitted.

He laughed. 'Good boy, Griff, you know. Sort of steady chap. Can't see why you didn't wed him. Always trust him.'

'Does it matter now?'

'No,' he replied good-humouredly. 'The thing is, did he bring the fifty quid?'

Blodwen felt her heart capsize. 'Yes,' she said shakily. 'Yes, he did . . .'

Her husband nodded. 'Good boy, Griff. Came in and asked me to lend it to him so he could get a real special ring for his girl Gwen. Nice girl. Said he'd get it from his savings when his dad came home from the pit and bring it up here.

'A good boy, Griff; yes, a good boy . . .'

How a Pub was Shipwrecked by a Sailor's Return . . .

W.W. JACOBS

In 'Dixon's Return' that canny Jacobs invention, The Night Watchman, relates the story of George Dixon 'whose mother owned a pub in Wapping and 'ad brought George up very quiet and genteel.'

When she died George was easy prey for a 'fine handsome young woman who had her eye on the pub.'

All sweetness and light to begin with, Julia quickly turns into the most impossible shrew.

Within a few months she has brought in her cousin Charlie Burge, his brother Bob and their father. And the family lead poor George a terrible life. Finally reduced to sleeping in the bar, George decides to quit. He runs off and goes to sea.

George writes home from various ships describing the hardships of life afloat and suggesting that if his wife would get rid of her relations he might come home. They find this amusing.

Soon afterwards his ship is reported missing with all hands.

Mrs George is now a widow – with a prosperous pub.

The Night Watchman takes up the story . . .

The only difference it made at the Blue Lion was that Mrs Dixon 'ad two of 'er dresses dyed black.

The others wore black neckties for a fortnight, and spoke of Dixon as pore George, and said it was a funny world, but they supposed everything was for the best.

It must ha' been pretty near four years since George Dixon 'ad run off to sea, when Charlie, who was sitting in the bar one afternoon reading the paper, things being dull, saw a man's head peep through the door for a minute and then disappear.

A'most direckly afterwards it looked in at another door, and then disappeared again. When it looked in at the third door Charlie 'ad put down 'is paper and was ready for it.

'Who are you looking for?' he ses, rather sharp. 'Wot d'ye want? Are you 'aving a game of peep-bo, or what?'

The man coughed and smiled, and then 'e pushed the door open gently and came in, and stood there fingering 'is beard as though 'e didn't know wot to say.

'I've come back, Charlie,' he ses at last.

'Wot, George!' ses Charlie, starting. 'Why I didn't know you, in that beard. We all thought you was dead years ago.'

'I was pretty nearly, Charlie,' ses Dixon, shaking his 'ead. 'Ah! I've 'ad a terrible time since I left 'ome.'

'You don't seem to ha' made your fortune,' ses Charlie, looking down at his clothes, 'I'd ha' been ashamed to come 'ome like that if it 'ad been me.'

'I'm wore out,' ses Dixon, leaning agin the bar. 'I've got no pride left; it's all been knocked out of me. How's Julia?'

'She's all right,' ses Charlie. 'Here, Ju . . .'

'H'sh!' ses Dixon, reaching over the bar and laying his 'and on his arm. 'Don't let 'er know too sudden; break it to her gently.'

'Fiddlesticks!' ses Charlie, throwing his 'and off, and calling, 'Here, Julia! He's come back!'

Mrs Dixon came running downstairs and into the bar. 'Good gracious!' she ses, staring at her 'usband. 'Whoever'd ha' thought o' seeing you agin? Where 'ave you sprung from?'

'Ain't you glad to see me, Julia?' ses George Dixon.

'Yes, I s'pose so; if you've come back to behave yourself,' ses Mrs Dixon. 'What 'ave you got to say for yourself for running away, and then writing them letters telling me to get rid of my relations?'

'That's a long time ago, Julia,' ses Dixon, raising the flap in the counter and going into the bar. 'I've gone through a great deal of suffering since then.

'I've been knocked about till I 'adn't got any feelings left in me; I've been shipwrecked, and I've had to fight for my life with savages.'

'Nobody asked you to run away,' ses his wife, edging away as he went to put his arm round 'er waist. 'You'd better go upstairs and put on some decent clothes.'

Dixon looked at 'er for a moment, and then he 'ung his 'ead.

'I've been thinking o' you and seeing you agin every day since I went away, Julia,' he ses. 'You'd be the same to me if you was dressed in rags.'

He went up the stairs without another word, and old Burge, who was coming down, came down five of 'em at once, owing to Dixon speaking to 'im afore 'e knew who 'e was.

The old man was still grumbling when Dixon came down agin, and said he believed he'd done it a-purpose.

'You run away from a good 'ome,' he ses, 'and the best wife in Wapping, and you come back and frighten people 'arf out o'' their lives. I never see such a feller in all my born days.'

'I was so glad to get 'ome I didn't think,' ses Dixon. 'I hope you're not 'urt.'

He started telling them all about his 'ardships while they were at tea, but none of 'em seemed to care much about hearing 'em. Bob said that the seas was all right for men, and that other people were sure not to like it.

'And you brought it all on yourself,' ses Charlie. 'You've only got yourself to thank for it. I 'ad thought o' picking a bone with you over those letters you wrote.'

'Let's 'ope he's coming back more sensible that wot 'e was when 'e went away,' ses old Burge, with 'is mouth full o' toast.

By the time he'd been back a couple o' days George Dixon could see that 'is going away 'adn't done any good at all.

Nobody seemed to take any notice of 'im or what he said and at last, after a word or two with Charlie about the rough way he spoke to some o' the customers, Charlie came in to Mrs Dixon and said that he was at 'is old tricks of interfering, and he would not 'ave it.

'Well, he'd better keep out o' the bar altogether,' said Mrs Dixon. 'There's no need for 'im to go there; we managed all right while 'e was away.'

'Do you mean I'm not to go into my own bar?' ses Dixon, stammering.

'Yes, I do,' ses Mrs Dixon. 'You kept out of it for four years to please yourself, and now you can keep out of it to please me.'

'I've put you out o' the bar before,' ses Charlie, 'and if you come messing about with me any more I'll do it agin. So now you know.'

He walked back into the bar whistling, and George Dixon, after sitting for a long time thinking, got up and went into the bar, and he'd 'ardly got his foot inside afore Charlie caught 'old of 'im by the shoulder and shoved 'im back into the parlour agin.

'I told you wot it be,' ses Mrs Dixon looking up from 'er sewing. 'You've only got your interfering ways to thank for it.'

'This is a fine state of affairs in my own 'ouse,' ses Dixon, 'ardly able to speak. 'You've got no proper feeling for your husband, Julia, else you wouldn't allow it.

'Why I was happier at sea than wot I am 'ere.'

'Well, you'd better go back to it if you're so fond of it,' ses 'is wife.

'I think I 'ad,' ses Dixon. 'If I can't be master in my own 'ouse I'm better at sea, hard as it is. You must choose between us, Julia – me or your relations. I won't sleep under the same roof as them for another night. Am I to go?'

'Please yourself,' ses 'is wife. 'I don't mind your staying 'ere so long as you behave yourself, but the others won't go; you can make your mind easy on that.'

'I'll go and look for another ship, then,' ses Dixon, taking up 'is cap. 'I'm not wanted here. P'r'aps you wouldn't mind 'aving some clothes packed into a chest for me so as I can go away decent.'

He looked round at 'is wife, as though 'e expected she'd ask 'im not to go, but she took no notice, and he opened the door softly and went out, while old Burge, who 'ad come into the room and 'eard what he was saying trotted off upstairs to pack 'is chest for 'im.

In two hours 'e was back agin and more cheerful than he 'ad been since he 'ad come 'ome.

Bob was in the bar and the others were just sitting down to tea, and a big chest, nicely corded, stood on the floor in the corner of the room.

'That's right,' he ses, looking at it, 'that's just wot I wanted.'

'It's as full as it can be,' ses old Burge. 'I done it for you myself. 'Ave you got a ship?'

'I 'ave,' ses Dixon. 'A jolly good ship. No more hardships for me this time. I've got a berth as captain.'

'Wot?' ses 'is wife. 'Captain? You!'

'Yes,' ses Dixon, smiling at her. 'You can sail with me if you like.'

'Thankee,' ses Mrs Dixon. 'I'm quite comfortable where I am.'

'Do you mean to say you've got a master's berth?' ses Charlie, staring at him.

'I do,' ses Dixon, 'master and owner.'

Charlie coughed. 'Wot's the name of the ship?' he asks, winking at the others.

'The Blue Lion,' ses Dixon, in a voice that made 'em all start, 'I'm shipping a new crew and I pay off the old one tonight. You first, my lad.'

'Pay off,' ses Charlie, leaning back in 'is chair and staring at 'im in a puzzled way. 'Blue Lion?'

'Yes,' ses Dixon, in the same loud voice. 'When I came 'ome the other day I thought p'r'aps I'd let bygones be bygones, and I laid low for a bit to see whether any of you deserved it. I went to sea to get hardened – and I got hard. I've fought men that would eat you at a meal. I've 'ad more blows in a week than you've 'ad in a lifetime, you fat-faced landlubber.'

He walked to the door leading to the bar, where Bob was doing 'is best to serve customers and listen at the same time, and after locking it put the key in 'is pocket.

Then 'e put his 'and in 'is trouser pocket and slapped some money down on the table in front o' Charlie.

'There's a month's pay instead o' notice,' he ses. 'Now git.'

26

'George!' screams 'is wife. ' 'Ow dare you. 'Ave you gone crazy?'

'I'm surprised at you,' ses old Burge, who'd been looking on with 'is mouth wide open, and pinching 'imself to see whether 'e wasn't dreaming.

'I don't go for your orders,' ses Charlie, getting up. 'Wot d'ye mean by locking that door?'

'Wot!' roars Dixon. 'D – n it! I mustn't lock a door without asking my barman now. Pack up and be off, you swab, afore I start on you.'

Charlie gave a growl and rushed at 'im and the next moment 'e was down on the floor with the 'ardest bang in the face that he'd ever 'ad in 'is life.

Mrs Dixon screamed and ran into the kitchen, follered by old Burge, who went in to tell 'er not to be frightened. Charlie got up and went for Dixon again; but he 'ad come back as 'ard as nails and 'ad a rushing style o' fighting that took Charlie's breath away.

By this time Bob 'ad left the bar to take care of itself, and run round and got in the back way, Charlie had 'ad as much as he wanted and was lying on the sea-chest in the corner trying to get 'is breath.

'Yes? Wot d'ye want?' ses Dixon, with a growl, as Bob came in at the door.

He was such a 'orrible figure, with the blood on 'is face and 'is beard sticking out all ways, that Bob, instead of doing wot he 'ad come round for, stood in the doorway staring at 'im without a word.

'I'm paying off,' ses Dixon. ' 'Ave you got anything to say agin it?'

'No,' ses Bob, drawing back.

'You and Charlie'll go now,' ses Dixon, taking out some money. 'The old man can stay on for a month to give 'im time to look round. Don't look at me that way, else I'll knock your 'ead off.'

He started counting out Bob's money just as old Burge and Mrs Dixon, hearing all quiet, came in out of the kitchen.

'Don't you be alarmed on my account, my dear,' he ses, turning to 'is wife, 'it's child's play to wot I've been used to. I'll just see those mistaken young fellers off the premises, and then we'll have cup of tea while the old man minds the bar.'

Mrs Dixon tried to speak, but 'er temper was too much for 'er. She looked from her 'usband to Charlie and Bob and then back at 'im agin and caught 'er breath.

'That's right,' ses Dixon, nodding his 'ead at her. 'I'm master and owner of the Blue Lion and you're first mate. When I'm speaking you keep quiet; that's dis-sipline.'

I was in that bar about three months afterwards, and I never saw such a change in any woman as there was in Mrs Dixon.

Of all the nice-mannered, soft-spoken landladies I've ever seen, she was the best, and on'y to 'ear the way she answered her 'usband when he spoke to 'er was a pleasure to every married man in the bar.

W.W. JACOBS *died in 1943 and is widely recognized as one of the very great humorists and story tellers of his time.*
P.G. Wodehouse was an ardent fan and wrote of him '. . . When I started out as a writer, W.W. Jacobs represented to me perfection . . .'

A Midnight Train to Nowhere

KEN FOLLETT

The driver was thinking about winning the pools, champagne, early retirement, a holiday in Jamaica, girls in bikinis. Through the mist of his daydreams he saw a station and touched the brake.

The guard was reading a paperback about a milkman's 'confessions'. The milkman had just been invited into a bedsitter by two girls in negligees when the train jerked to a halt. Automatically, the guard pressed the button which opened the doors.

He looked up from the book and realized his mistake. He closed the doors quickly.

The driver came back from Jamaica with a lurch. He, too, realized his mistake. His brow creased in puzzlement.

The train pulled away.

Janet stood on the platform, rubbing her eyes. She had wakened with a start and, realizing that she was well past Euston, jumped out just as the doors closed.

She muttered a curse as the lights of the train vanished. She had fallen asleep over a book of horror stories – the last station she could remember was Hendon Central. It was midnight. There should be one more train back.

Her heels tut-tutted irritably on the concrete as she walked towards the Way Out sign. The station lights seemed very dim, and she had to peer into the distance to see the end of the platform.

She followed the rusty metal signs to the northbound side.

The wooden bench was thick with dust. Typical London Transport, she thought. She searched her handbag for a tissue and cleaned a little space on the seat, then screwed the paper into a ball and dropped it into a litter bin.

They never provided enough litter bins, she thought automatically. If only they did, the stations would not get so filthy. But oddly enough there was no litter on this platform; just the thick dust everywhere. The air smelt musty.

She shivered again and looked impatiently at her watch; it was about time that train came in.

Something small scuttled across her feet, and she jumped up with a squeal. She saw a mouse disappear into a tiny hole in the brickwork. 'Oh! You little horror!' she gasped.

She looked about in embarrassment, but there was nobody on the platform to hear her shriek. She could not sit down again. There was probably a nest of the vile creatures. Where was that wretched train?

She felt hungry. She found a coin in her purse and went in search of a chocolate machine. There was one at the far end of the platform but it was empty.

There were cobwebs round it. That showed how long it had been since the thing had been filled.

A slight breeze ruffled her blonde fringe. At last – the train was coming.

The breeze turned into a wind and the train clattered into the station. As it slowed, she could see into the brightly lit, almost empty carriages.

In one a couple were necking; in another a man had fallen asleep under an open newspaper. A third carriage was filled with a grey haze from an old gent contentedly puffing a pipe like a small furnace.

She stepped to the edge of the platform. The train began to speed up.

Janet was flabbergasted. 'No!' she shouted. 'You haven't

stopped!' Her voice was drowned by the noise of the accelerating train.

'Stop!' she cried uselessly. The last carriage disappeared into the black throat of the tunnel and the noise died away.

Janet looked at the tunnel blankly. This sort of thing did not happen – even on the Northern Line. How could a driver simply forget to stop?

Suddenly the station seemed very creepy. Flyblown posters, dim lights, dusty seats, cobwebs – and now trains which did not stop. She fought down panic.

'I am not frightened,' she said aloud. 'I will simply go up the escalator, pay my excess fare, and take a taxi home. And I will write a very nasty letter to London Transport.'

She took out her ticket as she walked towards the exit. No, I won't pay the excess, she decided.

They can sue me for it, and I'll tell the court about the Northern Line drivers who are in such a hurry to get home they can't be bothered to stop at stations. It will get in the papers and cause a fuss.

Bursting with indignation, she turned a corner and stalked down the passage. She was brought up short.

The corridor was boarded up with planks. I must have taken a wrong turn, she thought.

She retraced her steps, looking for a way out. She ended up back on the platform. Suddenly she was terrified.

She ran back to the blocked exit, and returned to the platform. It was impossible – was there such a thing as a ghost station, a place in the supernatural limbo where lost souls wandered for eternity, clutching their tube tickets in their hands, cursing the driver who had stopped by mistake and the guard who had opened the doors before realizing the error . . .?

She screamed, very loud, and very long. She no longer knew what she was doing. She sat against the wall by the bench and shut her eyes tight, hoping she would wake up in bed.

After a while the mouse came out and stared at her.

In a dream, she heard a West Indian voice say, 'Trains ain't s'posed to stop here.' A hand shook her shoulder. She looked up, saw a black face and staring white eyes, and screamed again.

31

The man said, 'Quiet! Lady, do me a favour!'

Janet said, 'I'm in hell, aren't I?'

The man took a tube map from the pocket of his dungarees, put down his broom and pointed to the map.

Janet read aloud, 'Station closed until June 1976.'

The man said, 'You ain't in hell, lady. You are in the Strand station.'

KEN FOLLETT *began his journalistic career with the* South Wales Echo. *He then joined the* Evening News – *a well-remembered and respected colleague. His novels, such as* The Eye of the Needle, The Key to Rebecca *and a personal favourite* The Man from St Petersburg *have established Ken Follett, as* Time *put it, as 'an expert in the Art of ransacking history for thrills'.*

A Fine Sight

DENYS VAL BAKER

They lived in a small rather squalid row of houses in the East End.

It was a sad, run-down neighbourhood but the man liked being there because they were within earshot of the great docks. He could hear the endless tooting and wailing of hooters, the grinding of cranes, the puffing of tugboats.

It brought back to him those dreamlike days when he had been a merchant seaman, roaming the docks and harbours of the whole world. Now, as he listened to the familiar sounds of the past he would sit peacefully with a smile on his lips.

And because she loved him and wanted only his happiness, his wife accepted life amid the squalor.

Sometimes, though, the revulsion would rise up in her, and then she would consult their carefully hoarded savings and propose one of their infrequent outings.

Inevitably their outing would take the form of a day by the sea. But this time she felt adventurous, she wanted to break away from the too convenient trip down the line to nearby Southend.

She set the alarm for six o'clock, and they were out of the house before seven, joining the early crowds streaming to the centre of London.

An hour later they were at Waterloo sitting in a carriage on the Bournemouth express.

Only it wasn't Bournemouth she took him. She had chosen Lymington. She had looked the name up in a guide book and noted it was a small port and facing across to the Isle of Wight. It sounded right for what they needed – for her, escape from the prison of buildings to the sweet open brightness of the country; for him, a journey from the sound of ships to the smell of the sea.

By midday they were walking down the broad main street lined with oak-beamed Georgian houses.

'Ah,' he said, sniffing the air. 'Do you smell what I smell?'

She squeezed his arm and smiled. She was never so happy as when they escaped together upon these outings.

'I smell the sea, Jim. It's fresh and salty, I can taste it.'

'That's it,' he cried out, taking deep breaths. 'There's nothing like it in the whole world, my dear. Haven't I always told you?'

'Yes,' she smiled. 'You've always told me.'

She tightened her grip on his arm and they crossed the road and followed a path.

'Oh, Jim! Boats! Dozens and dozens of little boats, painted blue and red and white, some with sails fluttering . . . and the sea so very blue.'

He nodded wisely. 'Lymington. I must have been here some time or other. It's a port for yachts, really, lots of moorings – ah, a pretty sight indeed.'

He lingered over the phrase and she could feel him remembering. She went back down the years with him in memory. 'Did you ever go sailing, my dear?' she asked, turning into the towpath that ran out to the headland.

'Sailing?' He laughed, and for a moment it seemed she was hearing the carefree laughter of a young boy again. 'Of course. My old man built a twelve-foot sailing dinghy for my brother and me. We used to go out every evening, tacking down the coast.'

They came to the end of the path. There was a green field sloping up to the side. They climbed half-way up and sat to eat their sandwiches, and some biscuits, a glass of cider. There was nothing like it, sitting in a field overlooking the sea, picnicking.

'My word,' he said, smacking his lips. 'That was good – real good.'

He turned away from her and rolled over to lie lengthwise, propping his head up in his cupped elbow.

'You know, it all sets me remembering. The smell of the sea, the feel of the wind on my face again . . .'

She screwed up the wrapping paper and put it away, and came to sit close beside him, one arm gently across his shoulders.

'Go on, Jim,' she whispered. 'You remember. You tell me . . .'

So he talked, as they sat there in the afternoon sun. He talked with sudden animation, with life, with vigour.

Listening, she half-closed her eyes and she was carried away to strange places, across distant seas, into hot tropical lands bursting with the babel of voices, the flame of exotic colours: Cape Town, Madagascar, Port of Spain, Colombo, Singapore . . .

The names streamed across her mind as symbols of all the excitement and adventure that had once been his life, and for the moment she was not so much sad at what he had lost, but rather full of marvel at all he had gained.

'Go on, Jim, darling.'

When he talked like this, she knew, he became a whole man again. In his words and his memories he rekindled the fuel that fed his very life.

And as he did so, it often seemed as if he was refreshed physically as well as mentally.

He squared his shoulders, he stretched himself – even, his face seemed to lighten, as if the darkness was pushed away by the brightness of his inner thoughts.

When he was like that she knew that she loved him as much, more than ever. She regretted nothing, she could only marvel at the fact of the two of them together.

'Oh, Jim,' she whispered, her voice trembling.

He put out a hand gently, touching her cheeks, feeling the wetness of her tears. Without saying anything he drew her into his arms.

It was early evening before they stirred from the field. They had felt the sun and the wind falling upon them and their secret happiness and, smiling, they had fallen into a deep sleep.

When he awoke it had been time to start back, and hand in hand they had wandered across the fields to the towpath, and gently back into the sleepy town, past the painted boats and the lapping waters.

Just before they turned up into the town she paused and looked back, unable to resist a farewell glance at the scene of so much beauty. Beside her the man waited patiently.

'Is it a fine sight?' he said at last.

She turned away.

'Yes, Jim. It's a fine sight.'

They said no more. She took his arm and guided him steadily up the street.

Passers-by, turning to watch them, could only stare in mystification. How very sad, they thought. What a tragedy, they said. And they paused and stared with pity at the sight of a woman leading a blind man along the road.

DENYS VAL BAKER *has delighted thousands with his hilarious autobiographical books about bringing up his family in Cornwall; boats and the sea. There is a sense of compassion that weaves through his writing.*

Day to Remember

JAMES CLAVELL

The Colonel's wife was lying in the rubble of an old London house laid waste by a V-2.

The November wind squalled and cut as only an English wind can cut, and she felt the freezing rain on her face.

But she was glad of the cold. It deadened the hurt that now surrounded her.

Around there were screams and pain and the sound of flames nearby – and far off, the sound of approaching sirens.

I hope I don't burn, she thought, I don't mind dying, but I don't want to burn first. What's today? Oh, my, it's Sunday. Of course, I'd just got back from church. You're getting quite silly Maudie. Well, Sunday's a good day to die on. The little thought comforted her.

She tried to move. She could not feel her legs at all. Nor her right arm. But the left moved free, and she watched as it lifted itself above her, and the rain ran down her fingers across the little gold band and dropped on to her face.

The fingers touched her face then brushed a little of the rubble away and moved a strand of grey hair from her eyes.

She began to wonder about the other tenants. Did they get out of their bedsitters before the V-2 hit? And what about dear little Felix, the kitten, the joy of her solitude. Maudie remembered that she had had him in her arms near the stove pouring some milk, just before. 'Kitty! kitty!'

'No need to worry,' she said aloud for she had been alone so long she often talked to herself, 'kittens have nine lives.

'They're luckier than humans. Or perhaps unluckier. Perhaps it is better to have only one life.'

There was something that she had to remember. Something important. What could that be? Oh, yes. She'd left the gas fire on! Now that's a silly thing to do. Dangerous. And, oh yes! The rations! Her week's rations had been on the table. What a waste.

Such a lovely lamb chop that she'd saved her whole week's coupon for.

Maudie, that'll teach you a lesson. Eat your rations while you've got them.

That thought pleased her. And another; no more queues or ration books or being cold. She hated the cold and loved India. Ah, those were good days, in the Indian Army. The warmth and enough food and the servants and such lovely dances . . .

The rain fell harder now and she had to close her eyes. Somewhere there was an all-clear siren. The sound of fire was nearer. . .nearer than before.

Pain came and took her and used her, and then the terror of dying engulfed her and she shouted, 'HELPPPPPP!' But she made no sound at all.

Get hold of yourself, Maudie. There's no need to be afraid. There's a God in Heaven and, all in all, you've been as good as a human can be. So there is nothing to fear. Perhaps you won't die after all. You must be patient and wait and see.

So she gathered herself and settled to wait and as she waited she prayed.

Most of her prayer was for William, her eldest son, now part of the armoured horde that was sweeping the enemy away.

Blasted Germans. Twice we've had to fight them. Well let's hope we do a good job this time. I lost my father and my uncle in the Great War – and now in the Second – my youngest, my George, a Spitfire death, and my husband, my Richard, lost somewhere in the East, 'missing, presumed dead.' So many deaths. Dear God in Heaven, what for?

'Here, kitty, kitty.'

When the war began, Maudie had been glad for Richard. Peacetime promotion was so slow, and in war, well, he was trained for war. With luck, a General's crossed swords, like his father before him.

But he was captured at Singapore and promotions were being swallowed up by juniors.

Still – if he was alive, if he lived out the war – even now he could get his General's swords.

Those meant security, and the house that they had always wanted to buy – the house they had seen so many years ago, the house that was far above their means – the house that she bought two years ago.

'I just had to, Richard. The owner was leaving England, and it was so reasonable . . .'

An ancient Elizabethan house. Rolling gardens and lawns and oaks and a wisteria and a little bridge and diamond windows peeping out so prettily. Chadlott's Close. Their home.

She had taken out all their savings and the deed had been drawn up and she had promised to pay five thousand more pounds over years and years but that did not matter for there was all the time in the world.

And one day Chadlott's would belong to William and his children and his children's children.

Then a year ago she had come back to London to sign more papers and give more money, but that was good for she could just manage if she was careful.

And then she had gone home and got off the train and walked the four miles and all the yew trees were smashed down and the roots of the wisteria were torn from the earth and the house was no more and blown apart and the beams were gutted with fire and the swathes of lawn were holes, holes, holes, and over Chadlott's there was smoke.

Chadlott's was dead. Dead.

That night she had died too, sitting on a murdered tree, her tears watering the earth. She got up and never returned.

And, now thinking of the unnecessary obliteration of such

beauty, she screamed her hate at the devil's spawn who started the war and destroyed Chadlott's.

And she cursed them with her whole being for taking the life of Chadlott's and letting her live.

Curse you, curse you, curse you!

Not for my father or my uncle or my son, or my son-in-law or his son, or my husband, or for me – humans are expendable and it is right that men should defend these shores and women should suffer.

But ten thousand million curses for Chadlott's Close.

For nothing ever, ever, can rebuild or re-life that which had seen four hundred years of life. Nothing. Not even God.

'Kitty, kitty, here kitty.'

I don't mind dying, but I hate dying without seeing you all again. I wish I could see you again, all of my children and most my Richard – who is most my child, my old, old child.

Poor Chadlott's my dear one.

'Here kitty . . . here . . .'

She died in the rubble there under the rain and the wind, deep in the rubble. The kitten still nestled into the cradle of her shattered right arm. Cold long since.

JAMES CLAVELL *a half-Irish Englishman, was born in Australia and served as a Captain with the Royal Artillery during the Second World War.*

In 1942 he was captured by the Japanese and sent to the dreaded Changi prison in Singapore. His first bestselling novel, King Rat, *was based upon his experience there.*

After the war James Clavell wrote a number of short stories and screenplays. The highly successful film The Great Escape *is an example of his prodigious talent. Producing, directing, writing, other films followed:* To Sir, With Love *and* The Last Valley *are two personal favourites.*

King Rat *followed by* Tai-Pan, Shogun *and* The Noble House *made up a remarkable Asian quartet, and established James Clavell as one of the world's outstanding writers.*

Bigger Money, Dear

ANTHONY GREY

S he was sitting at the bar of the little Nachtlokal on the Savigny Platz.

She was holding her left elbow in her right hand, smoking a long filter-tipped cigarette and talking rapid French to the barman.

You could see that when she stood up she would be tall.

Short dark hair, those high, prominent cheekbones that give European girls classic eyes. Legs that were long between knee and ankle, strong-looking but beautifully turned.

I'd been in Berlin two years. But now I was leaving and since it had been a long, busy day showing my successor the ropes, we were grabbing a quick late-night drink near the office.

I sneaked the odd look at her as we sipped our whisky. Mark was doing it, too.

She looked round once. But clearly a girl as attractive as she had long grown used to frank appraisal.

Little floating islands of French conversation eddied around in the sea of German. We felt our English was immune to understanding so were talking and laughing a bit louder than we might have been – and exchanging appreciative adjectives about the girl.

It was a surprise when she turned and said to me: 'You're English, aren't you?'

I confessed I was. But she spoke very good English. I told her.

'Hardly surprising, is it? I am English,' she said with a direct look from those classic eyes.

We expressed incredulity and admiration for her perfect French and English.

Without a word she took a passport from the handbag slung over her shoulder and put it on the bar. Stiff blue cover, familiar lion and unicorn crest. Like a fool I didn't memorize the name. It might have helped. The mystery has nagged me ever since.

'Mummy was French, Daddy was English. I've spent a lot of time in Paris.' She spoke with the assurance an expensive education provides.

'What do you do in Berlin?' I asked.

'I'm a dancer.'

'Really? What, er, what kind of dancing?'

'I strip.'

At that moment a snake-hipped Latin fellow – she obviously knew him – came over and asked her to dance. They went to the little dance floor where couples were shaking and shuddering at each other to records.

The Latin fellow – I fancy he was a Cuban – was good. He did lots of tricky little steps, flicking his fingers, twirling round, laughing, swaying his tiny, narrow-as-an-arrow hips.

She seemed to flow across the little dance floor like a sensuous wave. The number was fast and on those long, strong legs she swept and jigged around the exiguous Cuban, hips twitching, eyes down, twisting, turning, absorbed in the rhythm. And in all her movements there was a subtle, erotic dignity.

Most of the other dancers retreated to stand and watch, washed from the floor by her fluid movement.

Then she was back on the stool again and the Cuban had disappeared. She wasn't breathless: she just picked up her cigarette and her drink.

'Where do you do your professional dancing?' I asked lamely.

'The Chez Nous.'

Mark said something goggle-eyed and drooling about the dancing we'd just watched. I heard myself telling her we'd like to take her to dinner. It was difficult, she said, not finishing until about this time. Well drinks, anything. I persisted, I was leaving Berlin soon.

'I've got to go into hospital tomorrow,' she said.

'Hospital,' I queried incredulously. That dance had convinced me that nobody in Berlin was more healthily, sensuously alive than she was. 'What for?'

'I'm having an operation – to enlarge my bust,' she said, matter-of-factly.

"But why?" I asked. She was by no means flat-chested.

'Bigger statistics, bigger money, dear!'

The bland delivery, the direct look from the high cheek-boned, classic eyes gave the remark stunning impact. A simple showbiz fact. A coarse fact, delivered with beautiful, sophisticated aplomb. The most memorable remark I've ever heard from a woman.

The Cuban came up again and they went to dance. We watched her once more, grinning and shaking our heads in disbelief over such superb femininity.

Reluctantly we gulped down our drinks and waited for the end of the dance.

I was hangdog. During my remaining days in Berlin she would be receiving exclusively the impersonal attentions of the cosmetic surgeons.

When she came back to her stool, 'I hope we'll meet again,' was all I could manage.

'You might find me here,' she said, a last faint smile creeping into that direct, challenging look.

We left and walked dejectedly across the foggy Savigny Platz without speaking. Then Mark turned to me: 'You do know what the Chez Nous is, don't you?' I stopped in mid-stride. 'Oh my God yes, I do. It's . . . It's the transvestite showplace.'

Of course. He was right. It was the night club where alluring striptease dancers bludgeoned their audience at the climax with the wig-and-bra revelation that they weren't women at all.

I felt numb. Then I saw a gleam of hope.

'Mark,' I said slowly, 'it's true isn't it – they do mix the acts, real girls in between to heighten the suspense and mystery?'

'Yea . . . s that's true,' he said speculatively. Then after a pause. 'What do you think of . . . ?'

43

The sentence trailed off. I had no answer. We walked on wordlessly across the deserted square.

That was four years ago.

I still don't know if the most memorable woman I've ever met was . . . well, one of the most memorable women I've ever met. Why didn't I take a closer look at that passport?

There are many reasons for the writing of a short story. For ANTHONY GREY *it was a matter of sustaining his reason. Anthony Grey was imprisoned by the Chinese in Peking for 26 months, mostly in solitary confinement. A Reuters correspondent, he worked on a group of short stories during his confinement.*

Company Requested

CARDEW ROBINSON

Alastair Campbell, a sandy-haired man in his mid-thirties, pulled up at the impressive door of the mansion.

He began to wonder if he had come on the right night: the whole place seemed so dark and still.

Switching on the car's roof light he reassured himself with a glance at the expensive-looking invitation card. The date was today's. The remainder of the card he knew by heart.

'You are invited to dine with myself and other fellow Scots exiles in the West Country. I can promise you an abundance of the food and wine of Scotland and, I hope, an interesting evening in the ancient tradition.'

There followed the date, the time, eight for eight-thirty, the address, The Manse, Little Bartock, and finally, the signature, Don Camdal.

When the invitation dropped onto the mat at his Devonshire cottage, Alastair had wondered how many other West Country-based Scots had accepted invitations from Mr Camdal.

He had finally decided to accept when he found that Little Bartock, although a Cornish village, was only just across the border and meant only a forty-five-minute drive.

It was twenty-five minutes past eight when he lifted the heavy knocker on the oak front door.

It was opened by a very old man, still quite erect and every inch a butler.

'Good evening sir. Please come in.' He had a strong Scots accent.

'I'm sorry I'm late. I had trouble with a flat tyre and also trouble finding your house.'

'Of course, sir. We haven't been here very long. Before we came, the house had another name, I believe. An English one.'

The reason for the gloominess of the exterior became apparent to Alastair as he followed the old man past room after quiet room, until they finally came to a high door, which the butler opened.

There were about thirty men already standing around, drinking.

'If you will be good enough to help yourself, sir, I will return to announce dinner in a few moments.'

As Alastair poured a whisky a man said, 'Hello. Is your name Campbell?'

Alastair said, 'Yes. How did you know?'

'Because mine is, too,' replied the other, a man about Alastair's own age, 'and I think you'll find that's the name of everyone else here.'

'But our host – his name is Camdal,' Alastair said. 'That's not even Scottish to the best of my knowledge. Though, of course, it sounds a bit like Campbell if you say it quickly.'

Conjecture was cut short when the butler came back to announce dinner. They crossed the hall to a magnificent dining room.

Standing at the head of the table was a man as tall as the butler and only a few years younger.

Camdal smiled, his voice with its slight yet definite Scottish accent was soft and pleasant. 'I hope you will enjoy this little repast. If you will in return do an old man the favour of restraining your curiosity until after dinner I will be pleased then to tell you the reason I asked you all here.'

The meal was excellent. Scots salmon. Delicious Highland venison. During dinner Alastair, who was sitting a few places away from Camdal, could hear their host chatting to his immediate neighbours – but only of trivialities. Finally when the Drambuie and cigars had been served, Camdal rose.

'Well gentlemen, I trust you have enjoyed your meal.' There were murmurs of genuine, grateful assent.

'Splendid. They do say, don't they, that the condemned should eat a hearty meal!'

At this, those heads not already facing the top of the table turned in surprise.

'You will obviously have wondered why I asked you all here tonight, strangers to me and to each other. All of you have just one thing in common, the name Campbell.

'It may help you to understand when I remind you that today is the anniversary of the massacre of Glencoe. The day when the Campbells accepted the hospitality of the Macdonalds and then repaid with murder.

'I thought the time had come to even the score. You will notice by now a distinct feeling of drowsiness creeping over you.

'In a few moments this will intensify and you will fall quickly into your last sound sleep. Your whisky had something added to it.'

He smiled grimly.

'I'm glad to see that Campbells though ye may be at least ye're no teetotallers!'

One of the diners struggled to his feet, his face ashen.

'But – why . . . ?' Then he crashed forward on to the dining table. The man on Alastair's right muttered hoarsely, 'My God, he's mad,' then slumped forward in his chair.

All round the table other guests were following suit. Alastair, fighting desperately against the overpowering lassitude invading him, was one of the last to succumb. Camdal surveyed the inert forms of his guests and chuckled.

'Well that will have given all those Campbells a very nasty moment,' he said, 'especially as they will all have thought it was their last. And when they awake tomorrow in the various situations we have arranged for them I'm not at all sure they won't wish it had been!'

His eyes twinkled wickedly as he pressed a bell and then to the six brawny men who entered the room detailed the places where they were to put each Campbell.

Some in cars, locked together in apparent head-on collisons;

47

some in conspicuous public places minus their nether garments; others in unfortunate private places even more heavily divested, and all sprinkled very liberally with whisky.

In each case appropriate phone calls would ensure certain discovery by the parties most interested!

'Now my bonny lads, work swiftly and by the time they're all discovered we'll be on our way to the Highlands and this house will be empty again. Empty and as desolate as that other house in Glencoe.'

'It's a pity, sir,' said the butler, 'that more of these Campbells didn't accept the invitations.'

'Heavens no, Alec,' said his master, 'we've quite enough to cope with. In any case I always thought it likely that even some Campbells would realize that Don Camdal is an anagram of Macdonald!'

CARDEW ROBINSON, *well known as a fine radio comedian and cabaret entertainer, was a frequent contributor to the* Evening News *short story page. His effervescent sense of humour had often a touch of the macabre, as in this story.*

Poor M Revoise

R.B. LAYLAND

'It is an affront to my honour.'

Madame Revoise, collected in spite of her anger, stood beside the fireplace and surveyed the bald head of her husband who was sitting in his favourite chair.

'There is nothing more to say,' she said, showing every sign of continuing for the next three hours. 'I have been gravely insulted. Before my friends; before the whole town.

'What have I done to deserve it? Have I not been a good wife? Have I not welcomed your desires? Brought your children up favourably? Kept your house in the manner of a wealthy man on the money of a tradesman's wife?

'Do I not dress well to reflect credit on you? And yet you are so ungrateful as to do this to me.'

M Revoise sat a mute, resigned victim over whom his wife disgorged her curdled rage.

'It is not unknown for a man to take a mistress,' she continued in precise but leisurely tones. 'It is even, after some years of marriage when a man wishes to recapture his youth, usual for him to take a mistress.

'It is also usual that the wife understands. The good-mannered, the honourable practice is that the mistress should be far enough removed to inflict no humiliation or distress upon the family. The core of the marriage, the home, is preserved. The man is happy, relaxed, and his contentment is shared by his family. There is no loss of dignity or position.

'But when after twenty years of faithful marriage M Revoise chooses a mistress, it is a woman from the butcher's shop three doors down the street!

'He at first takes her out in the car where she insists she will not exercise matters of love. She protests that she must have a bed.

'Now there are a million beds in the world. There must be a thousand within a short distance of this house.' M Revoise writhed. He sank a humbled head lower towards the plump wreaths of his torso.

'But no, M Revoise waits until his wife has prepared for a journey to see her mother and then carries his mistress across his own threshold and into the sanctuary of his wife's bedroom.'

Madame Revoise paused, breathing heavily from the exertions of her self-control.

'Having satiated themselves and violated the chastity of the marriage bed, they then look about themselves for fresh diversions.

'It occurs to them to have a bath. They move on to the bathroom for that purpose. They sit together in my bath, laughing like children.'

The logs ticked among the hot ashes. M Revoise sank into a shapeless heap of misery.

'To make matters worse,' Madame Revoise pursued his tortured spirit remorselessly, 'the mistress is not young and attractive, but old . . . old and the possessor of fat legs.'

After flinging those crisp words upon the room Madame left.

For some moments her husband stared unhappily at the fire. How could she know? How could she know of such a detail as the bath?

But how strange were women. Was it not the fat legs of Madame Denault which had filled him with desire?

His eyes watered with the joy of his reminiscence.

He remembered the voluptuous stir of Madame Denault at the moment of possession. Here was one who did not mock his manhood or lacerate his worthiness.

Wounded by his wife's scornful delivery, he longed to be with his mistress again to restore his self-esteem.

He rose sighing, and slipped out into the hall where he put on his hat and overcoat.

His steps led automatically in the direction of the house of his love. He rattled the letter box and was answered quickly by the sound of her step and the cautious opening of the door.

'Lise. Can you come with me for a moment?'

She stared at him unsmiling. 'I have things to do,' she said. 'And my husband is upstairs.'

'We are discovered,' he whispered. 'I must talk to you.'

She fetched a coat and secured the door behind her. They walked through the town to the river. There he took her into a café and ordered coffee.

M Revoise undid the buttons of his coat and leaned over the table. 'My wife knows everything,' he said, his eyes fond but unhappy as he gazed at his mistress.

Lise's eyes were lowered in attention to her gloves. She was a plump woman with untidy brown hair which had begun to go grey. She did not answer him.

'How could she know, Lise? How could she know all the details? I do not understand it.' He shook his head. 'It is, after all, possible that someone saw us go into the house together . . . it is possible that someone drew conclusions. But she knew about the bath – everything.'

He drank his coffee with hasty, distracted gulps and the liquid shone on his upper lip. Lise was silent. And she stared at him almost coldly.

There were students lounging and laughing about the room but her words came clearly to him. 'I told her.'

He stared over his glasses, astonished.

'You, Lise, told her?'

'Yes.' About the fine amber eyes of Lise Denault grew an expression of malignance and contempt. 'I told her. Everything. Every detail. I told her even where she kept her handkerchiefs and letters.'

'But why, Lise? Why did you do such a thing?'

'Because I hate her. I wished to see her humility.'

Her eyes swung about the room in impatience. 'Yes. I hate her. I've always hated her. I knew her as a child and I hated her.

'She was a pig to me that woman. I was never as fortunate as she and always she made me feel less than I was, even as a child.

'How she pranced to her private school with neat pigtails and new shoes. She went to dancing lessons while I scrubbed my father's shop.

'Then she grew up, tall and haughty with her white fingers and bony ankles. And she complained to me about a leg of mutton in front of a shop full of people.

'My father told me I must be nice to her or we would lose the custom.'

M Revoise was dazed. Always his Lise had dancing eyes and laughter. Tonight she behaved as though he were of no consequence.

A horrible thought suddenly consumed his attention. 'Lise, did it all mean nothing . . . were you only intended to make some sort of revenge? Lise . . . ?'

'How she shook when I told her! How she wished she could leave me. But I would not let her go. I made her hear. I told her everything and watched her face. I broke down her cold haughty strength with the things I told her. Now, every time she looks at me she will know that I despise her.'

M Revoise wandered sadly home. His wife had not yet gone to bed.

Her husband took off his spectacles and rubbed them slowly with his handkerchief. 'There will be no more, my dear, ever.' He turned wearily to go upstairs. 'I am no match for the treachery of women.'

Once in Love with Carla

STAN MOYE

This is the story of four people, all from this village.

First Carla, the most beautiful girl in the world.

Then Fidel, rich old goat and hard businessman. Next Rosa, fat and plain, daughter of the innkeeper.

And lastly me, Jose, a handsome, young man of athletic . . . oh pardon, perhaps I overstate my case.

The sad business begins with Carla the beautiful making a decision that was to alter all of our lives.

She wanted to be rich (born at the other end of the village as well. How did a perfect blossom grow from such weeds?).

So she set out to follow a well-worn path. Have you heard the wise saying: 'If you don't inherit it, or earn it, or win it, then marry it.' You haven't? It's not surprising, I just invented it.

And who was the only one with money? Yes, Fidel the crabface. What a waste. There was I, all that any woman could desire, waiting, eating my heart out, but she ignored me.

What did I have? I had Rosa the ugly, always at my elbow – 'Jose, take some wine, Jose, come for a walk, Jose, do you like my dress?' And all while the light of my life was throwing herself at a walking bank.

Forgive me. The thought of her beauty and his money brings tears to my eyes. I love both.

Next comes the most heart-breaking part. I must bring myself to say it, though. Came the day they married, there was bright sunshine. If there was any justice it would have snowed, with earth tremors.

Such rejoicing. Some danced. Well, to be truthful, all the village danced, but not me. There was singing all night but I did not sing. All I could do was be brave, hide my wounds, and drink wine. Of course, it was Fidel's wine and that nearly prevented me from taking it.

But I am a man of strong character and I forced myself. And so Carla, the woman I loved, went to live with the old skinflint in the big house on the hill.

I waited to see her become unhappy with her bargain but, as I sit here, I swear she looked, first of all, content. Yes, that is the word, content – and as time passed, even happy.

Sometimes, at the end of the day, she would meet him as he closed his office and they would walk slowly back up the hill in the cool of the evening.

How I watched them. The sight of her olive skin and white teeth as she threw back her head to laugh at something he said was agony to me. And he – he actually looked twenty years younger. No, I lie – ten years.

'If she does that for an ancient mummy like him, what could she have done for me?' I thought. And then came a thought to console me. To be married to Carla and be poor would be bliss. But to be married to the widow Carla *and* be rich would be paradise.

How long could he last? Surely she must kill him with love. A young, beautiful wife must be kept – happy, if you know what I mean. Think of his heart! While this was going on in my mind, Rosa was always there, 'Do you like my hair? Take me up the mountain (and I admit there had been some walks up the mountain). Papa wants to meet you!'

Meet me! All my life I have known him and now he wants to meet me! The woman was madly in love with me – desperate. But it is quite understandable. Woman are very weak. Then, my friend, one glorious day Fidel dropped dead. 'Hooray – God rest his soul,' I shout.

Now soon will be my chance. But I am a man of propriety. I

54

wait. One week, two weeks, three whole weeks. Then I make my move. She was more beautiful than ever in black. 'Good morning, Carla,' I say, 'may I extend my . . .'

'Good day,' she says, not even looking at me. 'Drive on,' and away goes the coach leaving me in a cloud of dust.

Me! – the one who has saved himself for her (well practically), fought off the advances of others (most of the time), left with shame in the middle of the village.

I suddenly see I have made a terrible mistake. This woman is not in love with his money, she actually loved Fidel. How can this happen? What can I do? How can I ever reach her? The woman is deaf and blind with grief.

Feeling I needed support I staggered into the inn. It was a black day, for there waited Rosa's father eager to discuss his daughter with someone.

We talked like civilized men. So intense did we become that, at the climax of our discussion, he buried a meat axe into the table in order to make his point. That man had an arm like a bull's leg. And then this big generous man, who did not know when to stop giving, gave me his most treasured possession, his daughter Rosa.

Now I am a very reasonable man and can understand the views of someone that size, so I accept.

That day I survived two momentous events. My beloved spurned me and I was given a wife.

The years have passed and we are all older. Carla still lives in the big house, the one with the iron gates. You see? From her radiates the same contentment and inner happiness.

She married for gain but found most unexpectedly, love.

I am now the landlord of the inn and live with Rosa and our ten children. Yes, it's true, ten. Rosa is still a very large, plain woman but she has many hidden attributes.

I, too, married and then found love later. Perhaps we are guided along life's path after all.

What? Is that all there is to my story I hear you ask?

What did you expect, family feuds, gunfire, horse whippings? This is a quiet village where a man has time to drink a little wine and watch his children grow. Nothing happens here – nowadays.

The Specialist

ROBERT QUIGLEY

Harry left Malaga in the heat of the afternoon.

He took a boat over to Tangier, hired a car, and drove through Casablanca to Marrakesh.

On arrival he checked into a small hotel on the Avenue Mohammed V.

He hung a few things up in the wardrobe and went over to the window. It was all orange-ochre coloured, with the overpowering sensuous scent of orange blossom.

A palm grove to the right guarded one of the city's red, sandy edges.

It was good to be away from England for a while; this was a solid, civilized arrangement he and Caroline had; taking their holidays separately.

That evening Harry changed into a new lightweight suit and left the hotel, walking down the avenue.

Half-way down he hailed a horse-drawn caleche, and they trotted down into the old city. It struck him then that it was all rather provincial French.

He was dropped off at the Ksar El Hamra, a typically Moroccan restaurant, where he ate couscous, washed down by Valpierre; afterwards he sat smoking over some sweet mint tea.

It was then he caught sight of her.

She was attractive in a sophisticated highbrow sort of way; her dark hair, darker eyes, dressed with a contrived garishness. In her early thirties, with an ample figure.

Their eyes met, and there was an instant rapport. He moved over to her table, and it was really no surprise to find that she was English. She invited him to sit down while she finished her brochettes.

'The name's Harry,' he said.

'Alone?' She nodded, then leaned towards him, smiling coquettishly.

'Before you grill me, I must warn you that I make it a golden rule never to tell the truth on these trips abroad. The truth is so dull. So no names, no pack drill. OK?'

Harry looked at her quizzically. She could be a shade mental, but if anonymity was to be the name of the game . . .

'Have it your way,' he answered, smiling. 'So what do I call you?'

'Just call me Fred,' she replied, with her mouth full.

They settled their bills and left the restaurant, walking slowly till they reached the huge El Fona Square in the old city.

Tatty orchestras of cross-legged old men twanged and wailed and thumped. Water-sellers in mad, triangular tasselled scarlet hats filled brass bowls to pass round the huge crowd.

Tumblers twirled like mediaeval jesters and snake-charmers charmed their snakes out of cane baskets.

The Medina hummed like a giant honeycomb. From its dark slits and alleys came the tap of bronze, the tinkle of silver, and the cries of vendors selling their dyed silks and leather bags.

They wandered about, Harry and Fred, till it was quite late; then he took her back to the Mamounia hotel, near the Jdid Gate, where she was booked in. After one drink at the bar, he left to return to his place.

In the days that followed they wandered about the souks; lolling like salamanders; browning themselves in the gardens outside her hotel.

At night they did a round of the clubs and restaurants, with the inevitable surfeit of Berber belly-dancers.

At first it was all pretty innocent, but towards the end of the week it wasn't.

They spent the last night in an hotel in Tangier on the way back home. It was then that he noticed the rash on her neck. She went to the mirror: 'Good Lord, it's German measles.'

'Is it catching?' he asked her.

'If you don't run fast enough,' she joked.

They said their final goodbyes in Malaga a few hours later. But he was still no wiser who she was. In a way it gave him a vicarious sort of thrill; a stab in the back to all things banal.

Harry got back to Caroline late the following evening.

They went through the usual rigmarole; exchanging notes. She'd been to Devon and as she raved on about Torquay, he, for the sake of expediency, watered down his tale of North Africa.

He returned to work on the Monday: the 8.25 to Liverpool Street and the import/export job. But his mind was way back in an hotel room, in Marrakesh. He wondered if he'd ever see her again.

It was about a fortnight later that he broke out in a rash behind the ears.

Caroline took one look at him that night when he got home.

'Better get along to the doctor. Probably something you picked up in Marrakesh,' she remarked tritely, not realizing how close she was to the truth.

'Is it the surgery in Laburnham Grove on Tuesdays?' he asked her.

'Yes, there's a panel of four. See if you can get Dr Morris. He's new.'

Harry sat reading magazines in the waiting-room. It was ages since he'd last been to a doctor. His name was called, and now he was sitting opposite Dr Morris, relating his recent experience abroad, trying to keep it flippant.

'It was this rather fetching creature I met on holiday in Marrakesh. Discovered she had the spots on our last night.'

'A Berber belly-dancer, no doubt?'

'As English as they come,' Harry corrected him. The doctor examined his spots, smiling cynically.

'Hmm, very interesting . . . the things that come out of a trip to Marrakesh, eh?'

He prescribed the treatment, and as Harry was knotting his tie the doctor spoke a few words into his intercom. Then he addressed Harry.

'Before you go, Mr Johnson, I'd like a second opinion. I have a specialist on the premises. My wife.'

A few moments later the door behind Harry opened.

'Ah there you are, Frederica darling. Have a look at this gent quickly will you? More down your street, wouldn't you say?'

The Lippi Madonna

JOAN FORMAN

I saw the man only once, but am not likely to forget the encounter.

It occurred on a late November day.

I was walking across the Ponte Vecchio, with a precious parcel under my arm.

The acquisitive instinct warps a man's nature, and so it was with me. All my life I have wanted to possess whatever was beautiful; I could not see without coveting.

Ally acquisitiveness to artistic taste and no money to gratify either, and you have a problem.

I lived in a one-room apartment on the outskirts of Florence. It wasn't sordid, but rich and comfortable, I stole what I wanted for it, and I have a talent for theft.

Quick as a cat from childhood me. And silent. Most of the stuff I pinched in other places – an altar cross from Sienna; a Della Robbia ceramic from Fiesole; a statuette from Pisa.

The usual household comforts I stole from every shop in Florence. I had no police record. I had never been caught.

I thought I knew every picture, every statue throughout my city, but this one I'd never seen – a picture by Filippo Lippi.

I guess the gallery had had it in a storeroom and just brought it out for an airing. They have a change around from time to time, so that the tourists don't get bored.

This was a beaut. A Madonna and child, with the Virgin wearing a look which was more mischievous than innocent. Don't know how Lippi could paint like that in the fifteenth century – Holy Church thought Virgins should look like virgins. Lippi's were a break with tradition.

I wandered round the Uffizi one rainy morning before the tourists had climbed into their sandals and raincoats, and there was this lovely thing facing me on the wall. I had to have it.

Never occurred to me otherwise. It was the work of a minute to nip out a sheath knife and cut round the head and shoulders of the girl. She had a real saucy gleam in her eye. I left the child where it was. Never cared much for kids.

So happened that I had a copy of Oggi with me. I tucked this bit of picture into it, rolled the lot up and stuck it under my arm. The picture fitted in nicely, being just the right size.

And then I went out. The only official I saw was in the entrance, and he was tearing a strip off some other guy in uniform.

Once in the street I walked. Saw a couple of cops, but they knew me. It was 'Ciao, Umberto!' and pass by. Too wet to stop and talk.

I meant to go straight home, make a frame for that picture, and hang it on my wall. I'd always wanted a Lippi, but somehow my feet took me another road.

To be accurate, I followed a girl. Now I'm not one for girls, except in pictures. Oh, the odd one comes along for a night occasionally and I have a list like any other man but I don't let them get regular.

This one, however, was different. She had lovely legs, neat waist, and swung her self along as though nobody else existed. Her hair was wheat-coloured, like the Madonna in Lippi's picture. Perhaps that was the attraction.

I followed her to the Ponte Vecchio, and she came to the bit which opens out on to the river, then she disappeared. No, I don't know where she went; into a shop perhaps.

Anyway, when I got to the embrasure the girl wasn't there, but this fella was. A tall, dark chap wearing clerical dress.

Now me, I'm not a good Catholic; I don't go to Mass more than three times a year, and not to Confession more than twice, but happening on that priest right after pinching the picture, then following the dame with intent – well. I can tell you it gave me a jolt in the conscience.

Couldn't get past him, either. He shot out an arm and grabbed me with a 'Ciao, Umberto!' Just like he was police.

He drew me over to the balustrade and we looked at the river. It struck me afterwards that there wasn't a soul on that bridge except us two; and that was odd, even in November.

He began to talk, about pictures mostly, and what he didn't know about fifteenth-century art could be written on a postage stamp. The way he went on you'd think he knew these Renaissance painters personally; told me about their private lives – most of it invented, no doubt.

I was in a hurry to get away. Saw an old enemy of mine at the far end of the bridge, and he'd started in my direction. A cop, of course – one Jacopo Menzi – who'd never liked me since we were at school together.

Didn't want to meet him at that moment, and this priest wouldn't let me get away.

Every time I took a pace off, his arm would shoot out and grab me again, with a 'Just a minute, this'll interest you.'

The only thing to do was get so deep in conversation that Jacopo wouldn't have the nerve to interrupt. I tried to listen to what the clerical guy was saying.

'Of course, the early painters painted all religious subjects, and since the church was paying, she dictated the way it should be done. Madonnas like bits of wood – holy wood, but solid just the same; no life, no reality. You couldn't believe in women like that.

'They could never have felt, thought, or borne children.

'Oh they didn't distract the congregation, of course, and that was why they were painted as they were. It took old Lippo Lippi to break the mould.'

I was startled by his mention of that particular name.

'What do you know about Filippo Lippi?' I asked.

He grinned. 'He was a monk, my boy – a monk with a roving eye. He painted all the girls who flitted in and out of his bed. Oh, don't look shocked! In those days monks were men, you know.

'Unfortunately, the abbot didn't like to see Madonnas looking

62

like Lucia the serving-wench, so they kicked Lippo out of the order.

'But his paintings – they showed Madonnas who were flesh and blood.'

'Yes,' I said. 'I know.' I glanced over my shoulder. Jacopo was three yards away. I didn't wait to make excuses I left.

Somewhere I must have dropped the Oggi. I didn't have it when I reached home.

I found a portrait of Filippo Lippi the other day – Fra Filippo Lippi, the monk. His face was that of a clerical gent on the Ponte Vecchio. I remembered an odd thing then: I'd been able to see the bridge through the priest. Not behind him, you understand, but through!

I remember I was late on duty that day, and my boss ticked me off. 'Punctuality is one of a policeman's essential qualities, Umberto,' he said. 'It is second only to honesty.' I agreed with him, of course.

Key to the Question

STEPHEN PHILLIPS

M y name's Quail.
Robert Quail.

At the time I'm talking about I was roaming around the South Seas with the financial backing of a rather obscure research council, studying rare tropical diseases.

On a morning when the sky had ribs of gold in it I hit this little island, Waikua, lonely, beautiful somehow out of this world.

A tiny fishing-craft put me ashore. My colleague, Dr Grange, was on his way out for a spell of leave.

'Well, best of luck, Quail,' he said, giving me an odd kind of look. 'By the way you've a problem case on your hands – a Nick Mordaunt and his wife. Poor devil's on his way out. Ought to be in hospital. That's right, a terminal case. But his wife won't hear of it.

'She insists on doing almost everything for him herself. Even resents the native nurses I've been sending along.'

He threw his bag on to the boat. 'More than once I've washed my hands of the case. I don't know if his wife realizes it, but she's killing herself by inches! But what can a poor penniless quack like me do about it?'

He jumped on to the boat, glad to get away. Later that day I sat studying Mordaunt's history. And gradually the feeling got into me that this fellow, Mordaunt, was a bit of a swine – selfish, weak-minded, hard to handle.

And that, even before he'd been stricken down, he'd never really been a lot different.

And then the door of my tiny surgery swung open and my receptionist – a pretty young native girl – smiled at me.

'Mrs Mordaunt to see you, doctor,' she said.

I motioned to a seat. I studied her furtively. Almost girlish-looking; and really quite attractive.

But my God how tired – sick – she looked!

'I . . . I wondered if you could call as soon as possible, doctor . . . ?'

'Of course. This afternoon. The nurse has been?'

'Yes. This morning.' She stood up. 'Well, I must get back to him. He doesn't like being left . . . alone.'

I stood up, too: looked at her.

'When was the last time you had a real night's sleep, Mrs Mordaunt?'

'It . . . doesn't matter,' she said.

'It does matter. I'm your doctor, too. Remember that.'

'Oh, very well,' she said listlessly, and turned away.

In the next few days I learned things that surprised me quite a lot. Dr Grange had been prescribing tablets. Three a day, when the pain was bad. Not more than three, though, taken one at a time. Those tablets were lethal.

Mrs Mordaunt kept the little bottle of tablets locked away in a small cupboard. Round her neck she wore a thin gold chain, with a key attached, the key to the cupboard where the tablets were kept. The key, she told me quietly, never left her possession.

I tried, as young Grange had done, to make her realize that she couldn't go on much longer the way she was doing. It wasn't much use, though. Eva Mordaunt had a quite savage disregard of herself where her husband was concerned.

She just wouldn't listen to reason. Sometimes she was so worn out, physically and mentally, she could scarcely stand on her feet or keep her eyes open.

And once, the district nurse told me Nick had yelled at her, sworn at her demanding to be given more tablets . . .

65

I began to realize what young Grange had been up against. And then, one morning, this island schooner, the *Sea Witch*, glided into the tiny harbour below my surgery.

The skipper, Ross, was a tall young sailorman, with Scandinavian yellow hair. A good-looking, laughing, careless sort. And pretty soon he was hanging around the Mordaunt bungalow. Apparently Nick had roamed around a lot before he was suddenly struck down. And this handsome young fellow Ross, knew most of the places Nick had been to. That, on the face of it, was the reason why Ross was so much at the Mordaunt place.

Only, pretty soon, the nasty talk started – about Ross and Nick's wife. The gossip spread like wildfire.

Late one evening Eva Mordaunt came running – 'For God's sake, doctor, come quickly . . .' I went at once. Nick was lying on the floor dead. Beside him lay the little bottle. It contained only two tablets. My shirt collar was suddenly sticky. There'd been ten tablets in that bottle that morning.

'I . . . fell asleep,' she whispered. 'On the couch over there. I . . . I tried to stay awake. Oh, God, how I tried!' she sobbed; dry, harsh sobs. 'He . . . he must have got out of bed, taken the key off the chain . . .'

A terrifying thought hit me. Was it true about Ross? What people said? Had she deliberately let herself fall asleep? Or . . . or perhaps it wasn't Ross after all. Perhaps her last conscious thought had been one of pity . . .

'My . . . my brain,' she whispered, 'it . . . it's always so confused . . .'

I gave her a sedative and had Nick taken away. There'd have to be a P.M. of course. But questions chased around in my brain . . . Deliberate murder? Murder for love of another man? This fellow, Ross? Or . . . or sudden wild compassion for her suffering husband?

Or was it like she said sheer exhaustion? A form of euthanasia, something I had often asked myself if doctors should do?

Then, startled, I noticed the *Sea Witch* slip away. As dawn burst like a wild flood of fire, Eva Mordaunt came walking swiftly towards me. I stood and stared at her – at her face, deathly pale, her wide-open startled eyes. I said roughly, 'You're too late! Ross has gone! Run out on you . . .'

'It doesn't matter,' she said, and the strange smile on her lips haunts me still. 'Just now, when I . . . I woke up, my thoughts were crystal clear, you see.' She raised small, trembling white hands. 'It was you I was thinking of when I fell asleep,' she said. 'Ever . . . since you came here it's . . . always . . . been you . . .'

Hot South Wind

EDWARD RICHARD ROSSET

'Thomas, are you going to eat your supper?'

The old woman eyed her son, a worried expression on her wrinkled face.

Outside, the gusty wind raised blinding dust in the deserted alleys of the little Spanish village.

Thomas grabbed the bottle of wine and had a long pull at it. 'I'm not hungry tonight, mother.' He wiped his mouth with his sleeve. 'I'll go to my room and lie down . . .'

Thomas's mother raised dark apprehensive eyes from her garlic soup. 'It's this cursed wind. I know it. Every time the wind blows hot something evil happens here. Remember last year when Pepe was found dead . . .'

Thomas spat into the fire. 'Bah, they all slipped on the ice down the Devil's Gorge, that's all . . .'

'And the year before, Maria was found stabbed to death in her bed . . .'

He shrugged his shoulders. 'A tramp was caught by the Guardia Civil later.'

A sudden strong gust made the old house tremble. The doors and windows moaned and creaked.

The frightened woman crossed herself quickly. 'Something is going to happen tonight,' she whispered, 'I can feel it. It's in the air . . .'

She was quite right. Something sinister was going to happen. Something as sinister as the death of the town mayor.

Thomas stretched himself noisily, 'I think I'll go to my room,' he said to his mother.

The lone yellowish electric bulb in the landing upstairs cast a grotesque wobbling shadow against the decaying smoky walls as he climbed the creaky stairs.

Outside the unpaved village streets were deserted.

Thomas checked his old pocket watch. Nine o'clock. Rodriguez shouldn't be long now. Every night Carmen's husband passed in front of the balcony to see his sheep before retiring.

Thomas remembered Carmen's long dark raven hair brushing her slender tanned shoulders. He saw in his mind once again the undulating soft movements of her hips, as she swayed along the path.

As he noiselessly slid open the balcony windows he shivered in the cold air.

He took a broken tile from the outjutting roof and carefully weighed it in his hand, tiles fall on windy days, don't they . . . ?

Thomas was quite confident that he wouldn't miss. He had always been considered the best stone thrower in the whole valley.

Suddenly, there was a shadow moving towards his house. A faint pale beam peeping timidly from behind a dark grey threatening cloud glittered for a moment on Rodriguez's bald head.

Thomas crouched against the protective darkness of the balcony. As the unguarded man briskly walked under the balcony Thomas took careful aim, then tossed the heavy tile.

It didn't miss. As Thomas carefully peeped over the railings he saw Rodriguez lying spread-eagled on the dusty ground, motionless.

He smiled, grimly, pleased with himself. That was it, now to bed. People would think it was an accident.

'What are you doing on the balcony, Thomas?'

Thomas whirled around to face his old mother standing on the landing. Concentrating on his deed, he hadn't heard the creaking of the stairs.

'I . . .' He stammered nervously. 'I thought I heard a cry or

69

something, but there's nothing down there. It must be the owls . . .'

The old woman seemed satisfied with the explanation. 'I came up to see if you're all right . . . You've had nothing to eat yet.'

Thomas waved her aside impatiently. 'I told you I wasn't hungry, I'm just going to bed, *buenas noches.*'

He watched his mother slowly climb down the steep stairs to her own room and he breathed a sigh of relief.

It must have been almost eleven o'clock when he heard the scream. Slowly he got up fully clothed and descended the stairs taking his time.

As he opened the heavy door he saw several neighbours gathered around the fallen body of the ex-town mayor.

'*Qué pasa?*' he shouted at the gathering.

A voice answered back. 'Old Rodriguez. He's dead. A tile fell from your roof. It hit him right on his head.'

Another voice broke in. 'It was that *maldito viento*, it is a curse that wind.'

Thomas nodded. Now to wait for the Guardia Civil. They'd just write it off as an unlucky accident and that'd be the end of it.

The young *teniente* of the Guardia Civil was adamant. 'I have to make a full report that's all,' he insisted. 'Now tell me, your mother said that you heard a cry about nine o'clock. Is that not so?'

Thomas swallowed hard, 'Yes, I heard something but I didn't see anything, it was very dark.'

The *teniente* fixed alert blue eyes on him. 'I gather from my questioning of Señor Rodriguez that you two were very close friends . . .'

Thomas felt cold sweat trickling down his brow. Inwardly he cursed the inquisitive *teniente* and his twisted mind. 'We're friends, that's all,' he said. 'There's nothing more to it . . .'

The *teniente* tapped on the mayor's desk with his pencil. 'Just good friends, hey?' He kept silent for a moment, gazing absent-mindedly at Thomas's thick red frayed pullover.

Then he asked suddenly. 'It was cold last night when you opened the balcony, was it not?'

Thomas looked uncertainly at the man in the smart green uniform sitting behind the large oak desk.

'Yes,' he said, hesitatingly. 'I think it was a little cold.'

The *teniente* stood up. 'Do you know why, Thomas?'

Thomas frowned and shook his head. 'I'll tell you why.' The *teniente* paced the room with his hands behind his back. 'It was cold because the wind changed. The warm south wind stopped blowing last night a little before the . . . accident.'

Thomas felt the colour drain from his face.

'Yes,' the *teniente* continued, 'at the moment Señor Rodriguez passed in front of your house the wind was blowing from the north.'

The *teniente* looked for a moment into the greyness of the morning mist swirling around the limewashed houses. 'How then, can you explain that the tile went against the wind . . . ?'

Just a Peasant

PLICHTA HALL

Sehr geehrter Herr Doktor Sonnenstrahl,

Have thanks for visiting me today.

I am not a double murderer.

I mean, suppose you saw a man jump off the Reichsbruecke. Would it not be a joke if the police charged you with murder, just because you know that the Danube flows at two metres per second?

Of course, Berger and Schwartz did not jump into the Danube, but it is the same thing, is it not? You are a lawyer. You understand these things. Maybe I am a stupid peasant, but, a murderer? Oh, Jesus, Maria and Josef!

It was a good idea of yours to let me write this all down. My stutter is very embarrassing I know and the more nervous I am the worse it becomes.

I did not like Berger and Schwartz. Truly. But I would not murder them. They meant to cheat me of half a million of the Schillings we robbed from the bank. That is how the police caught me. When they searched their bodies they found the money.

Berger and Schwartz were criminal types. Without honour. They did not intend to share fairly with me. They thought I was a stupid peasant.

Of course I will plead guilty to robbing the bank. I was caught. I knew the risk, but please make it clear to the court that I did not know Berger was armed. I do not believe even Schwartz knew about the automatic.

He was a good-natured fellow, Schwartz, with a lot of muscle, but not much brain.

Berger could be pleasant when he wished. He was friendly and flattering at first, because he needed a good driver for the robbery. Anyone in Vienna will tell you that I am a wonderful driver.

I wanted the money from the bank to modernize my father's farm. It earns too little for our large family. You know how badly paid the vinyers are. That is why I had to come to Vienna.

If only I had stayed honourable. Berger was right, I am a stupid peasant.

It was a shock for me when I saw Berger carrying a gun as he ran out of the bank. The gendarmes were very quick.

As we drove out of the village and headed for Vienna their Volkswagen was right behind us, and Berger wanted to shoot them, but I hit him on the head with my elbow and he dropped the gun out of the window.

It was awful in the car, Berger went crazy and tried to strangle me, but big Schwartz soon shut him up.

I was very cool. The car I had stolen was a Mercedes 300 SEL and it was a wonderful feeling to be driving it, I let the gendarmes draw level at over a hundred, then I knocked them, arrow straight, between two cherry trees and into a cornfield.

I did not wish to hurt the gendarmes and I am glad they were not injured.

I have shown the police where we dumped the Mercedes into the Danube. First we transferred the booty to Berger's old Fiat 4CV of course, and then we split up. Berger took Schwartz in his car and I rode my Sunbeam.

That is an English motorcycle and the English name means the same as your name, Herr Doktor. A great coincidence is it not? It is a wonderful machine.

We joined up again in Bruck-an-der-Leitha which was a clever idea because everyone would think the robbers had gone to hide in Vienna. Ha-ha-ha!

I led the way down into Burgenland and out to the back of

Mikula's vineyards where it is very quiet. There we hid our vehicles under the trees.

We had plenty of sausage, bread, paprikas, and peppers with us, and Berger opened the lock on Mikula's field-cellar and brought out four litres of wine. I do not care much for Mikula's wine.

Berger was recovered. He did his imitation of my stutter to make Schwartz laugh. Swine. He said there was a table in the cellar that was big enough for him and Schwartz to sleep on. He said I would have to sleep on the cellar floor because he was going to lock the car with the money in it.

I said I would sleep under a tree because I did not want a rheuma, and Berger said it was all right by him because he would not want to smell my peasant feet all night, which is a rotten lie, all my family wash their feet. Every night, Herr Doktor.

Berger locked the car and hung the keys on his watchstrap. He and Schwartz carried their blankets into the cellar and slammed the door behind them.

It was almost dark as I walked between the vines, looking for a bunch of grapes for dessert. They had already been harvested so I had no luck.

Mikula has a very early harvest and puts a lot of sugar in the grape juice. That is why I do not care for his wine. You have a head like a water bucket the morning after drinking it. Surely we need not mention this at my trial?

I slept under a tree and awoke at six as usual. I opened the cellar doors, then went into the vines again. By the light of day I did manage to find two small bunches of grapes that the harvesters had missed. I ate them for breakfast.

I dashed down into the cellar, took the keys from Berger's watch-strap and transferred the money from the car to the panniers of my Sunbeam. I went again into the cellar and replaced the keys. Ugh!

An hour later I was at my father's farm having a proper breakfast. It was there that the police arrested me later the same day.

It never occurred to me to search the bodies. The police found five hundred thousand Schillings in their pockets, and they soon found out that I had been seen in their company. Ergo, I was the third man.

Yes, yes, I am a stupid peasant, Herr Doktor.

But I am not so stupid that I would sleep in a wine cellar where thousands of litres of freshly pressed grape juice were fermenting and pouring their poisonous gases out through the open bungs.

Ah no. No peasant would be that stupid.

Give a Man Enough Rope . . .

FRANK BROADBRIDGE

'*Buenos días, Padre.*'

The priest, who had been walking slowly, lost in thought, stopped. The pack-mule, which he led by so short a length of rope that the animal was almost treading on his heels, stopped also.

A few yards away a very fat man was sitting on a horse as unconcernedly as if he were on the open plains and not on a narrow ledge of rock 2,000 feet above the tree-tops. The priest's dark eyes gazed unblinkingly at the horse.

'*Buenos días,*' repeated the horseman, his eyes narrowing at the priest's flat stare. Then, taking off his hat he smiled genially; but the priest, who was half-Indian, looked into his eyes and shivered.

'*Buenos días, Señor,*' replied the priest at last and took off his large black hat to fan himself.

The horse backed suddenly and with an oath, the fat man reined him up. A few loose stones rattled over the edge of the path.

'Be careful,' warned the priest, his voice low in order not to startle the quivering animal, 'this is no place for tricks.'

The rider sat back in the big hand-tooled saddle and lit a cigarette.

'I am a *vaquero* from Brazil.' His voice was proud and at the same time a little mocking. 'I was born on a horse,' he added.

'Perhaps,' said the priest, mildly, 'but not that one. That is the horse of Geronimo de Caqueza.'

The *vaquero* gently let his breath out. Slowly, he reached up and took the cigarette from his mouth, crushed it out and put it into his shirt.

His hand lingered there and the priest felt himself tense, as if to take a blow. Then the fat man smiled at him and the hand came out again, empty and harmless, to pat the horse's neck.

'You are right, father. He is not my horse.'

The priest said nothing.

'I found him standing just a little way back along the path,' explained the rider, 'but of the man who rode him, I saw nothing. Perhaps the horse took fright at something and threw him.'

The priest's face now was wholly Indian – calm, almost contemptuous in its stillness.

'Geronimo always *led* his horse along this ridge,' he said, 'for he was an old man.'

'Then I cannot account for his disappearance, father,' replied the fat man smoothly, 'but one thing is certain – he must be dead, since neither you nor I have seen him.'

The priest returned no answer to this. His eyes were following the wheeling buzzards planing down into the valley.

The fat man urged his mount forward. It passed the mule without any demonstration, picking its way cleanly over the loose stones.

'Go with God, father,' called the *vaquero* mockingly without turning his head.

Then the rope dropped over him.

For all his bulk the man twisted round like a cat whose tail had been stepped on.

But before he could raise the pistol which had appeared in his right hand, the noose ran up under his armpits and he was jerked out of the saddle.

He hit the path on one shoulder and went out into space.

Sun, mountain peaks and jungle whirled about him for a brief moment, then he was spinning slowly on the end of the rope, alternately facing the rock face below the path, and the tremendous mountains which hurled their summits fifteen thousand feet or more into the sky.

A dozen feet above him the priest's face was peering over the ledge. Beside the priest was a gaunt tree stump, around which the rope was looped once; and he held the spare quite easily in one hand.

To the priest, lying on the rocky path, it appeared that the man was standing on a strip of green grass, although two thousand feet of empty air were beneath the bare toes.

The priest said: 'You will tell me what has happened to Geronimo – and you will not lie to me.'

'It is the moment for truth,' agreed the fat man. 'I killed him, father. He was leading his horse – as you said. I took the reins with one hand, and pushed him with the other. That was all.'

With his free hand the priest made the sign of the cross.

The fat man grunted and tried to ease the rope's pressure by lifting himself.

'Geronimo was a good man who had harmed no one,' said the priest sorrowfully. 'It is hard to understand why God let him die.'

'Perhaps the Señor God turned his back for a moment,' suggested the *vaquero* seriously.

He began to sing softly, beating time with one bare foot.

'I need a sign,' whispered the priest. He closed his eyes and began to pray. After a while the *vaquero* stopped singing.

'Listen, father,' he said impatiently, 'do not trouble God with this little matter. No doubt this good Geronimo is with Him at this very moment.

'You do not fear to meet God after what you have done?' asked the priest in horror.

'Why should I be afraid? If God did not like what I did why did He not prevent me?' asked the *vaquero*.

'To tell the truth, father, I suspect that God is not so concerned with our affairs as you priests seem to think.' He threw back his head and laughed; and the echoes came back hollowly from the tremendous rock faces above him.

The priest closed his eyes and tried to pray.

The bullet hit the path a foot from his face and showered him with splinters of stone. He almost let the rope go with the shock of the explosion.

The *vaquero* put the pistol inside his shirt and then came up the rope slowly, hand over hand. 'You cannot let go,' he said mockingly, 'it would be murder. You must wait for a sign.'

The priest could see his eyes glittering as they came closer. 'Pray for your sign, father. Pray!'

There was a sudden crack – and the rope burned like fire through the priest's fingers. The tree stump had broken cleanly in two. Without a cry, or sound of any sort, the *vaquero* had gone wheeling down into the valley.

Geronimo's son laid his head upon his arms, and wept.

Games People Play

DAVID HUNTER

Beneath a glowing orange sunset, Marcus walked silently across the hardened earth of the training ground.

He was grateful for the deep shadow of the barracks spread out before him. It gave his eyes some relief from the blinding sunlight.

Once inside, he rested the heavy iron helmet on the table and looked down at the inch-deep cut in his arm.

The wound, the outcome of his only mistake of the afternoon, was still open but the blood had had time to start to congeal.

He knew that left uncauterized the wound would soon become infected from the dust and dirt blowing around in the arena. There was only one thing he could do.

Roman doctors had been known to bleed a man to death and he trusted none of them.

Instead he looked to the corner where a brazier stood full of red-hot coals and embers. Three iron rods were sticking out from the grating in the side, each firmly embedded deep into the blazing centre.

Carefully he eased his shoulder epaulette down over his arm, but a sharp corner of the metal caught in the jagged wound.

Gently he eased the epaulette over the hole and threw it away in anger. Beads of perspiration broke out on his forehead and ran down his temples as he wiped round the throbbing, bleeding wound.

With a piece of knotted cloth between his teeth to relieve the pain, he touched the wound with the red-hot metal.

In an instant the agony of the burning flesh exploded in his arm, and sent his mind reeling. For seconds, after he'd dropped the iron on the floor, he remained dazed, staring out into the empty space in front of him.

His mind was floating in a swirling delirium, his hold on reality so slim that he barely remembered bandaging the wound and falling into his bed. But in the nightmare that followed he relived the contest over and over again.

The programme had followed the usual pattern. Late in the afternoon, just after the preliminary contests between animals and captive slaves, they had all marched into the arena to the sound of blaring trumpets.

Suddenly the trumpets stopped and the crowd ceased to cheer. Silently they all waited in the baking heat of the afternoon sun for the address by the Prefect of the Games.

A grey-haired old man sitting to the left of the Emperor, stood up and looked down at the handful of men gathered before him.

'You are here', he began in a frail voice, 'to fight well and to die for your Emperor.'

'Those who fight well will be paid well in gold. Those who die well, will be given a decent burial. Now let the games commence.'

The salute was soon given and Marcus carefully eyed his opponent. The Greek was wearing a large helmet with a visor that hid his face. The only thing that distinguished him from the many others in the arena was a deep blue scar on the back of his hand.

From the start Marcus felt the weight of the foreigner's sword against his shield and the crowd cheered.

For what seemed hours, the Greek watched his every movement with eyes hidden by the helmet, attacking at any point of weakness. Suddenly, in a split second, he feinted to the left and lunged to the right.

Marcus tried to sidestep the attack, but the sharp point of his adversary's sword dug deep into his arm.

The crowd cheered as they saw him wounded, but with the strength brought from the need to survive, Marcus attacked. The Greek was caught off guard, and fell back.

Marcus saw his chance, attacking and lunging, not allowing the Greek time to balance. On his retreat from Marcus's blows he tripped over a discarded shield and sprawled on the ground.

Silently he waited for the decision of the Emperor. The crowd was with him, but Nero, not known for his mercy, turned thumbs down.

Marcus thrust straight at the heart. His sword cut through cloth and hardened skin with ease, sending a bright red stain out across his defeated opponent's tunic.

Then the whole episode would start again.

Three days later the fever had passed and Marcus felt fit to travel. Before dawn, while the stars still shone brightly in the sky, Marcus mounted his horse, and set out for the gates of Rome.

The guard at the gate was commanded by a shortish, stout soldier with the rank of Decurion.

'It's not wise, sir,' he said looking up at Marcus, 'during the hours of night the roads are full of robbers. They lie in wait for travellers such as yourself. Could you not wait till daylight?'

Marcus smiled. 'I've travelled these roads before at night and no harm has yet befallen me. Come, guard, open the gate, I'm already late for the Games of Augustus in Gaul.'

The heavy wooden gates swung slowly open and Marcus rode out into the barren lands beyond the city limits.

An hour's ride saw him leave Rome far behind. Still the sun was not above the horizon, but the sky was light as the time for dawn drew near. Suddenly Marcus heard something move. His keen eyes scanned the road ahead and caught sight of a dark figure moving out from behind a boulder.

In a second the words of the guard ran through his mind. Instinctively he reached behind him for the sword he kept hidden under his cloak.

His hand resting on the hilt, ready to draw it in a second if need be, he reined his horse to a stop and waited. The sky was already becoming light and streaks of sunlight began to beam over the horizon giving all around him form and shape.

Boulders on the roadside became visible, white fluffy clouds showed up in a deep blue sky, but nothing could be heard except the breeze blowing across the open land.

The figure, dressed in a dark cloak, moved out into open view and looked up.

'Gladiator Marcus, hail!'

Marcus remained motionless with his hand still on his sword.

'I am not a greedy man, I want only half the gold you won at the games.'

Marcus threw down the gold in front of the man. Carefully the figure picked up the bag and weighed it in his hand.

Immediately Marcus saw the deep blue scar on the back of his hand.

'And next time, Marcus old friend,' the Greek smiled up, 'it's your turn to wear the pig's bladder filled with blood. I'm running out of unstained tunics.'

It is Called Love

BARBARA CARTLAND

'Please, please Papa, do not make me do this.'

'I have told you before, Selina, that I will have no arguments and that you will do as you are told. You are an extremely lucky girl to marry anyone so important as the Marquess.'

'But, papa . . . he is old, and when he comes . . . near me I feel as if there was a . . . snake in the room. Please let us . . . turn back before it is too . . . late.'

'I have no intention of doing anything of the sort!' Sir Mallory Westcott said.

He looked at his step-daughter sitting beside him noting that she looked extremely beautiful, if fragile, in her wedding gown. He could understand why the Marquess of Chorley desired her.

There was silence, then as the coach rumbled on over the rough roads Selina said with a piteous little cry, 'I cannot do . . . it, Papa! I would rather . . . die than marry such a . . . man!'

'I thought I had beaten such nonsense out of you,' her step-father replied sharply. 'Behave yourself! You will marry the Marquess and go down on your knees and thank the Almighty that anyone so unimportant, penniless, and with no assets except a pretty face should have taken his lordship's fancy.'

'I cannot! I cannot . . . marry him!'

Selina's voice was little above a whisper.

There was a sudden jerk, a cry of alarm, and the coach came to a standstill.

'What the devil is happening?' Sir Mallory exclaimed.

'Stand and deliver!'

There was a masked face at the window and a pistol pointing directly at Sir Mallory's heart.

'God damn you!' the nobleman ejaculated.

'Alight!' a voice replied firmly. 'My men wish to look under the floorboards where I am quite certain you keep your valuables.'

Cursing, Sir Mallory stepped from the coach and Selina followed him.

'A bride!' the highwayman exclaimed. 'This is unexpected!'

'Get on with your thieving, felon!' Sir Mallory snarled. 'I will see that for this work you hang on Tyburn Hill.'

Selina glanced to where two other masked men were holding up the coachman and the footman on the box. Then because her step-father's oaths disturbed her, she moved away on the mossy ground under the trees.

She wondered desperately if she could run away where no one could find her. The idea of marrying the man her step-father had chosen for her was a horror beyond expression.

He was old and debauched, and even in her innocence she realized that the feelings the Marquess had for her were not those of love but something evil and unspeakable.

There were tears in her eyes and a voice said beside her, 'I will not be so ungallant as to ask the bride for her valuables.'

She looked up and realized that what she could see of the highwayman's face was young and handsome. In answer she pulled the huge diamond ring from her small finger and held it out to him.

'Take this,' she said, 'and I hope I . . . never see it . . . again!'

'You sound as if you were not happy at the idea of your marriage. Who is the lucky man to whom you have promised yourself?'

For a moment Selina hesitated, then he heard the horror in her voice as she said, 'The Marquess of Chorley!'

The highwayman stiffened.

'That swine? It cannot be true!'

'It is . . . true!' Selina answered. 'And I am afraid . . . very afraid!'

'It is not surprising!' the highwayman said. 'How can your father . . .'

'He is not my father!' she interposed. 'He is my step-father and he is glad to be rid of me. I think, too, he wishes to please the Marquess.'

'You will certainly please him,' the highwayman said grimly.

He looked at Selina's large eyes misty with tears, at the trembling of her small mouth, at the delicacy of her heart-shaped face.

'How old are you?' he asked.

'I am seventeen.'

'It is unbearable!' he said. 'Is there no one who can help you?'

'No one! My mother is . . . dead.'

He stood looking down at her and as their eyes met instinctively, as if it was an impulse she could not prevent, she put out her hands towards him.

'Save me!' she whispered. 'Please . . . save me!'

For a moment he was very still.

Then as he would have spoken one of his servants who had been ransacking the coach came to his side.

'There's not much money, m'lord,' he said in a low voice, 'but plenty of what I thinks be wedding presents.'

'They are,' the highwayman said briefly. 'Divide the money, Jeeves, between you and Tom for your trouble. Let the gentleman keep the rest and set the horses free. It will take time to catch them.'

He turned to Selina.

'You really meant what you asked me? You are prepared to trust yourself to me?'

'I know I can . . . trust you,' she said softly. 'I do not know how I know . . . except that you are different . . . very different in every way to the Marquess.'

'I should hope so.'

He gave a low whistle and his horse, which had been cropping the grass under a tree came towards him.

86

'You are still sure you will not regret coming with me?' he asked.

'I am quite . . . sure,' she answered, and he saw the light in her eyes.

He lifted her on to his saddle, and as he did so she heard her step-father give a shout of fury, but she did not look back.

The highwayman swung himself up beside her and as he did so he pulled off his mask and flung it into the bushes.

'I have won my wager!' he said. 'Sir Mallory has boasted for years that he has never been held up by a highwayman.'

'He will never . . . forgive you, and he may . . . harm you.'

'I think it unlikely,' the highwayman answered, 'although I have robbed him of something very precious!'

For a moment she did not understand. Then as a flush stained her cheeks he rode his horse away into the wood.

'Very precious,' he said again, 'and I have a feeling it is something I have been looking for for a very long time.'

'It is . . . perhaps what . . . I have been wanting . . . too,' she whispered.

He smiled down at her as he said softly, 'I think, in fact I am sure, we have both been seeking the same thing. It is called love!'

Every Woman Needs to Have a Secret

LINDEN HOWARD

I watched him pile strawberry jam on top of a scone, and said, 'You'll get fat!'

He shook his head. He was the lean, energetic type that never gathers flesh.

Outside snow flurries feathered in an icy wind; inside central heating wrapped us in warmth. As I watched him, I recalled vividly a day last July.

We had a lovely summer – remember? Not that I saw much of it – as personal assistant to Greg, whose beautiful designs in glass were beginning to be noticed in the right quarters, I had a tough job.

Greg was impatient, demanding, generous, kind and stubborn. I was going to marry him – when we had time. Lately, I had begun to wonder whether I was really in love with this human dynamo, or perhaps I had been bewitched by him. I needed a breathing space to decide.

I decided to take a day off. Greg said, 'Do you good, Rhonda. Go and have a shopping spree. Have a fabulous lunch, and a new hairdo.

'Isn't that supposed to be the perfect pick-me-up for any girl?'

I didn't want attentive waiters, new clothes or the cool dimness of a beauty salon. Instead, early next morning, I put on frayed jeans and an ancient straw hat and drove south.

When eventually I turned off the main road, I found what I was looking for: a jagged piece of cardboard with a chalked message – 'Pick your own strawberries. First turning right.'

The turning was a lane, snaking upwards to a well-holed road that petered out into a rutted track beside a vast field of strawberry beds. There was a van and a bored-looking woman sitting beside scales and baskets.

Below me, Southampton Water shimmered in the heat. I crouched happily on my heels, working methodically along the rows among the glistening, rosy fruit. I thought I had the place all to myself, until a voice beside me said, 'Somebody's going to make a lot of jam!'

I looked into a pair of blue eyes. A lean, tanned young man with fair hair was working the row beside mine.

'Jam?' I looked at my well-filled baskets. 'I never thought about that, I just decided to pick strawberries. It's something I've always wanted to do. I'll probably eat them when I get home.'

'All those?' He shook his head in mock reproof, his face creased into a smile and we both laughed.

That was how I met Kevin. As we picked, we talked, easily, as though we had known each other for years.

The country town in which he lived was a few miles inland. With his sister he ran a bookshop there. She was a great jam maker and he was combining a day off with strawberry picking.

'Strange,' he said slowly, 'we should both have decided on the same sort of day off. Do you believe in Fate?'

I made some light-hearted reply but my heart beat faster and when he said that there was a pub nearby where they did a ploughman's lunch, I murmured yes, it sounded fine.

So I parked my baskets in the car, and walked down the hill with him to a tiny pub that had everything – atmosphere, the privacy of high-backed settles, ice-cold beer.

I sighed blissfully, knowing I didn't want the day to end. I talked about my job. I didn't tell him then, that I was engaged. After all, Greg's ring wasn't on my finger, because there hadn't been time yet to choose it.

After lunch, Kevin said, 'I often come here. I'll show you around.'

There was a stream, a straggle of thatched cottages, a grey church amid crooked tombstones. We paddled in the stream, read epitaphs on the tombstones and bought ice-cream cones from a tiny, front-parlour shop.

A perfect day filched from the busy world, a day full of enchantment – and the enchantment included Kevin.

Time was running out too fast. We sat hand in hand under a vast, shady oak and Kevin said, 'You'll love my home town. It has the Rip Van Winkle touch – you know, antique shops, old houses with potbellied windows, funny little streets. I'm going to take you there. You're not just going to walk out of my life. I've never met anyone like you before, Rhonda.'

I saw it all as clearly as though I stared into a crystal: time to read and walk, to dawdle and live slowly. It wouldn't have any of the hectic social round that was part of my life with Greg – going to the right places and meeting the right people.

I knew I could choose, then and there. I could follow the lazy road with Kevin, who attracted me because he was a quiet person at heart, as I was; or I could race down the long straight road with Greg.

So then I told him about Greg.

'That kind of life isn't for you,' Kevin said. 'You'll have to tell him. When you have, I'll be waiting.'

We walked back to the car in silence. He held my hands and kissed my lips gently. Always when I catch the scent of strawberries I shall remember today, I thought. With Kevin I could have a lifetime of such days.

There was just time to put the strawberries in the fridge, have a scented bath, change into a sleek, expensive dress and brush my hair, a new way, before Greg arrived.

He looked at me approvingly.

'It has done you good!' he told me. Suddenly, surprisingly he caught me close in a fierce embrace.

'You're . . . different, Rhonda! There's something special about you tonight. I never realized before just how much I love you.

'I work you too hard. I work myself too hard, trying to prove to myself that the kid from the Children's Home can make it right to the top if he wants to. Only – you have to be there with me. It's no use without you.'

I saw the look on his face and I knew then that I should never tell him about my day. It would never belong to anyone but me, and every woman is entitled to one secret, one stolen day in her lifetime.

Oh I knew what I was letting myself in for – being part of the rat-race. But it didn't matter any more because I had found an answer to my questions.

I had discovered that you can be happy if you're in the wrong place with the right person but never if you are in the right place with the wrong person.

Kevin was like me; but Greg was the only person for me.

I made several pots of strawberry jam and gave them to my mother to sell at her summer fete. I kept back just one pot as a reminder of summer magic.

As this is the first day back from our honeymoon, I opened it for Greg this afternoon.

'One day,' he said determinedly, 'there's going to be plenty of time for all the things you like – the quiet, country things. I promise you that, Rhonda. You shall walk along country lanes, bake your own bread, make your own jam. And I bet it'll taste good!'

I looked at him sharply.

'What do you mean?' I asked.

'Oh, this is very good jam. Strawberry is my favourite but yours is superb. You can't beat the home-made stuff, can you?'

'No, darling,' I agreed. 'You certainly can't.'

Postscript to a Marriage

KAY HARRIS

Charles insisted on going home alone after the funeral.

His partners' invitations he had declined brusquely; Margaret's more gently.

'I'll have to face it alone sometime, and I'd rather do it now. Besides, there is so much to see to, papers to go through.

'I really would prefer to be alone just now, my dear. Don't worry about me, I'll be all right. I'll phone you tomorrow.'

It had been easier to persuade Mrs McGarry that there was absolutely no need for her to change her evening off and after paying her respects to her late mistress, and muttering a few words of condolence to her employer, she had set off to visit her sister.

Charles's partners had willingly taken over his surgeries and hospital duties, and the answering service would re-route all his telephone calls, so that he would not be disturbed.

His partners had also urged him to go away for a few days, but he doubted if he would take their advice.

He drove home, put the car away and, letting himself into the house, went into the lounge and poured himself a whisky.

Then, dropping into his own comfortable chair, he sipped his drink and settled down to read the letter Sybil had left.

Dear Charles,

I have wanted to tell you for a long time, and now that I know I am going to die I can do it without fearing your anger or dreading what you might do.

You never knew I had a lover, did you? We had only been married a couple of years, but already I felt you regretted our marriage. Then you bought me my first car, and I fell in love – with the car salesman.

Did you never wonder why the car had to go back to the garage so often? What a scandal there might have been! The doctor's wife and a car salesman, and he one of your own patients, too!

But much as Tony loved me, he could not desert that dull little wife of his. She could not even give him the child he so dearly wanted. But I could! And I did!

Do you understand, Charles? Your precious Margaret is not your daughter at all. Tony fathered her, not you. When she was growing up you used to say, over and over again, that she had your *eyes,* your *hair,* your *smile; that she was one hundred per cent* your *daughter. I wanted to shout the truth at you, but I always held back, because I had promised Tony that I would not tell you.*

When I first told Tony I thought I was pregnant his only concern was to protect me and the baby.

He thought it best to go right away, so that you would never suspect and no stigma would attach to our child.

He gave up his job for my sake, and decided not to tell me where he was going, in case you ever found out and tried to trace him.

Charles took another sip of his drink.

'Poor Sybil,' he muttered. 'Little did you know I had to buy the car business by proxy in order to boot him out. Then, of course, the discrepancies came to light and he could be dismissed without notice. He didn't tell you why he was leaving his job, did he? And I couldn't.'

He turned over the page and continued to read.

All the time Margaret was growing up I hugged the knowledge to myself. Sometimes I thought you must surely suspect something when you kept on and

93

on about how like you she was, but Tony always said the thought would never enter your head, you were too self-centred, too egotistical.

I didn't mind at all the little economies I had to make, so that Margaret could have the best of everything – expensive toys, a private education, her own pony, a year in France and all those expensive clothes, because it was all for Tony's child. You would never have let me had you known the truth.

Charles changed his position in the comfortable chair.

'Poor foolish Sybil. All Margaret's expenses were more than paid for from the profits of the car business, but I could hardly tell you that, could I? Your petty economies were totally unnecessary, as I tried to tell you many times.'

Wearily he turned again to the letter and read on.

I am now convinced that Tony must have died some years ago, otherwise he would have been in touch with me to learn how his child was developing.

He was so very delighted at the thought of becoming a father and I would have liked him to know that his sacrifice had not been in vain.

He had wanted a son so badly, but I am sure he would have been pleased with his daughter. I must say that Margaret has turned into a very beautiful and poised woman, even if you have won her affections away from me with your adulation and expensive presents.

I don't think you will disinherit her now that you know the truth. You'll keep the knowledge to yourself (though you'll squirm inwardly) rather than be made a laughing-stock, so I think Margaret is safe enough.

I can't even apologize for deceiving you all these years. You never really loved me, not the way Tony did. Your patients have always meant more to you than I did. I am grateful to you for fostering Margaret, so please accept the grateful thanks of Tony and Sybil.

Charles put down the letter with a sigh.

'Poor Sybil. You deluded yourself all those years. Your precious Tony could never father a child. It was all there, in his medical records. The tests proved it conclusively, but he would not accept it.

'He blamed that poor frightened little wife of his, and insisted on test after test, which only proved her fertility and his sterility.

'He was quite frantic, I remember, but the consultant convinced him in the end. Oh! yes he knew all right – months before you ever met him.

'Your affair meant nothing to him. He collected women as a Red Indian collected scalps. And he fooled you completely. Poor deluded Sybil. You were a born loser.'

He picked up the cigarette lighter from the table and, kneeling before the fireplace, set alight the letter and watched it burn to ashes.

Bartram's Book

PETER WALLACE

While Toby was getting the next round in, I glanced at the morning paper.

When he came back I greeted him with 'The bookies are complaining again. They say that each-way betting is ruining them.'

Captain Toby Bartram, lover of thoroughbred horses and underdone beef, smiled jovially. He sat down in his usual manner – controlled to half way and then hope the springs will stand it. 'They are always complaining, my boy. The Bahamas echo with their lament. But when did you last see a bookie on a bicycle?'

'True,' I said, 'but . . .'

Toby in full spate, steam-rollered over me. 'Done properly it is almost impossible not to make money as a bookmaker. I saw Mungo Raferty in town this afternoon.'

I blinked, but showed no other reaction. There is a technique for dealing with Toby when he makes this sort of remark. Under no circumstances do you say, 'Who is Mungo Raferty?'

'Where did you meet him?'

'I said I saw him. Great difference. We don't meet; we don't talk.'

'You quarrelled?'

'A blazer! All over the Derby: the year Kilcreggan won it.'

I did a rapid spot of calculation. 'But you were only about sixteen the year Kilcreggan won the Derby!'

'Yes, Mungo and I were at school together and we shared a study. Same interests, you know: his father had six horses in training, good ones, too.'

'Boyhood chums!' I said, sentimentally.

Toby took a sip and smiled sardonically. 'When the Derby drew near, Mungo and I agreed to run the sweep – on one condition.

'The prefects hadn't got time to do it themselves and it was usually run by a couple of fellows in the fifth. Mungo and I were the obvious choice. I laid down the conditions myself. *Tom Brown* gave me the idea. You ever read it?'

I admitted that I had.

'Yes, well, they ran a sweep in that and you can see just why I don't like them. Some junior draws the favourite while the ones who are really interested draw an outsider or a blank.

'So I said we wouldn't do a sweep but we would make a book, and that was what we did. Heavens, it was fun!'

Toby sighed reminiscently, and I caught the waiter's eye. As our glasses were refilled he went on, 'Pretty near the whole senior school got involved. We had our odds chalked up on a board in my study and we changed the odds as the money came in.

'Most of the info came from the papers and so our odds were on a par with the big fellows, but I remember that a lad called Alan de Villiers had a private tip for Coleraine and we had it backed down to four to one while the papers still had it at a hundred to eight.

'Everyone in the place had a bet on with us except Percy Farmer, and he was only out of it because he was broke. He was mad keen and had worked out the form by a patent system of his own which is maybe why he was broke.

'He had decided that Logroller would win and used to come in and stare at the board until his specs misted up.

'Logroller was at fifty to one and steady, nobody fancied it at all. Then he'd ask if he could bet on credit. We didn't allow that, of course, so he'd go away until the next day.

'I've never known anyone so convinced that he'd got the winner. But everyone had their half-crowns or quid on with us – our assistant housemaster even stopped me in the passage and asked what odds on Coleraine but when I told him he grinned and said he'd put it on outside.

'The night before the race Mungo and I went through our books for the final check. It was a perfect operation. If Kilcreggan, the favourite won, we would make £2 each. If one of the outsiders won we could clear anything up to the full £44 in the kitty. Our only loser was Coleraine but even there we stood to lose a mere 30 bob.

'I slept well that night. What an operation! An assured profit. Marvellous! After breakfast I staggered over towards the school block and then I heard a shout behind me. Dashing towards me was Percy Farmer, waving what looked like a couple of pound notes.

'Now, two quid on Logroller would muck the whole book up, so I dodged. We were in different forms so there was no problem there, but I had to go into lunch late and get out early, and I couldn't go near my study.

'In the end I holed up in the library and he didn't find me. Nobody came near the place and I listened to the race on the wireless in there. Kilcreggan won, of course.

'Then I went back to the study and Mungo and I paid out. I checked the tickets and he gave the cash. As the favourite had won there were plenty of successful punters! At last they'd all been paid off and Mungo and I divided up.

'I looked at my share – £3. "I thought it would be two each," I said, "Or did someone forget to collect?" "No," said Mungo. "There's an extra one each from Percy Farmer. I heard he'd been sent some cash and I managed to find him before the start."

'"Managed to find him? You mean you looked?"

'"Course I did. I knew he'd plonk it all on Logroller and it hadn't got an earthly."

'"But what if it had won? How would we have managed to pay him?"

'"No danger. It couldn't have won."

'So I told him that he hadn't got the brain of a pea and we started to fight.

'They separated us, of course, put us in different studies. We never spoke to each other the rest of our time at school.'

'Well!' I said. 'So that's Mungo Raferty! What does he do now?'

'Oh, he's in the City; stockbroker, I think.' A waspish gleam came to Toby's eye. 'I hope they check their books carefully.'

Dented Dignity

PETER WALLACE

'Don't be ridiculous, Toby,' I told him.

'I fail to see why the word "ridiculous" should be waved at me!' Captain Toby Bartram replied. 'No reason why I shouldn't have a canter in the Row.'

'The RSPCA would throw a fit!' I cried. '"Canter" indeed! The horse that could break into a trot with you aboard hasn't been foaled yet.'

'I don't understand your attitude.' Toby was getting plaintive. 'I know I'm the wrong side, slightly, of twenty stone. But a good weight carrier could . . .'

'Toby!' I interrupted, 'for years you've been saying that horses are not just mediums for having a bet. You claim you love them.

'Now, just because your doctor suggests that you are overweight, you propose to put some gee gee through the hoop.'

Toby carried on as if he hadn't heard me. 'It will be the first time I've ridden since '62. Far too long to be out of the saddle.'

''62,' I mused. 'I thought you settled for armchairs and a padded shooting stick in '58. So you've always led me to believe!'

'Well, I did retire from active participation in '58 but I had one last ride in '62. You were in France at the time; I never mentioned it, can't think why.'

His eyes gleamed in the direction of his empty glass.

When Toby tells me a story he thinks I may use, I am duty

bound to keep the drink coming. Heaven help me the day he feels a novel coming on!

When the barman had done the necessary and we were settled in our seats . . . 'What did you get up to while I was in France, Toby?'

'Well, Robby Valence had a big grey gelding that never made the grade at "chasing" . . .'

'I remember, Jugears!'

'That's right. He gave me the brute as a present and I sent it to Jack Nichols' stable up in East Hopshire. Jack hunted him with the local hunt and lent him to friends for exercise . . .'

'Them or Jugears?'

'Both. I went up to stay a few days and see the local hunt's point to point. Jugears was entered – to be ridden by Porky Middern. Very old friend of mine, Porky, almost as big as I am but nowhere near as heavy. I have very heavy bones, you know.'

'I doubt if an X-ray could penetrate that far,' I said, staring at his waistcoat.

He went on hurriedly, 'Well, they were starting a book at the local and Jugears was ten to one on the ante-post list.

'I wasn't too flush but I raked up fifteen quid and plonked that on. I couldn't let Jugears go unbacked.'

'What was the opposition like?'

'Five of them. Nothing special. The East Hopshire was a "wear and know" hunt.'

'Eh?'

'Well, hunts are divided into two categories – the "what you ride, and how you go" are the real working hunts.'

'What are the others?'

'"What you wear and who you know" – social clubs really.'

'Oh.'

'Yes, well, the East Hopshire wasn't noted for hard riding.

'I reckoned a big brute like Jugears was worth a flutter.'

'What happened to the odds?'

'Very good point, Peter. Nothing! I put my £15 on at ten to one and next day the price was still ten to one. The day before the race I scraped up another tenner and that morning I put it on as well.

By evening when I went down to the local to check the price was still ten to one.'

'You'd have thought your money would shorten the price at bit!'

'You would indeed! I knew at once what had happened.'

'Tell all!'

'Lord Queensberry had the same trouble once. He poured money on a horse, the price never shifted. The bookies took all his bets without wincing.

'They knew that the jockey had agreed to lose the race!

'On that occasion Lord Q. waited till they were in the paddock and then took off his coat to show he had his racing silks on under it. "I'll ride it myself," he said. The bookies ran to put the price down to evens but it was too late. Q. won in a canter and the bookies weren't half sick!'

'Toby! You didn't?'

He smirked. 'Yes, I did.

'After breakfast I dashed up to "get my shooting stick" I told 'em, and put my silks on. Then I put my overcoat on and joined Jack Nichols' party. Blistering hot day. I was baking in that coat but I couldn't remove it.

'Still I had a word with the stewards before the race and then came to where Porky was getting ready to mount.

'Just like old Q. I said, "I think I'll ride it myself, Porky!" He stood there and gaped.

'Then the announcement came over the loudhailer that Jugears was to be ridden by the owner and not by Sir George Middern. Jack Nichols came flying back from the ring with his mouth open.

'"This true, Toby?" he demanded.

'"Yes," I said. "Has it affected the price?"

'At this point I turned to Porky and said "I'll see you after I've won, miscreant!" and punched him on the nose. Then I climbed aboard and off to the start.'

'What happened in the race?'

'I won all right. Not without some difficulties. There were jumps, you see, where every other horse wasted time going up in the air. Jugears took the lot by the roots.'

'Couldn't you control him?'

'I lost my whip at the first – my stirrups at the second, and the reins at the third. I spent the rest of the race clutching his neck and watching the ground flying by under my nose.

'I fell off some three yards past the winning post. It was the biggest laugh they had enjoyed in East Hopshire since Clive climbed the church tower. Did you ever hear what local legend says he left flying from the weathervane?'

'Don't change the subject! What did Jack Nichols and George Middern say?'

Toby blushed. 'I was the hero of the hour. George forgave me, and Jack let me off Jugears' feed bills! They got their money on at starting price.'

'Eh? but wasn't that less than . . . ?'

'Everyone but me seemed to know what Jugears was like. When it was announced that Middern wasn't riding the price didn't half change. Thirty-three to one, I was! But my bets were still at ten to one!'

'Poor old Toby! Still, I can see why you never told me when I got back from France.'

'Well,' Toby admitted, 'I had a bashed bowler, a bruised bottom and one hell of a dent in my dignity!'

Pay Time

JOHN RENWICK

V ic Gold stared at the phone, the clock, the phone again, and lit another cigarette.

The instrument was strangled immediately by Vic's eager sweeping hand, its mouthpiece caressed by nervous fingers.

'That you Gordon?' he snarled.

'No, it's Whistler's Mother.'

'Gordon?'

'Listen, I'm only saying it once. Problem Boy in the three-thirty. You got that.'

'I've got it,' Vic said, lips working feverishly. 'Gordon . . . you wouldn't happen to have . . .'

'No,' the other voice cut in abruptly, 'nothing.' There came a fervent sigh, and then, 'Will you ever learn?' Disgust heavy, like icing on a cake.

'It's just that my luck's such a bitch these days,' Vic tried to explain.

'Luck doesn't exist,' Gordon snapped. 'Only these calls of mine twice a year, and the fact that you're my brother. You been messing round the dog-tracks again?'

'Something like that, you see . . .'

'I don't want to hear about it. Sad stories cloud my glasses. Why you can't wait and act on my calls is beyond me!'

'I try to,' Vic said. 'But they're only now and then.'

'Have I ever let you down? Ever given a loser?'

'No.'

'Has Joan left you?'

'No.'

'You're lying through your teeth, but I don't want to be involved. How much cash've you got?'

'Six quid.'

'That's sad. This one's worth more than that, but then you're always at the wrong place at the wrong time – namely at the bottom of the ladder. One thing, Vic. You'll never get dizzy. Or rich.'

'Gordon . . . if you could see your way, just this once!'

'I'm getting off this line before I burst into tears!'

'Gordon . . .'

' 'Bye Vic.'

A click, final and terrible, from afar. Dismissed. Like the flushing of a cistern. He saw a picture of Gordon leaving the booth at the racecourse to rejoin his gleaming wallet-upholstered friends for another round of cocktails . . . perhaps a quick chat about what the Stock Exchange had to offer on the morrow. Nothing serious. Just pleasant camaraderie until the first race.

Vic Gold shifted in his seat and rearranged the working of his mind to form a tattered shawl around himself.

There was this question of absent capital causing a draught.

He glanced at the open paper and was startled to see Problem Boy listed at odds of tens. Which was astonishing because Gordon's tips usually romped in at short odds. It suddenly became clear what his brother meant by saying the move was worth more than Vic's pittance.

Vic pitched his thoughts an octave higher.

Joan was good for some cash but getting it from her was like pulling teeth. And she had been known to keep eighty pounds or so hidden somewhere around the flat. His eyebrows clashed together as he sprang out of the chair.

To search the place systematically was out, because there wasn't time, and Joan was an erratic squirrel. He tried all the old favourites first; under carpets and linoleum, in sugar and flour tins, saucepans, coffee-pots, behind pictures.

Then he improvised. The letter cage, kids' room, pelmets, medicine cabinet, inside the vacuum and even the toilet cistern.

Nothing. The drawers were to be ignored because Joan couldn't think that way. One had to reason illogically or not at all. There was no prize for logic.

He ripped through the flat like a cyclone, the spur of the clock jabbing him on. Whimpers of frustration escaped from his lips as each wifely citadel fell barrenly before the onslaught.

The curtain of time fell bleakly, ever nearer, like a shroud.

Vic's head buzzed. There was this horse, you see, and the hairy-chested fact that it was going to win at tens, Gordon never failed. He had the real Midas touch to go with the name. Gold.

Joan's eighty at tens would top eight hundred quid!

Vic went into a last desperate frenzy that got him nowhere but on his knees in front of the fire. He was defeated, and knew it. With only one ploy left.

He put on his jacket, got a carrier bag and swept the radio into it. Gleaming and trendy, it was good for a tenner at least in the pawn.

In fact, Vic knew it was – he'd had it there twice before, with hell to pay as well as the pledge. Joan hated hocking almost as much as she hated gambling.

'Sign here, please,' the pawnbroker said.

'Now I'll be back within the hour,' Vic Gold said without looking up. 'Keep it in the bag exactly as it is – no messing about with the batteries or anything. Got to get it back on the dresser before my missus opens the door.'

'All right, Mr Gold,' the man said, as Vic pocketed the notes and left in a hurry.

There were ten minutes to spare when he reached the nearest bookmaker, and he was lucky to get on Problem Boy at eights. Five minutes later the horse was fours, and by the time it had won by five lengths it was a two-to-one favourite.

After deductions, he left the place over a hundred pounds richer and vaguely happy. He called back at the pawn, then took a taxi home. The radio was scarcely enthroned when a breathless Joan came through the door, making unerringly for the dresser.

He watched with interest as she pounced on the radio, took the back apart and held up a sheath of twenties.

'This lot had me worried, I don't mind telling you,' she said. 'Nearly two hundred of the best I've been putting by for the rainy day that's just arrived. Silly of me to be nervous really.'

'Joan,' Vic said, 'why is it you cannot trust me?'

Horses? I've found the Magic Formula

RAY KINROSS

I could have sworn that Jed Kitts was blind drunk when he won the two-thirty. In a photo finish it would have been his nose that got the verdict, not the horse's.

He was half over her ears by the time they passed the post. He wasn't much better in the winner's enclosure: slid off with a bump, made a mess of unsaddling, wobbled off to the weighing room.

'He looks a bit pooped,' said a woman beside me.

I could have suggested another word for it.

Jed was down to ride in the four o'clock, but he didn't show up. One of the apprentices took his place and did well to finish third. If Jed had been up, he'd have walked it.

He was that kind of jockey. Punters bet on him, not the horse. Five Derbies, two Arcs, a couple of Laurels and champion five times: he'd got the world on a short rein. Owners and trainers begged him to ride their mounts and every crowd was behind him the moment the stalls clattered open.

So what the hell was he doing knocking back a bottle of Scotch in the car park at four-thirty?

I didn't like the look of it at all.

I liked it even less two hours later when I walked into my local and found him buying drinks all round. Doubles too. He was perched up on a bar stool, cocky as if he was riding the last of a winning treble. But you could see straightaway from his eyes that he had a load of trouble under him.

The hangers-on made the most of it, did their best to drink him dry. I bided my time. Eventually the good cheer died, the wallet stopped flashing, there was just me and a jockey looking anything but champion.

I moved in quietly. 'What's the trouble?' I asked.

He looked up at me, boss-eyed with booze. 'She's left me,' he mumbled.

So that was it. He'd married Judy three years ago and she was as nice a little number as you could hope to see parading her talents on the stage.

The press made a big thing of it at the time. Unfortunately, Judy didn't know one end of a horse from the other – and that's not much good if you're married to a top jock, he won't be trotting home every night. It's ride at Salisbury on Friday afternoon, fly to Newcastle for the evening card. Stay overnight then down to Yarmouth – and maybe off to Paris on the Sunday. Either a woman understands that and lives racing, or it's no go.

And it was clear before very long that Judy wasn't the type to sit pretty at home day after day.

'That's rotten,' I agreed, eyeing his glass. 'But you're riding at York tomorrow, remember?'

'The hell with York!' he snapped. 'Barman!'

I sat there quietly and let him take his time. It all came out in the end – from the first quarrel. Soon it was hard to tell tears from whisky. I put him in my car and drove him home.

Still, it wasn't York that was bothering me, it was the June Cup meeting at Newmarket next Wednesday that I was beginning to sweat about.

Jed didn't make too much of a fool of himself at York but he didn't win either. There was a bit of talk about him being off form, but already funny rumours were creeping out of the weighing room, too.

I spent an uneasy weekend.

I saw him again on the Tuesday evening. He was back in the

pub buying doubles. The word was getting around town and there were a couple of real floozies there that I didn't like the look of.

'How about that ride tomorrow?' I asked when I got to his elbow.

'Worr ride, eh?'

'Axeman in the June Cup. A lot of money on you, Jed. A lot of hopes, too. Not going to let 'em down, are you?'

He straightened up. 'Think I can't ride, eh?' he challenged me. 'Who says I can't ride? Drunk or sober, I can ride 'em. Just like Charlie Marlow.'

'Come again?'

'Charlie Marlow. They say he was stoned when he got aboard the Flying Dutchman for that match with Voltiguer in . . . when was it . . . 1850? If he can do it, I can. I can win 'em all, mate!'

I daren't tell him that Marlow had gone under by half a length. Still I had my own plans for Jed.

I took him to my own place that night, let him sleep it off. But he wanted more booze in the morning. I went along with him, feeding him by the glass and not the bottle. When it was time to leave for the races, he was pretty high again.

Fortunately, his first ride was the big one – the three o'clock. All the time Jed was niggling at me to give him a snort. Why he couldn't go and get his own I didn't know, but I suspected that he daren't. I was his only source of supply – and it certainly made things easier for me.

He was still yapping when he came out of the weighing room. 'Come on, come on,' he snarled, 'Just one more won't hurt me.'

One more, I knew, could send him over the top.

'Here.' I uncorked a hip flask. 'Take a really good one from that.'

He drained it to the last drop. Somehow he still managed a bit of the old swagger into the paddock. I went and leaned against the rails and prayed.

Axeman seemed to know the way to the start, which was just as well, considering Jed's condition.

There's always this long, slightly breathless pause between their cantering down the course and being loaded into the stalls. This time it seemed even longer.

Finally, just as people were starting to look at their watches, the commentator announced, 'There's been a bit of a delay, it's Axeman, I think, Yes, Jed Kitts has dismounted.' There was a long pause.

'I'm not too certain if it's Kitts or the horse which is receiving attention ...' Everything went dead for two minutes. Then, suddenly, 'They're under starter's orders ... they're off!'

I suppose that in my heart I never doubted Jed. Whether he'd forgive me for what I'd done to him was another matter. But when he rode, white and shaky, into the winner's enclosure he managed a faint, watery smile. And that even included me.

'That Kitts,' said the fellow next to me. 'Dunno how he does it.'

'Brought Axeman through like a dose of salts, didn't he?' said his mate.

Cough mixture, actually. Because that was what I had given Jed a really healthy slug of, thinly disguised with Scotch, just before the race.

The stall loaders told me afterwards that they'd never seen a man so sick in their lives. But not so sick that he couldn't get back on his horse like the real pro he was and ride to win.

Axeman started at two to one. But I'd got seven to two a fortnight before, ante-post. When you're putting on a cool thousand there's a bit of difference between those two figures when collecting from your bookie.

And you think a professional gambler doesn't work for a living?

A Very Simple Job

PETER WALSH

'What we lacked,' snarled Matrellis, 'is simplicity. We've always been too complicated.'

He hammered on the desk to emphasize his words.

'I don't get you, boss,' groaned Jersey. Jersey is solid ivory from the eyebrows up.

'Listen here, boneheads,' he pointed the large cigar, unlit of course, at the three of us. 'If you could have planned one decent job over the last twelve months I could have afforded to buy a cigar I could smoke instead of these two-penny bangers!'

Dudley Corner and I looked at each other. One of us had to ask. Dudley saw I wasn't going to and so he did the necessary. 'You got something in mind, boss?'

'Yes, Dudley,' answered Matrellis. 'Not only do I have a mind, which puts me one up on you and Peter. But I have got something in it, which makes me two up.'

'Point taken,' I said, 'but what is it you want us to do?'

'I shall be coming with you on this job . . .' he began. Dudley and I nearly fell off our chairs. Mr Matrellis never actually comes with us; he always stays at home.

'. . . You see,' Matrellis went on, 'I feel that this job is absolutely foolproof, so I shall be quite safe on it. On the other hand, you three have blown so many cast-iron jobs that I want to be around to see how you manage to mess this one up.'

'Aw, boss . . .' Jersey began.

'Shut your cauliflower face!' ordered Matrellis, trying desperately to sound like Humphrey Bogart.

'I shall now explain the job so that a child of five could understand it. If you concentrate you lot might even get it.'

Jersey looked baffled. 'Concentrate' was a word he knew vaguely.

Matrellis leaned forward. 'Throgmorton Smith retired to South America last month, one jump ahead of the Fraud Squad.

'Now the rumour is going around that to finance the getaway he sold a wad of shares at a bargain price to an old friend. Me.'

'I haven't heard that rumour,' objected Dudley.

Matrellis favoured him with an icy smile. 'I'm not talking about East End pubs. Several feelers have been extended from the octopus of crime and I have agreed to sell my holdings for two thousand quid.

'Big gangs are always on the look-out for genuine investments to stow their loot legally.'

I was puzzled. 'Throgmorton Smith wasn't all that friendly. How come he flogged you those shares?'

Matrellis beamed at me. 'He didn't. Slush Moran has been up for three nights printing me some forgeries. But when I sell them to the Stokesay gang I shall be in the clear; they'll blame Throgmorton and not me!'

Dudley grinned. 'They'll take the money back!'

'No they won't. This is the story. I owed the Mafia two grand. I had it saved up when Throgmorton needed help. I gave him the money for the shares. Now I turn up with a lawyer,' pointing at me, 'a bodyguard,' pointing at Jersey, 'and a member of the Mafia,' Dudley's turn.

'They'll never dare try to get the money back from Cosa Nostra.'

'Brilliant, boss!' cried Dudley.

'Superb!' I echoed.

Matrellis preened himself.

'You call that simple?' asked Jersey, wistfully. 'It's too hard for me!' He brightened. 'But I heard the words "two thousand pounds"!'

'You did indeed,' beamed Matrellis, 'and it's money for old rope.'

Two days later we arrived at Paddington Station where the switch was to take place. Matrellis was his usual self; I was spruce with a bowler, black pinstripe and briefcase; Dudley had a false moustache, dark glasses and an Italian accent.

Jersey was large and muscle-bulging. As we came into the station we lost Jersey for a moment but he soon caught us up smiling. 'Sorry, boss; just saw Simon Sopwith, I haven't seen him for ages. Had to have a word . . .'

'We're on a job!' snarled Matrellis. 'Save your social life till later.'

Then we saw the Stokesay gang's messengers and introductions were made. The station was crowded but the commuters were so concerned with their trains that we could have been wearing stocking masks and robbing the bookstall and nobody would have noticed.

The Stokesay boys checked the impressive scrip which Slush had prepared for us. Matrellis checked the bulging envelope and agreed that there were two hundred tenners. Goodbyes were said and off we went. The whole operation took less than ten minutes.

'Right,' said Matrellis. 'Off you go, Dudley. Change in the gents and become your normal self.'

Dudley slipped away. Matrellis carefully printed his name and address on the envelope and put some stamps on it. Then he dropped it into a nearby letter box.

'That's that!' he said. 'Two or three days from now the postman will deliver us a nice little nest egg!'

'I have to admit,' said I, 'that this has been the smoothest operation I have ever been on!'

The letter did not arrive the next day. Nor the day after. In fact, a week later Matrellis called us in to discuss whether we should write to the GPO and complain.

While we were waiting to see Matrellis, Dudley and I made conversation with Jersey.

'Seen your pal Sopwith lately?'

'No,' said Jersey. 'I heard a rumour that he'd had a good touch and had gone to Spain to spend it.'

'What was his line?' I enquired.

'Oh, dead easy.' Jersey grinned. 'That was why he got the nickname "Simple" – it was so simple.

'He makes a fake letter box and puts it up somewhere. Then he clears it – wears a false uniform. Anything worthless he posts, but anything worth having he . . . What's the matter?'

Dudley and I were staring, mouths wide open. 'You saw him on Paddington?' I cried.

'And he's "had a good touch"?' Dudley quoted.

'Yes. Why?' Jersey was baffled.

Dudley and I looked at each other and nodded. 'We won't wait for Matrellis,' said Dudley 'you just tell him about Simple Simon.'

'I don't get it!' Jersey was still puzzled.

That was a fortnight ago. The postman hasn't been. Matrellis has another ulcer coming on and 'Simple' Simon must be on the way to becoming the Suntan Kid.

Wolf at the Door

—

PETER WALSH

Jersey, Bonger, 'Lord George' and I are the present Matrellis gang.

The others have been caught on other jobs and are all doing time.

Matrellis' wife runs the café, Tonio's, and we are guaranteed at least one good feed a week. This is one of the things that keeps us loyal to our boss; the other is his ulcer.

We feel that Matrellis always having Scotch and cigars when he would prefer milk and herbal ciggies is a primary cause of his ulcer.

He does try so hard to live up to the film version of a gang boss.

Matrellis was in fine form this particular evening. He chewed the end off his cigar and spat the pieces in the fireplace.

'Right,' he snarled in his Humphrey Bogart voice – the one that sounded like a querulous Stan Laurel. 'Let's get down to cases!'

Jersey looked worried. Perhaps he was remembering the hours we'd spent at Paddington in our bag-snatching days.

'Not those cases fool!' Matrellis had seen Jersey's 'bloodhound' look. 'I'm going to spell out our next job for you. It's so foolproof that I confidently expect us to make a bomb.'

'I'm having nothing to do with political assassination,' warned 'Lord George.' As soon as you heard his accent you knew where the nickname 'Lord' had come from.

'Not that sort of bomb. I mean money. Cash. Loot.'

Our eyes lit up. As full-time members of the Matrellis gang we had rather forgotten what real money looked like.

'I have it on good authority,' said Matrellis heavily, 'that "Spoons" Wilson is lifting the Casemount pearls tomorrow and selling them to Fencer King in the evening. We shall roll up as he is let in and take the pearls and the cash.'

'Pearls is poison!' warned Bonger.

'We won't keep them.' Matrellis was in high good humour and glad to show his cleverness by explaining, 'As soon as they offer the reward – which can't be less than £200 – we'll "find" them.'

'So we get £200?' I inquired.

'Plus the £2,000 which Fencer will have ready for "Spoons" Wilson.'

'Brilliant!' said Jersey.

Matrellis smirked his agreement.

'I suppose Fencer and Spoons won't object to parting with the pearls. Oh, no, not by any means! Not likely.' Lord George was heavily sarcastic.

'Look out of the window, twerp.'

We all looked. Outside there was a smart blue car with a flashing sign bolted on to the roof. 'Taxi' it proclaimed.

'One touch of a switch on the dashboard and that sign revolves a turn. "Police," it says. You'll be disguised as cops.

'Grab Spoons and Fencer with the loot, let Spoons wriggle away and give chase in the car. Forget Fencer. Peter will make you up so you'll not be recognized, can't miss.'

'What about you?' asked Bonger.

'I'll stay here in case you need bailing out.'

'Thought you said it was foolproof?'

'It is. But . . .' said Matrellis, 'I sometimes think my gang is composed of specially selected morons.'

'It does sound workable!' agreed Lord George.

'So workable,' said Matrellis, 'that the restaurant has made a profit last year, and you lot have got your annual bonus.'

'Eh?'

'I think of everything. You're gonna have money to burn. We

don't want to have awkward questions about where did you get it. I've faked the restaurant's books to account for it.'

'You think of everything, boss,' said Jersey; and certainly we all felt that the nail was truly hit on the head.

Next evening we were waiting in Ballard Street. 'Taxi' the sign proclaimed over our heads. I had made the lads up a treat. Their own mothers would have screamed 'Copper' at the sight of them.

Spoons Wilson slinked down the road and stood nervously clutching a brown paper parcel on Fencer's doorstep.

As the door opened we drew up. A quick dab on the switch and we piled out. Lord George had the speaking part. 'I warn you, oh the usual, Fencer, you know the drill. Take the evidence from him, Sergeant.'

I took about £2,000 of 'evidence' off him.

'Constable, Spoons seems to have a little something for us – relieve him of the weight, will you?'

As Bonger did so, he added, 'We'll give you a receipt at the station. Now, if you'll come with us to the car . . .'

That was the only hitch in the proceedings. As we turned to the car we saw the sign. Half of it had jammed and we were showing a large flashing 'POLAXI'.

As we gaped Spoons took his chance and made off like the wind. We leapt into the car. 'After him, Sergeant!' And off we shot, leaving Fencer gaping on the pavement.

We got back to Matrellis in triumph.

He put the notes, a hundred tenners and two hundred fivers, all nicely worn, on the table in front of him.

'Er . . . sorry about this lads.' He was almost weeping, 'I have to deduct expenses.'

'Sure,' we all agreed.

'Fifty for Lennie for fixing the sign on the "taxi".'

'Okay.'

'Four-fifty for Mary King.'

'Fencer's sister?'

'That's how I got the inside info!'

'Okay.'

'Er.' He cleared his throat. 'This is the hard bit. I'm sorry, chaps. Just when you go and do a good job I have to muck it up.'

'Eh?'

'The cover story! I had the income tax people down today, it appears I now owe them £1,487.'

'Oh, no! But . . .'

'So we have £13 between us.' He gave us £2.60 each. We regarded it with horror. 'I shall leave London for a few weeks,' he went on, 'I am a broken man. Oh for such a thing to happen to me . . .'

We tiptoed out, respecting his grief.

That was last week. The full horror of the situation didn't hit me till this morning.

You will remember that Matrellis faked his café books to invent a profit that would explain the affluence we were all going to have.

Well he can't unfake them.

Which means that some horrible tax man has me down for some improbable amount I didn't get and haven't got and I am now about to be done for tax evasion.

After all, that's how they got Al Capone.

The Thing That Went Scratch in the Night

DANIEL FARSON

'Sure you'll be all right? We'll be back in the morning.'

His son sounded anxious, but so determined not to feel guilty that his tone was almost accusing. They were on holiday – the older man, his son and daughter-in-law – in a rented bungalow on some sand dunes near the sea.

It had not been a success. The weather had been oppressive; the nearest village was miles away; the young couple were bored. This was why they were driving to Plymouth that evening. The young man was restless with anticipation, but he lingered – 'Of course we could drive back tonight,' he said lamely. 'If you'd like us to. But it's a hell of a journey . . .'

'If you're going for God's sake go!' exclaimed his father impatiently. 'I'm fine, just tired by this damned humidity. I'll have my dinner and go to bed. There's a play I want to listen to on the radio.'

'Your plate's in the fridge,' said his daughter-in-law, as if she was speaking to a child, 'a nice cold chicken salad. Granta's bowl beside it.'

'Good,' he said, 'Granta will look after me, won't you?'

Recognizing her name, the gentle, light honey Labrador thumped her tail with pleasure on the floor.

'Now off you go and enjoy yourselves.'

He was relieved when the noise of their car vanished into the distance. It was a bad idea going on holiday together, always on top of each other. No wonder they wanted to escape. A hotel might have been better.

Next year he would stay at home and encourage them to wander off on their own somewhere. Trouble was, they felt responsible for him – helpless widower all on his own – and guilty. He sighed.

Ironic about the weather. Not the English summer drizzle they feared, but white and overcast and stifling, day after day, close to the sea, but airless.

He gave Granta her meal and went to his bedroom carrying the chicken salad and a glass of cool white wine. He undressed and stretched out on his bed, naked except for a sheet covering him.

Granta lay on top, beside him, panting from time to time for she found the heat insufferable too. The warmth of her body, folded against his own, was uncomfortable, but there she was, protecting him faithfully and he did not have the heart to shove her away.

He was absorbed in the play when he sensed, suddenly, that the dog was alert – tense. He listened in case there was someone outside, approaching the house. Nothing.

She jumped off the bed and bounded towards a far corner of the room, whining. Then she barked, a furious, warning bark of alarm.

'What is it?' he called out to her, but he could see nothing.

She leapt back on to the bed. He could feel her fear as he stroked her, the hairs stiff, the hackles risen. 'What is it?' She jumped off again. She barked. She howled.

It was such an agonized sound that it made him shiver.

'What is the matter with you?' And he *did* hear something, or at least he thought he did, a sort of . . . he had no idea what it could be and still he could see nothing.

In the next moment her howls ceased. She growled instead at the thing in the corner, preparing to attack whatever was there, or was not there.

Infected now by her own panic, anxious to calm her too, he got out of bed and grabbed his stick. A furious din as if she was fighting something – 'Stop it Granta!' he cried, 'there's nothing there.'

Pulling the dog aside, he hammered down blows on the invisible thing in the corner.

'There,' he said, soothingly, 'there was nothing there.'

She seemed reassured, at least she was quiet, but when they lay on the bed again he could feel the beating of her heart. Neither of them slept well that night.

When his son returned from Plymouth the next morning he started to tell him – 'We had an awful time. The restaurant we'd picked out was fully booked and . . .' but he was interrupted by his father who seemed strangely agitated.

He announced he was going home.

There was just enough time to drive him to the station. 'I know it's daft,' he said, in answer to their questions, 'but I think this hideous place is haunted, I wouldn't spend another night in that room for anything. Anyhow, it's too damned hot . . .'

He was ashamed to mention he had struck at something in the corner that wasn't there, but he told them about Granta – 'and at one moment I was sure I heard, well it's hard to describe, but it was like the noise of someone writing something in pencil, on wood . . .'

'A scratching?' suggested his son.

The young man and woman looked at each other, with private smiles. When they returned from the station they talked about 'Granta's ghost'.

'I suppose I'd better tidy his room,' she said later that evening. They would bring his luggage with them when they returned home. She took the sheets off the bed.

At first she didn't notice 'it' lying in the corner. Then she did.

'Oh!' she stepped back quickly, putting her hand to her mouth.

'Steve!' she called out shrilly, and ran out of the room.

'Good God!' he exclaimed when he saw the mangled shape in the corner. 'How did it get there?'

A gap in the floorboards explained that later. When he was certain the snake was dead he picked it up carefully in a newspaper and carried it out of the house and flung it into the grass of the sand dunes.

'Odd that,' he remarked as he poured himself a drink afterwards, 'but it looked as if it had been bitten *and* beaten to death. Could Granta have attacked it? I suppose dogs do attack snakes . . . yet it seems to have been hit by something too.'

He shook his head unable to understand it, and poured himself another Scotch.

'Should we tell him?'

'The old man? I don't think so, do you? Might have forgotten all about it, probably has by now, anyhow.'

That was true. At that moment the old man was back in his village looking forward to the welcome familiarity of his local pub. No 'things' lurked in corners there. As they waited to cross the road, Granta looked up at him expressing absolute sympathy.

She had defended him; he had defended her.

No cars in sight – so she led the blind man forward and they went into the pub together.

DANIEL FARSON *is a well-known journalist of noted environmental issues. A regular columnist for national newspapers, he is the author of a number of country associated books and animal related articles.*

A frequent broadcaster, his love of nature is at the heart of much of his writing.

Fat Cat

BRETT ROBERTS

The fat cat sat on the mat.

Correction; the fat cat sprawled on the spotless Wilton rug, warming his snow-white belly before the synthetic log-fire, stretching his well-groomed tabby limbs.

His name, absurdly, was Edward K. Pulvermacher, so called by Mr and Mrs Barry Harkup, 24 Dene Close, shortly after they had opened their front door to a wet, mewing kitten a year or two before and had taken it immediately to their childless bosoms.

Ed (for short) stirred in his dreams of poached mice on anchovy toast, awoke, arose, stretched both forelegs to an incredible length, meanwhile arching his elegant back.

Time for din-dins.

In a moment, he was in the kitchen, softly stropping his left flank, then his right, against the slim, nylon-clad ankles of Moira Harkup, who was half-way through preparing a *Gostolette di vitello alla Valdostama* for the evening meal.

The veal cutlets, half-stuffed with Fontina cheese and canned white truffles, had to wait while Moira minced Ed's fresh liver (it was Tuesday) and poured the top off a bottle of milk into a bowl simply inscribed 'His'.

Ed sat, curled his tail round his rump, and ate. You would think that a well-balanced fat cat, treated like the first-born son of a wealthy duke, would sit around and enjoy the luxury of life, twenty-four hours a day.

Not so. No sooner had the last shred of liver, the last whisker-drip of cream, disappeared into that delicate pink maw than Ed was at the kitchen door.

Moira looked at him, shaking her head sadly, 'Edward,' she said, 'aren't we doing enough for you? We give you a lovely home, haddock fillets, calves' liver, the top of the milk, my best brocade cushion to sleep on? What else, for heaven's sake?'

But Ed, as ever, had made his mind up. His schedule was immutable. 'Out!' he shouted over his shoulder. So out he went, as every evening after dinner, every morning after elevenses.

'Really!' said Moira, as Ed took off from the herb garden, scarcely touched the top of the six-foot fence, and disappeared with an insolent flick of his tail.

An hour or so later, the *Gostolette di vitello* settled comfortably within, Barry and Moira decided to go along to the nearest Classic to see a film.

But they never got there, because Barry wanted a quick half-pint first, because the film finished after closing time. They made a brief detour towards the Lame Duck, but again they never got there because half-way along a short, narrow road called Pickens Court (former artisan cottages converted, at enormous expense, to bijou town houses), Barry stopped dead, grabbed Moira by the upper arm, and shouted, 'Great heavens, Moira, look!'

Moira looked towards a window back-lit by the discreet, orange lighting of somebody's through lounge. On the ledge inside the window sat a fat cat, tabby with white under-carriage.

'Am I seeing things,' asked Barry, 'or is that Ed?'

'It is Ed,' said Moira, simply, but with feeling. 'It could only be Ed.'

By this time Barry had his thumb firmly on an illuminated bell-push, and melodious chimes were repeating themselves faintly but urgently within.

'But Barry,' said Moira anxiously, 'what are you going to say?'

'Leave it to me,' said Barry. 'We shall have to play this thing by ear.'

The door opened, but not widely, and a thin man in very casual gear raised his eyebrows at them.

'Sorry to bother you,' said Barry, 'but the cat in the window . . .'

'Not for sale,' said the thin man, bristling slightly.

'I should think not!' shouted Moira. 'It's our cat!'

'I beg your pardon,' said the thin man, bristling much more. 'That cat is Percy and he's definitely our cat . . . And,' he began to close the door firmly, 'I wish you a very good evening.'

It was Moira's foot that got in the doorway first, though Barry's was beaten only by a short toe-cap.

The thin man, being a civilized citizen and realizing that the matter was serious, invited them in.

In a few moments the thin man and his wife (who was not thin) had introduced themselves as Arthur and Ruth Hellingly, and in a few moments more the Hellinglys and the Harkups were standing in an awkward, perplexed group looking at Edward, alias Percy, who was unconcernedly cleaning up.

'I do assure you,' said Moira, 'that this is definitely Edward, our cat.'

She groped in her handbag and produced a dog-eared colour snap of a fat cat, 'Look – that heart-shaped white patch on his shoulder . . .'

Ruth Hellingly moved swiftly over to an Art Nouveau bureau.

She produced another, almost identical colour snap, showing the unmistakable heart-shaped white patch on the shoulder.

'Snap,' said Ruth triumphantly.

Crisis point. Clearly, Edward (or Percy) was leading a double life. 'We need,' said Arthur 'an independent referee. Somebody who can decide, impartially, whose cat this is.'

'Somebody like Mr Gorringe?' suggested his wife.

'Exactly,' said Arthur, and turned with an explanatory gesture to the Harkups. 'Mr Gorringe is a lawyer friend of ours. There will be no question of a fee. We know him well.'

'George Gorringe?' interrupted Barry. 'I know him, too – an excellent man. Judgement of Solomon and all that.'

'That sort of thing,' said Arthur. 'Might as well settle it now.' He reached for the telephone.

'Hello! That you, Gorringe? Hellingly here. Got a sort of legal problem we want to settle on the spot . . . No, no. Nothing really legal. Just a little domestic matter that will appeal to your basic interest in jurisprudence . . . Yes . . . And I'm just opening a couple of bottles of Pouilly-Fuissé . . . You'll come right away? Good!'

The first bottle was empty when George Gorringe rang the chimes and was admitted.

He joined the Harkups and the Hellinglys, standing round the hearth-rug, wine glasses in hand, at their feet a fat cat who was washing his nether fur with a long, pink tongue, his left leg hoisted skywards, so that he appeared to be playing a miniature cello.

Mr Gorringe looked at the cat, astonishment shining in his pale blue eyes. 'Fred!' he said. 'What the hell are you doing here?'

The Promise of Four Vital Blue Notes

HERBERT HARRIS

Ruth was brushing her long blonde hair at the mirror when the doorbell rang, and for a moment she sat frozen, fear in her dark-ringed eyes.

Going to the door, she called out in a trembling voice, 'Who is it?'

The answering voice called back, 'It's me – Mary.'

Relieved, Ruth opened the door to admit her neighbour from the flat opposite, a slim dark girl who contrasted strongly with Ruth's blonde hair and well-built figure.

'Haven't you still got the key to my door?' Ruth asked.

'Yes, love,' her friend said, 'but I only use it when you aren't here. Ruth, you're shaking. Has something happened?'

'No, just too many late nights I suppose.'

'Don't kid me, Ruth. I know what it is. Joe's been back, hasn't he?'

Ruth eyed her friend sharply, and Mary went on, 'He's out of gaol. He's been into the Red Lion. He doesn't remember *me*, but I remember *him* all right.'

'I was forgetting, you're barmaid at the Red Lion now!'

'He's hitting the bottle, Ruth, and that's when he's most dangerous.' She noticed Ruth's fingers shaking as she lit a cigarette. 'He's been pestering you for money again, hasn't he?'

The blonde turned away. Mary went on, 'You're my oldest friend, Ruth and I can't bear to see you terrified of that creep. How much did you give him?'

'Just the rent – twenty quid – all I had.

'He wanted another fifty to get somebody off his back, he said, then he'd let me alone.'

Ruth hasn't always been as low as this, Mary reflected. Once she'd been a bright intelligent girl. Then that charming ruthless no-good Joe had introduced her to that club.

From a first spell in gaol, Joe had emerged more vicious than ever. Yet somehow he maintained his strange hold over Ruth.

Mary looked at her watch. 'I've got to go now, Ruth. But try not to let him get you down. And don't worry about the rent money. I'll be back and I'll bring some money to help you out.'

Ruth's eyes filled with tears, and she gripped the barmaid's hand. 'Mary, I'll never forget how good you've been to me . . .'

Mary paused on her way out. 'If that rat so much as lays a finger on you, Ruth, I'll pay him out – I promise!'

When she'd done some shopping Mary returned to her own flat and from her dressing-table took out her National Savings book. It showed fifty pounds deposit.

With an hour still to spare before she went on duty at the Red Lion, she went to the nearest Post Office and withdrew twenty pounds. Then she headed for Ruth's flat.

When she had mounted the first flight of stairs she heard a door bang and looked up.

She caught a glimpse of the back of a man's head – curly black hair, grown thick at the nape – and heard the sound of feet descending in a hurry.

The caretaker's walk-in broom cupboard was at her elbow and the door ajar. She stepped inside and pulled the door to.

The hurrying feet came closer. Through the gap left by the partly open door she saw Joe dash past, panting.

She stood for a moment till he was out of the building then, sick with fear, she ran upstairs, scrabbling in her handbag for the key to Ruth's flat.

Her heart pounded as she opened the door.

Ruth lay behind an armchair, her body making a half-crescent as if she had curled up to go to sleep. The once attractive mouth was open, now taut and ugly in a kind of snarl.

There were purple-yellow bruises on her neck and her eyes stared lifelessly at the wall.

Mary's grief was huge and uncontrollable, but tears refused to come – perhaps because sorrow was competing with hate for the man who had done this.

And Joe would feel he was safe, wouldn't he? Nobody had seen him kill Ruth, and of course Ruth had mixed with other men at the club. They would have to *prove* that he did it . . .

As she dropped the key into her bag, she saw the money she had brought – the four five-pound notes. She took them out and stared at them. No use to her friend now, or were they . . . ?

Mary pushed the Scotch across the counter of the Red Lion. She took Joe Zolla's one-pound note and stood with her back to him as she hesitated over the till.

'That fiver you gave me is torn,' she told him.

'No, love, I gave you a p – ' he pulled himself up short, beaming. 'Wait a bit. I'm going round the bend. It *was* a fiver I gave you, now I come to think . . . it's torn, you say?'

'Yeah. One corner torn off. Still, there's a number in the other corner, so I suppose it's okay.'

'Sure it's okay,' he said. 'Banks are used to damaged notes.'

'I'd better ask the boss all the same. Fussy type,' Mary said. 'He's just out the back. Only be a tick.'

Joe smiled. Tender a quid and the silly bitch gives you change for a fiver! Oh well, every little helps . . .

In a room behind, Mary phoned the police.

HERBERT HARRIS *first contributed a story to the* Evening News *in 1951, and by 1978 his century of stories was logged up in the paper.*

His phenomenal output of short fiction earned him a place in the Guinness Book of Records in 1978, with over three thousand five hundred stories published in thirty years.

His stories have been published in twenty-nine countries and sixteen languages. Hundreds have been broadcast.

A founder member of the Crime Writers' Association, he has edited more than twelve crime anthologies and is the author of a number of novels.

When Sisterly Love is at a Premium

G.M. KARHUNEN

The two elderly sisters faced each other across the supper table. Vera, the elder, sat stiffly, angular and arthritic. Mollie, the younger, gazed mildly through her thick-lensed spectacles at the empty space in front of her.

She addressed her sister diffidently: 'Vera, d'you think I might have a little more?'

Vera sat upright, her eyebrows arching before she even opened her lips. 'No, you might not! For two reasons. Firstly, because there isn't any more. And, secondly, because I think you're becoming greedy!'

'Greedy!' said Mollie with spirit. 'I'm not greedy, I'm hungry . . . just plain hungry. You never give me enough to eat.'

Vera pursed her lips. 'Do you think our pensions are elastic?'

'Oh Vera, if only you'd let *me* do the shopping sometimes,' said Mollie, 'I might manage to . . .'

'That would be a fine thing,' snapped Vera. 'You'd be spending all the money on luxuries and there'd be nothing left for necessities.

'Don't forget . . . we've got to be prepared for a rainy day and . . . there are always the funeral expenses.'

Mollie sighed. Not long ago she had suggested they might have a colour television, but Vera had vetoed the suggestion on the spot. Mollie sometimes wished she could have her pension all to herself and go and live somewhere else.

She rose to clear away the supper things. 'I think you're just mean, Vera, mean, mean, *MEAN*! I'll finish clearing later. I'm sick of it all.' She left the dining-room and shut herself up in her bedroom.

Vera still sat at the table, looking grim. There was a knock on the garden door and Mr Brown came in. Mr Brown was their next-door neighbour and he helped the sisters with the gardening.

'Good evening, Miss Vera. Just to let you know I've cleared all the weeds from the left-hand border. I'll start on the rest tomorrow. Where's Miss Mollie?'

'My sister is in her room at the moment. She has a headache . . .'

Mr Brown scratched his head. 'Well, you know, I think, she's got a bit thinner of late.'

'I'm quite sure my sister is not thinner, Mr Brown. I'll not ask you to stay for coffee this evening, it's not convenient.'

'All right, if you say so. See you again. Goodbye.'

Mollie reappeared. She completed clearing the crockery, apparently her usual self again, but she turned and addressed her sister quietly. 'You know, Vera, I'm seventy-five now and you're older. Haven't we had all our rainy days? We need a bit of sunshine now. As for the other, well, we both have our money put aside for that.'

'Let us not discuss the subject any further!' said Vera. 'I object to being called "mean" when I spend hours working out how best to manage our money . . .'

During the week that followed, there was little communication between them. They didn't even exchange details of their personal mail as they usually did.

It was shortly after this that Vera began to notice the change in her sister.

Mollie no longer got up early in the morning and there were days when she was still asleep at breakfast time. She had also taken to retiring to her bedroom every afternoon 'for a short rest', which had begun with an hour and was now nearer three hours.

When she did put in an appearance she seemed listless and not a little vague. Her appetite, especially for the sweet food she used to like so much seemed to have gone.

Vera was worried. She began to think that Mollie was going to be seriously ill and begged her to see the doctor.

One afternoon, when Mr Brown came in, Vera broached the subject. 'Mr Brown, I'm afraid my sister is heading for something serious. Could be a stroke . . . and she won't see a doctor.'

Mr Brown showed no surprise. 'Well, I can't say I've noticed anything very much, she just looks a little thinner.'

'Mollie's far from well.'

Mr Brown looked sympathetic. 'Perhaps she should have medical advice.'

The situation did not improve and one day Vera said, 'Mollie, there is something wrong with you and I'm going to call the doctor.'

Mollie turned on her sister. 'Well, if he comes, I shan't see him. I shall tell him to go to hell . . . and you too!'

Vera couldn't believe her ears. This Mollie was a stranger. Even her appearance had altered. Her hair was in disarray and her clothes were untidy.

The climax came. Vera had been trying to carry on with some of the work Mollie was neglecting. She'd been vacuum-cleaning the whole house that day and done a wash in the washing machine.

When Mollie did come down she stood in the doorway in her dressing gown. Her hair hadn't been touched, her face was flushed and her eyes looked strange.

Vera was angry. 'What do you mean, Mollie, appearing like that at four o'clock? You're becoming a disgrace. Suppose anyone came in . . .'

Mollie answered in a slurred voice, 'I don't care who comes in . . . or who sees me.' She swayed a little. Her sister looked at her in horror. She said, 'Mollie, you're drunk! I do believe you're drunk!'

Mollie laughed. 'And what if I am? I like being drunk.' She came over and fell into a chair. 'You sit down too, Vera. I'm going to tell you something. I've been on a spending spree. D'you know that Continental food shop in the High Street. They sell the most gorgeous cheeses and pâté and cream gateaux! And I've become very fond of wine, too. It's added colour to my life.'

The older woman sat rigidly, pressing her hands on to the wooden arms of her chair.

Mollie continued, 'I've managed to do my own shopping – with a little help from Mr Brown.'

Vera began to breathe unevenly. Her lips refused to form words. She just managed to gasp, 'And where did you get the money?'

Mollie stood up and taking from her pocket a Post Office Savings book, waved it and said, 'I've spent the lot.'

Vera jerked out in horrified amazement, 'And . . . what . . . about . . . your burial expenses . . . ?'

Mollie sniggered. 'Well, that'll be your funeral, won't it. I won't be here to care!'

Vera stared helplessly. Her eyes became glassy, her face convulsed and her lips twisted. She made a series of staccato grunts, tried to rise, then slumped and fell to the floor.

Mollie rushed forward, sobered by dreadful fear. Her sister was staring beseechingly up at her. Mollie put a cushion under her head then ran to phone their neighbour. 'Oh Mr Brown . . . Mollie . . . can you come . . . something awful's happened to Vera . . . Yes, the doctor, I'm calling him now . . .'

Mollie knelt by her sister and took her hand; it was limp. The arched eyebrows and staring eyes gave an impression of pained surprise. There was a tap at the side door and Mr Brown came in. He looked at Vera for a moment then said, 'Oh dear, this is bad.'

Mollie turned to him. 'I'll never forgive myself, Mr Brown. I should have told her when I won five hundred pounds on the Premium Bonds and put it into my Post Office book.'

Feeding Their Every Need

SUSAN MUIR

You could always recognize them. They came from the Primrose Parlour with a furtive air, obviously burdened.

Guilt burdened them, as patently as the excessive flesh with which they were encumbered.

If you were cruel, if your sense of humour had an acid edge to it, you could extract a good deal of amusement from the spectacle of those who were more than averagely visible, demonstrating so plainly a desire for invisibility.

Miss Leech, who liked to be known as Miss Primrose although her baptismal name was in fact Doris, prided herself on the purely benign quality of her own sense of humour.

Of course she was not cruel, not acid. Fun-loving she was, certainly, but she believed she was sympathetic and full of humanity – particularly overweight humanity.

She was also a good business woman.

The woman entering now was obviously One of Them. She was stout and upholstered in vertical stripes.

No doubt she had read somewhere that horizontal stripes were taboo for those in the Extra-O-S category.

But even vertical stripes with their undulations in critical places seemed an unfortunate choice.

They were unfortunate on aesthetic grounds, and also in the cause of inconspicuousness.

Unless, of course, they were seen as camouflage, bearing in mind the zebra or the tiger. The lives of the hunted, Miss Leech thought, observing the woman's scared expression without surprise and giving her a sweetly welcoming smile.

'Would you like this table?'

Tables in the Primrose Parlour were carefully placed; few stood starkly in the centre of the room. There were little alcoves and little screens which looked as if their innocent intention was to exclude draughts.

The aim was to give an impression of cosiness, of withdrawal, of privacy.

Miss Leech *was* a good business woman.

'Oh, thank you. Yes – yes, I think this will do.'

The woman ensconced herself, after many nervous glances about her. She was safe, wrapped by the kindness of Miss Leech, in an exquisite privacy.

The fat man in the corner – the man whom Miss Leech suspected of being Another of Them, although he had not so far descended to confidences – and the two fat women near the window, who had already come clean, not only to their dear Miss Primrose but also, obviously, to each other, could not see her.

She let out a large creaking sigh as she sat down, a sigh of relief and of tension subsiding.

'And what would you like? Tea? One of our Special Teas, perhaps?'

Miss Leech employed a waitress, a comely girl called Sandra but when they were not too busy, she preferred to attend to customers herself.

It made her feel benevolent, hostess-like; and to mingle with people taught her, she often said, a great deal about human nature.

She might just as well have said that it satisfied a natural inquisitiveness, since that was what she meant, but she did not allow even her thoughts to run so crudely, let alone her tongue.

Nor did she care for the word customer. She liked to regard them as guests. Only when her famous sense of humour was in its merriest mood did she refer to them as fugitives.

The striped lady's eyes were very expressive, very eloquent. The shadow of guilt was in them still, but they responded with a limpid look of yearning to the mention of Special Teas.

'Sandwiches,' Miss Leech murmured, making music of the word. 'Home-made scones, with cream and jam. And pastries. I think you'll like our pastries.'

It was a little song, an exquisitely moving little song. Her visitor was visibly moved.

'It sounds very nice,' she said faintly, the expressive eyes now half-closed in a sad sweet ecstasy.

Miss Leech transferred the order – the unuttered but obviously desired order – to Sandra, and lingered. They were confidential sometimes, sensing a sympathetic ear, longing to unburden themselves.

'Of course,' she said in a rallying but still gentle voice, 'we do little grills too. If you felt like anything more substantial. Sausages on toast, that sort of thing. Perhaps another time?'

She sounded, as indeed she was, confident that there would be another time. The Primrose Parlour was rather oddly sited if the intention was to attract the passer-by.

It was not on a main road, nor were there many local residents likely to form a regular clientele.

Its situation nevertheless had been carefully chosen. There were those who came, and came again. It was expensive, very expensive, but it gave value for money.

The sound emitted by the striped lady was more than a sigh, almost a groan. 'I shouldn't,' she whispered. 'I really shouldn't. You see . . .'

Miss Leech smiled encouragingly. She knew what was coming.

'You see, I'm at Thorncroft Hall. Taking the course there – Dr Mossop's course. Reducing. Well, naturally I *do* want to get my weight down – but really . . .'

'I know,' Miss Leech cooed. 'So drastic. I *do* understand. Lettuce . . . ?'

'And orange juice.' The voice had something like tears in it. 'I'm starving.'

'It costs the earth, and I'm starving. They encourage us to go for walks, and I couldn't resist it – so attractive, I suppose you think I'm *quite* dreadful?'

Miss Leech protested, she did not think her dreadful at all. It was only human. Nobody could be expected to starve – and a little something at teatime or for elevenses, couldn't do any harm.

The cure would take a little longer, that was all – and how much pleasanter it would be.

Sandra appeared, staggering under the weight of a Special Tea.

Miss Leech smilingly withdrew. She had every reason to smile, because the Primrose Parlour was doing very well.

When that evening she saw her friend and partner, Dr Mossop, she would have an excellent report to give of how their venture was succeeding.

Its success was a source of great satisfaction to them, because they were both good business people – and what, after all, is the harm in that?

A Modern Christmas Carol

MONICA DICKENS

Marley was dead, to begin with. That's the start of my great-grandfather's *Christmas Carol*, and I'm going to borrow it for mine, because I can't think of a better one.

Well, then, Marley was dead and his widow lived on in the ugly narrow house with the gargoyle door knocker. One of those houses that make you think as you pass, 'Ugh! I shouldn't like to live there.'

Three people did live with Mrs Marley, and they didn't like it at all. Two of them were children, for Mrs Marley augmented her income by acting as a foster-mother.

The word mother sat as incongruously on Mrs Marley as her Christian name of Evangeline. She was pinched and sour, with a bitten-in mouth and eyes which had more of the devil in them than of angel.

The third person who lived with Mrs Marley was not much more than a child, either. A girl of sixteen, with huge, despairing eyes in a washed-out face, and skinny legs and arms. You noticed Betty's legs and arms particularly, because her cheap overalls were shrunk above her knees.

She hardly ever had time to play with the children. Mostly Ronnie and Nell were alone in the cold, bare room at the top of the house, where they listened for the creak of Mrs Marley coming up the stairs to be cross about something.

And now it was Christmas Eve, and Mrs Marley was very cross indeed.

'No,' she was telling Betty, 'you may certainly not have tomorrow off. You may not take the children home to your mother's for dinner. You must be quite mad.'

'Well, it's just because it's Christmas Day, see.' Betty fiddled with a grubby apron, whose strings went twice round her where they would have gone only once round a more buxom waist. 'I thought it would be a Christmas treat for them, like, seeing as you've got nothing planned . . .'

'Christmas treat!' Mrs Marley had a way of repeating your words jeeringly. 'You know quite well I don't believe in Christmas, and I'm not going to have them brought up to all that superstitious nonsense. I had to smack Nell this morning for asking again about hanging up a stocking.'

Triumphantly, she clamped her mouth so tightly that you might have thought a chisel would be needed before she could speak again, but it flew open to revile a head of matted yellow hair which a small boy poked round the door.

'Please, mam,' said young Ronnie, 'there's a lady called at the door.'

A cheerful young voice called out from the hall, and a cheerful girl's face appeared in the doorway over Ronnie's head.

'Caught you this time, Auntie Eva!' cried the girl, undaunted by Mrs Marley's expression. 'You wouldn't come to my wedding, but you shall come to my Christmas party. All the family will be there.'

'Christmas party, indeed!' she snorted. 'Waste of money and food.'

'Do come,' wheedled Mrs Marley's niece. 'Do you good to get out and see a bit of life.'

'Thank you,' rasped Mrs Marley. 'I see as much of life as I want to. I don't like it, if you want to know.'

Mrs Marley was disturbed twice more that Christmas Eve. First by some waifs, who were scared into the next street by her shouts, and then by some nuns, collecting for an Old Folks' Party.

Mrs Marley was just reflecting that she'd scored off them all right by telling them that she paid income tax to the State to attend to Old Folks, when she heard scuffles outside the door and Nell was pushed in by her brother.

She wouldn't look up. 'Please, mam,' she whispered, 'couldn't we go with Betty tomorrow?' Then, with an inspiration, 'We'd be out of your way, like.'

Cunning little devil, thought Mrs Marley.

'They're having a party!' burst out Nell. 'They're going to have a tree – a real tree 'un – and a pudden and a duck what Betty's uncle gave 'em. Oh please, mam. There ain't going to be no fun 'ere.'

'Fun!' exploded Mrs Marley, 'when you should be on your knees thanking me for food and clothes and shelter. Get up to bed, and if I hear any more about tomorrow, I'll smack you both – hard.'

When Ronnie and Nell had gone sobbing up to their room, Mrs Marley put the cat out and glared up the street towards the glow and noise where the cinema and dance hall were.

Merry Christmas – bah! Was there no escaping it? As she turned to go indoors, Mrs Marley suddenly thought that the gargoyle on the door knocker looked like her late husband which showed what an upset state she was in. Even Jake had not been quite as ugly as that.

She went back to the parlour – and there was Mr Marley, looking just as he had in life; and really, there was not much to choose between him and the gargoyle.

He didn't look dead. He still wore his sagging grey cardigan and his knitted tie.

He didn't sound dead either. He began at once to grumble at her, just as he used to, 'Well here's a nice mess you've got yourself into.'

'What do you mean, Jacob? I get along all right. I've done better than you, anyway. At least I'm still alive.'

'That's what you think,' said the ghost, as rude as ever. 'But you're not, any more than I ever was – God pity me. You're dead to the world, that's what it is; locked away from humanity in a coffin of your own making. And when you die, you'll have to pay for it, same as I'm paying now.'

'Are you in Hell then, Jacob?' asked Mrs Marley.

'Torment and unrest!' he groaned. 'If you only knew! Don't you see, woman, that if your spirit never goes out in Christian kindness to anyone while you're alive, after you die it has to wander, wander, goaded from place to place by remorse that comes too late.'

'You're to have one last chance,' he told her, in a voice that was scarcely more than a sigh. 'Spirits will come to you tonight. Learn from them, oh, Evangeline, learn, before it is too late!'

And then he was gone and there was only the brown dado, and a nasty chill in the air.

To prove to herself that she was shivering from cold and not from fright, Mrs Marley blustered her way up to bed. 'Spirits come to me, indeed! I wish they would. Fat lot of chance, with gin the price it is.'

When she opened the bedroom door, her equilibrium was completely restored because she thought she had caught Nell red-handed.

But when the figure standing by her bed turned, she saw that was no human child but a creature half little girl and half old woman, with a wrinkled face under soft, fair curls, and gnarled hands coming from the sleeves of an old-fashioned pinafore.

'I'm the spirit of Christmas Past,' said the child – or was it an old crone? 'Come with me.'

And now Mrs Marley knew it must be a dream, because suddenly it was daylight, and they were walking down a country road that she remembered.

Good Heavens – there was her old schoolhouse! Mrs Marley looked in, and saw, sitting at a desk, with long, thin legs twined round the chair leg – herself!

Herself at ten years old, with all the hope of the future in her face. She was looking, not at her books, but up towards the ceiling, where there flew and hovered all the romantic dreams and fancies that every child knows and too quickly forgets. Then she got up and went out eagerly, and Mrs Marley knew that she was going home, and that there was a treat for dinner.

For one sickening, heart-breaking moment, Mrs Marley wished desperately that she were a child again.

She turned away, and found herself back in her own parlour in the ugly, narrow house. But it wasn't her parlour as she had ever seen it.

Who had dared put up all that holly and coloured paper? Who had piled coal on the fire in that extravagant way? Where had all that food and drink come from? Someone, thought Mrs Marley, tight-lipped, had been playing about. Was it this stranger, lolling in her armchair in the ridiculous red flannel and cotton wool costume of a toy-fair Santa Claus?

Before she could challenge him he had shouted that he was the spirit of Christmas Present, and with a roar of most unseemly laughter, had whisked her into the crowded street.

She ducked into a shop and came out with a toy motor boat and a vast yellow teddy bear.

Then she found herself, first at her niece's Christmas party, where she blushed to see someone doing a comic of 'Old Aunt Eva'. Then looking in at a house rather run down, where Betty's family were having their Christmas dinner.

The floor and walls were mouldering with damp. A tin bath in one corner caught the ceiling drips. Two of the chairs were wooden boxes, and Betty's youngest brother lay coughing before the meagre fire in a packing-case cradle.

And Betty and Ronnie and Nell were there, tucking into duck and sprouts and roast potatoes, with a light in their eyes which Mrs Marley had never seen.

'Wasn't it kind of the old girl to let the kids come?' Betty was saying.

'Kind?' said Betty's mother, scarlet and shining, after taking the cloth off the steaming pudding. 'If that old devil's kind, I'm the Angel Gabriel.'

'My dear,' said the husband, mildly. 'The children! Christmas day.'

'Kissmas Day!' echoed the little ill child in the packing-case crib.

'Ah, bless 'im,' they said, and shook their heads sadly as he started his choking cough again.

'That child will never live,' said Mrs Marley austerely, to disguise the fact that she cared whether he did or not.

'Not unless he's taken out of that house he won't,' said the ghost. 'Now look at this.' He brought before her two great-eyed little living skeletons, and their faces were the faces of starving children all over the world.

'Who's responsible for this?' cried Mrs Marley, who by now had become quite righteous.

'You,' said the spirit. 'You and the rest of mankind, whose ignorance, greed and indifference make suffering possible.' And vanished. Leaving Mrs Marley to face a hooded spectre, who showed her Christmas Yet to Come. A tombstone in a deserted churchyard and Evangeline Marley's name on it, and no one to cry for her, except those who cried with relief.

On Christmas morning Mrs Marley opened the door for the cat and saw the street transformed by a sparkling fancy dress of snow. Now that the buses were hushed you could hear the parish church bells more clearly, which was a good guide for Mrs Marley who had never been there before.

When she got back, behold her in the larder recklessly opening hoarded tins for her Christmas dinner, for she has asked Betty's whole family to save the duck and come here, and she means to press them to leave their damp ruin and settle into her basement flat.

And behold young Ronnie scudding up to the High Street to find a stall still selling holly and mistletoe, and Nell skidding round to the convent with a pound note for the Old Folks.

And, talking of parties, behold Mrs Marley that evening, dancing 'Knees Up Mother Brown', at her niece's house.

Everyone rejoiced at the change in her, although they couldn't explain it. Of course, they didn't know about the dream. But was it a dream? What about the toy motor boat and the vast yellow teddy bear found on the end of Nell and Ronnie's bed? How do you account for them ?

Last of the Lady's Wine

TERRY TAPP

'Are you ill?' she asked.

'What?'

'Ill. I asked if you were feeling not good. My English is . . .'

He looked up at her, creasing his face against the hot, midday sun. 'I'm all right,' he said as he attempted to get to his feet.

'Let me help you,' she said as she saw him lurch forward. 'My house is just over there. You must sit down in the shade.'

He didn't reply, content to allow himself to be steered across the dusty road into the cool, fragrant room. It was so quiet . . .

'Wine,' she said. 'you must have some of our wine.'

'I think not,' he replied with a wan smile. 'I have not eaten for two days.'

'I thought it is like that,' she said. 'Your face is whiter than the walls of my house. Sit there and rest while I get you something to eat.'

He sat back on the rough wooden chair, closed his eyes and breathed in the cool air. He was thirsty for air in that fierce heat.

'What is your name?' she asked as she sliced a knife through a fat loaf of bread.

'Thomas,' he told her, adding as an afterthought, 'Tom.'

'Well, Thomas,' she said firmly, 'you need food and you need it now otherwise I would take the time to cook you some spaghetti.'

He watched her slice the cheese and the sausage, his eyes hungrily fixed upon the plate.

When he had eaten the salt sausage and cheese and washed the delicious meal down with rough, bitter wine, he felt better.

'Thank you,' he said. 'That's all I can do . . . thank you.'

'It is enough,' she told him simply. 'Now speak about you. What are you doing in Italy? Why have you not eaten for two days?'

'Money. I have no money to buy food. All I have had to eat are a few peaches.'

'You have no money to return to England?' she asked.

'How did you know I was English?'

'English or German,' she said. 'I do not speak German so . . . you were English! But you haven't answered me. Have you no money to return to England?'

'I don't want to go back,' he said. 'I came here to get away from . . .'

Suddenly he appeared to be wrestling with his words, his tongue lying thick in his mouth. 'Must be the wine,' he grinned, 'I have never tasted wine like this.'

'It is very good wine,' she told him. 'Was it your work which made you leave England, or was it a woman?' She laughed at that, a loud, rasping laugh.

'Work,' he said. 'I left because no one would listen to me.'

'What work did you do?'

'Experiments mostly,' he said. 'Experiments with animals.'

She made a face, poured wine to hide her distaste, then pushed the glass over to him. 'Drink wine,' she said. 'No wonder you left your work. It is evil to experiment with animals.'

'Oh, no,' he laughed. 'You have the wrong idea entirely. I do not mistreat them. I study the behaviour of animals so that I may learn about human behaviour.'

'There is a connection?' she asked. 'Animals behave like humans?'

The wine warmed him and he took out a crumpled cigarette, his last one, lit it and inhaled the smoke. The wine was pulsing through his body and his stomach was now full. What better than to talk?

146

'I have found,' he said, 'that certain animals inherit the tendencies of the parents. It is a genetic thing, really.'

'But this we know!' she cried. 'You spend your life indoors, making your face so white, so that you can tell me this? Does not the son look like the father?'

'No, no,' he said impatiently. 'This isn't a question of looking alike. Nothing at all like that. What I am saying is that parents pass on much more than just appearance to their children.'

'Tell me about it,' she said once more filling the glass with the red wine. 'I still do not understand.'

'Beethoven,' he said. 'You have heard of Beethoven?'

'Certainly,' she laughed.

'And Hitler and Abraham Lincoln? Well, it seems probable, from the experiments I have made, that the genes of the parents are passed on to the child and those genes contain certain patterns of behaviour – of action.'

'Now you have flown away into the sky like a bird,' she said sorrowfully. 'I do not understand.'

'The squirrel,' he said, taking another gulp at the wine and leaning forward in his chair. 'The squirrel buries nuts using his forepaws and snout. So how does he know what to do?'

'He watches his parents,' she replied. 'He learns these things.'

'That is what everyone thought,' he cried. 'But I took a squirrel when it was very young and I kept it in a cage and fed it only with soft foods. A year later when I gave the squirrel his first nut, he knew precisely what to do with it. You know, he tried to bury it in his cage!'

'The knowledge was already there,' the woman said. 'Of course, I see it now.'

'So, after many more experiments I discovered that the human child is born with similar knowledge. He has the tendency towards music if his father was a composer. If he were the son of Hitler perhaps there would be the tendency towards tyranny.'

'And the sins of the fathers are . . .' she searched for the quotation, '. . . visited upon the children and their children's children.'

'Pardon?'

'It was nothing,' she told him with a sigh. 'Drink your wine.'

By now the wine had loosened his tongue as he sat on the chair feeling very relaxed and sleepy. 'Perhaps you are right,' he said. 'Maybe I should not have spent so long working upon my theories.'

'No,' she said, 'I do not think that now. I think, perhaps you have discovered an important thing. Tell me, do you think that evil is inherited also?'

'I would think so,' he replied, stifling a yawn as the wine swept lazily through his body.

'And would the children's children inherit the same traits?'

His eyes were almost closed as he replied. 'Yes, the children's children would inherit the same tendencies. Forgive me, I am so tired.'

'Sleep,' she said. 'I talk too much.'

'And I . . . I don't even know your name,' he said. His eyes closed tight as she replied.

'Maria,' she said bitterly. 'Maria Lucrezia Borgia.'

London Interlude

MICHAEL DAWES

The meeting over, Manuel rose.

'Then it is agreed. We speak with Don Carlos.' And the four men trudged up the hill to the hacienda.

Don Carlos, taking his ease on the cool of the verandah, rose courteously to greet the deputation. They seemed apprehensive. '*Buenas tardes amigos*. Everything all right, Manuel?'

'*Si, señor*,' but Don Carlos was unconvinced. He called for wine, a tongue-loosening vintage. When the goblets had been filled for the third time Manuel spoke.

'We face a difficulty, *señor*, and you are the only one in whom we dare confide – the only one indeed whose help we would seek.'

'You flatter me, Manuel.'

'You remember the recent illness which afflicted some of us in this district, *señor*?'

'Of course, Manuel, and happily you have all recovered.'

'*Si, señor*, except that it has impaired our capacity to father any children.'

'Although, fortunately,' Pedro intervened hastily, 'it has by no means impaired our ability to make love.'

'That at least is splendid news,' said Don Carlos. 'Your wives are lovely women. But how may I assist?'

'*Señor*, you must realize that all our honours are at stake.'

Don Carlos understood fully. In the village great store was set on virility and these men might well become objects of ridicule. Manuel continued. 'We have talked with our wives and we should all regard it as the highest honour if you would consent to be the father of their children.'

They watched Don Carlos furtively, keenly aware of his weakness for women and that, because of his position in the community, he would also be very discreet. Presently Don Carlos spoke.

'*Amigos*, yours is a terrible dilemma, but I can promise to do all I can to lift this burden from your shoulders.

'Next month, after the harvest, the village will not take it amiss if you and your wives were to visit relations.'

'Most people go away for a while then.'

'I myself am visiting London, and Maria, Juanita, Carmen and Dolores can be my guests. We sail from Bilbao where you will meet me with the ladies, and there you will remain until our return. By then everything should be in order.'

The voyage from Bilbao was devoid of ship-board romance. The weather frowned on the little steamer and everybody was relieved to escape from the gangway at Southampton.

But by the time the boat train arrived at Waterloo, Don Carlos and his little troupe were in the best of spirits.

Don Carlos had had the foresight to fit the girls out with elegant clothes from the best shop in Bilbao, where, for the first time in their lives, they also had their hair styled and hands manicured.

They all looked lovely, especially Carmen, with her beautiful Madonna profile. It was difficult to remember them in their peasant dresses.

Their Bayswater hotel, though not listed in any tourist guides, more than adequately fulfilled its purpose, and to the girls it was like a palace, even though they all shared one large room – with the exception of Don Carlos who had his own directly across the corridor.

Day followed day in a happy dream. When Don Carlos was attending to his wine business in the City, the girls were fortunate in being befriended by a shrewd, motherly, widowed lady, Mrs Clarke, whose fluency in Spanish dismantled the language barrier.

If she was suspicious that Don Carlos should have so many delightful sisters whose cultural attitude so clearly differed from his own, she was diplomatic enough not to mention it. She simply kept vigilant watch on the party.

As host and diplomat Don Carlos was magnificent. He showed no preferences and every evening he wined and dined each of his ladies prior to fulfilling the obligations bestowed upon him by their husbands.

But despite everything, at the end of the holiday some inner stirring in their blood made the girls yearn to be back home again with Pedro, Manuel, Roberto and Miguel, to the simple life which was all they really desired and understood.

On the final evening Don Carlos threw a dinner party for all of them including Mrs Clarke, and the girls all cried when they said goodbye.

The voyage back to Bilbao was a lot calmer and if Carmen felt sick her indisposition was unconnected with the weather.

After the mildness of the London summer the plains of Andalusia were overhot.

Don Carlos relaxed once more in the cool shade of his verandah and life was back to normal.

Everyone remarked on the sparkle and vivacity of Carmen, Maria, Juanita and Dolores. It was just as though they had returned from a honeymoon.

Manuel and his compadres could hardly wait to tell the world of their prospective fatherhood.

But sadly, after a few weeks, it materialized that it was only Carmen of the Madonna profile who would justify the gallant efforts of herself and the courtly and chivalrous hidalgo.

The pride and joy of Manuel at his piece of good fortune was, however, totally overshadowed by the bitter disappointment of the others who, understandably, could not bring themselves to speak to Don Carlos.

But, little by little, as everybody came to accept that Carmen alone had been blessed, the wounds of resentment gradually healed and first Pedro, then Miguel, and finally Roberto discovered some pretext which allowed them once more to take wine with Don Carlos, who, as they all agreed was really more to be pitied than blamed.

But happiest of all, when the baby was born, he was with unanimous approval given the name Carlos.

His reprieved namesake graciously consented to be godfather and after the christening an enormous reception, to which the whole village was invited, was held up at the hacienda. Much wine was enjoyed, and late into the night the verandah echoed to the twanging of guitars, stamping of heels, and clicking of castanets.

A year later Don Carlos sat by the river, his little 'godson' on his knee. Nearby, Carmen pounded the washing. They talked as they often did of their 'London Interlude'.

Carmen was saying, 'Mrs Clarke was such a kind lady, though she once did something I never properly understood.

'One night she handed me a box of tiny pellets saying that if we each took one every day we would be perfectly safe.

'Well, I was afraid to take any but the others weren't.'

With a shout of laughter Don Carlos threw his arms round Carmen and ran off to find Pedro, Miguel and Roberto.

The Evening News *gave its own awards in special short story competitions. Michael Dawes impressed the judges not only for the originality of the plot idea and for the gentle ironic treatment, but also for the effortless light touch which he brought to his writing. His story won a first prize in 1973.*

City Encounter

PHILIP SAGAR

From London Bridge to St Paul's and thence to Covent Garden is no great distance for a Londoner, even with the streets more crowded than usual for the time of year.

For a healthy young man from the West Country, fresh from the harvest, and with a deep tan and knotted forearms as evidence of his vitality, the walk should have taken no more than fifteen minutes or so.

For Jeth Tregowan, however, it took considerably longer to make his way to London's great marketplace.

The journey from Truro had been as tedious as they'd led him to expect; but now, surrounded for the first time by the bustle and excitement of England's capital city, he felt that the discomfort of the journey was a small price to pay.

After two days here he was gradually becoming accustomed to the noise, the sights and the crowds. Not that he minded the crowds; their colour and urgency served only to add to his feeling of well-being. So much so that he would have been truly surprised if he'd heard some of the acid comments which the odd London native made under his breath: 'More damned visitors.'

Covent Garden was something that he, as a countryman with knowledge of market produce, was keen to see. Amidst so much strangeness he looked forward to the familiarity of things within his experience. He was also interested in seeing for himself the evidence of rising food prices about which he had heard so much complaint.

From the Bridge, therefore, he crossed into Lower Thames Street, aiming to take in St Paul's on his way to Ludgate Hill.

Jeth first saw the girl as she turned towards him from the direction of the Royal Exchange.

It was only a fleeting glimpse, but the halo of auburn hair was in itself sufficient to excite his interest.

So far, he had steered clear of what London had to offer in the way of feminine attractions – not so much from lack of interest as from respect for the warning they had given him back home.

Her face (what little he had seen of it) seemed pleasant, and as he quickened his pace he had already made up his mind that this was a 'nice' girl from whom no danger of 'fleecing' need be feared, and of whom he would certainly not feel ashamed.

His exact method of approach was something of a problem. What was acceptable in Truro might not, he feared, go down well in sophisticated London. Before his worries had time to build up, however, he found himself beside her, blurting out, 'Good morning, and a fine one . . .'

The smile she flashed him cut off the end of his hardly memorable or original opening. She was in every respect all he had hoped for.

The red of her hair and the paleness of her skin combined to present a picture of such beauty that Jeth found himself, for the first time he could remember, robbed of speech.

Her open face and frank smile at his inability to find the right words presented such an image of vitality and joy in living that they had already reached and passed St Paul's before he became aware of their surroundings.

No matter, St Paul's could wait. This delicious smiling, happy – and above all friendly – creature filled the whole of his present moment.

London and all its sights could vanish forever so long as she remained with him.

During their walk she must have gleaned some knowledge of him, either from his country clothes and awkward air, or from his own words; though what precisely he told her he couldn't for the life of him remember.

Certainly she was now treating him as a visitor, describing the eating places, the theatres, the sights, even the Royal Family – all part of the London which she so clearly loved. No wonder London became more popular every year with visitors from the provinces and abroad.

As they walked, he felt that he had to find some way of continuing the relationship.

An outright offer of a drink or an invitation to a meal might be taken as presumptuous at this early stage, and besides, at London prices any rash extravagance might well play havoc with his carefully planned holiday budget.

Clearly, however, they would not be likely to continue to share the same route indefinitely, and he racked his brains to think of something better than a 'may I see you again?'

Before long St Paul's and Ludgate Hill were left behind and they were half-way along the Strand.

He found his decision made easier as she chose to turn with him away from the river and upwards towards Covent Garden. Perhaps their paths were not to separate so soon after all.

At the corner of Drury Lane his mind was made up. To hell with the expenses! This was the girl for him, he felt sure. To lose her now could be to lose her for good.

Surely an invitation to have a drink would be taken only in the spirit in which he gave it – in genuine friendship and in the hope of prolonging an acquaintanceship which – dared he hope? – was becoming attractive for her, too.

Her look of incredulous amusement at Jeth's invitation was like a slap in the face.

Her laugh, and the swirl of her dress as she turned away, turned his stomach to ice.

As she moved towards the tall dark man who, he now noticed, was clearly waiting for her outside the theatre, he realized that his feelings, dreams and hopes had all been built on no more than a simple West Countryman's romantic imagination.

To make matters worse, he saw her point him out to her companion, who turned and gave a sardonic smile in his direction.

Why? Surely he had not misjudged her? Surely even in that short walk she had felt something for him? Disconsolately, he turned into a tavern on the corner. Perhaps a drink might steady his whirling thoughts.

Stepping through the door, he was, to his surprise, greeted with guffaws and back-slappings.

A foaming tankard was pressed into his hand, but before his questions could be formed into words, they were answered by the landlord.

'Aha, my boy! I see Mistress Nell has been up to her tricks again. 'Tis a shame the way she leads on some of you young visitors! But 'tis just as well His Majesty was in a good mood!'

A Gentleman of the Road Smells Death

PAUL STUART

Beneath the last dying light of a cold autumn sunset Matthew Redford slowed his exhausted horse to a walk.

Wrapping his sodden cloak tightly around his shoulders he tugged the brim of his hat down to shield his eyes and attempted to ignore the stabbing ferocity of the pain which was setting his right knee on fire.

He knew the ball was still embedded deep in the wound and that he alone would have to make the effort to remove it if he was to have any chance at all of evading capture.

The long leather boot soaked in blood was helping to keep his foot in the stirrup but each movement of his horse jarred the shattered knee, sending fresh spasms of pain throughout his entire body.

Spattering rain stung his lean pitted face, a face reflecting a cruel nature with little feeling. But he could still bring himself to extend a chilled hand along the animal's neck, lean forward and whisper in its ear. 'My beauty, you have earned your rest.'

Matthew slid from the saddle, collapsing into the rank heath grass. The horse ambled to a dark peaty stream, there to drop its head and drink.

Matthew's eyes burned like coals; his head was an aching,

beating anvil. But survival against all odds was his stock in trade and, with a tenacity fuelled by cunning, he dragged himself to the support of a lichen-stained rock, unhooked his cloak, rummaged in his bulging pockets and found the blade.

A knotted kerchief gripped between his yellow teeth was the only pain-relieving ruse that he could think of, but it was barely enough as the probing steel grated on the flattened lead ball.

Three times he probed, his face a watery grey mask as sweat and rain combined to pour from his forehead in rivulets down the hollow of his throat.

His head swam in delirium, but there in his hand lay that which had undone his plans. He threw it from him, cursing the woman whose aim, lucky or otherwise had brought him to the brink of death.

The robbery had followed the classic pattern. In gathering darkness the tiring team of horses had slowly breasted the rise of Ridgeway Hill. Matthew, riding through the quagmire of mud and filth which constituted the highway, had come up from behind to avoid presenting his silhouette against the still-light horizon.

No one had given trouble, least of all the guards. Seven passengers had stepped gingerly from the coach attempting to avoid soiling their fine silks.

Matthew did not dismount; he preferred each person to come to him. It had been a rich haul – they were all passengers of quality.

He beckoned the last of the seven to come towards him. She was extremely old and finely dressed and had fixed him from the beginning with a steady gaze from eyes which had made Matthew uneasy.

Her refusal to advance had left him nonplussed, in a battle of wills she had calmly stood her ground, and Matthew had been forced to change his well-tried methods of parting travellers from their valuables.

He spurred gently forward, harness clinking. His voice came quietly with menace. 'Madam, should you not comply as the others have complied I must resort to means which I would not normally wish to use.'

The eyes bored into his. An equally measured, quiet voice replied, 'Your means are of little or no interest to me. I am old. I have known much. Both my sons were lost in war, my husband as a young man.

'You hold me no fears, you pock-marked young man.'

She spat the insult with calculated venom. Matthew sprang from his horse and with a bound struck her full and hard in the face with his riding crop. She fell without a sound into the mud, a rag doll figure with twisted limbs.

Her purse was full and from gnarled fingers rings were roughly pulled. A necklace was ripped from her throat.

His haul included a silver snuff-box of exquisite workmanship which even he stopped briefly to admire.

She stirred and for the first time a look other than defiance crossed her sensitive face. 'No, please, not the snuff-box, it belonged to my eldest son.'

Her entreaties fell on deaf ears; he had stayed too long already.

His left foot found the stirrup, his right leg swung up across the saddle and at that moment from the ground beneath him came the flash and roar of a small pistol, the agonizing impact jerking a screech from his lips.

The horse reared and twisted but he kept his seat. He raked the animal's flanks and bounded forward towards the open moor and escape.

Now clinging to the rock, Matthew softly whistled the horse. Gripping its mane with both hands he found the stirrup and, from somewhere, the strength to hoist the useless right leg across the animal's back.

Again the swimming head, the eyes that failed to focus on a scudding moon, the slow cold night, the boot filling with blood, ebbing strength, the swaying body barely able to remain upright.

Chill dawn found him some twenty miles from the Ridgeway Hill gazing down from his lofty viewpoint, across a panorama of open heath, fields and woods.

But why red dots, why green fields covered with red dots, and why so many? His vision blurred. Twenty, fifty, twenty again.

Then, not three hundred yards from where he sat, a red-coated Trooper yelled his name, and drew his sword, swung it aloft and spurred his horse straight for him.

Matthew found his pistol. He searched frantically through his overloaded pockets for his powder box. By instinct alone the pistol was loaded and primed.

The Trooper came on screaming at Matthew to surrender, his blade glinting and shimmering in the morning light. Matthew raised the flintlock with both hands and, as the Trooper aimed the final stroke, he pulled the trigger.

Misfire! A second pull and again a misfire. The death blow fell swiftly between the angle of the neck and shoulder.

The Trooper approached the silent figure with caution, kicked the pistol away and then handed it to his officer.

'Young man, that was a brave act and for this man's head you will be well rewarded.'

A familiar scent caught the officer's attention and raising Matthew's pistol to his face he sniffed it gently.

'Trooper, you are luckier than you know. Collins' number seven Turkish blend, I'd say. Your capture primed his pistol with snuff.'

That First Week

JOHN ASTON

It was fantastic. Impossible.

Harry Whiteman just could not believe that here she was. Now. Sitting in Victoria Tower Gardens.

His startled mind reeled back two years, to the time when his world crashed and he witnessed in a daze the funeral of his old way of life.

But it was Anne all right, sitting near the tree playing with a toddler – a toddler who had to be Brian. Harry remembered a baby boy that had such an amazingly strong grip with its tiny fingers.

Trembling slightly, he also recalled how, almost two years ago to the day, there had been a row.

It had been coming for some time – ever since Anne's father had died. Little things had gone wrong, so many of them, and all with their details blurred by time. Just little things.

Then it was the day to discuss that week's holiday he always liked to spend in London.

Anne wanted a change. Friends in the West Country had offered them the use of a holiday cottage.

'I know you love London – but let's go to the country, just this once,' she had begged.

He argued, 'We went to Portugal in the spring because you

wanted to go there, and that was on the understanding that we had my week in London – first week in July.'

He had since decided, on looking back, that he should have given in. Anne had loved her father deeply. His death had thrown her off balance. She was bewildered.

But Harry was a creature with deep regard for old and trusted habits.

After the death of his wife's father, he had done all he could to comfort her. But, as she became increasingly petulant, ever more easily upset by trifles, he eventually decided it was time to take a stand. And so that week's holiday was to be in London, or there would be no holiday . . .

Standing by the entrance to the gardens for those first few moments, watching the wife and son who were now strangers, he remembered the fury of the parting.

He had said, in a low, quiet voice, they were going to London, or nowhere. She had screamed. For the first time since he had known her, she had screamed hysterically, uncontrollably.

'You're like a robot! A bloody, selfish robot!' How her eyes had burned, the muscles in her neck bulging.

'Every year since we've been married – and heaven knows how long before that – you've gone to London for the first week in July. Always! Always!'

'And what do you do for at least one whole day of that awful week? You sit in Victoria Tower Gardens like a fool. Just sit! Sit! Sit!' she screeched. 'Nobody else is like that. There's something wrong with you. I'm not the one who needs the doctor – you are!'

Yes, he did sit in those gardens some of the time. Why not? He did lots of other things, too.

In the gardens, he could let the world go by. Yet, with the pinnacles of the Houses of Parliament nearby, the thunder and grind of hurrying traffic on one side and the casual slipping by of the river on the other, he still felt at the heart of life.

'You're a nine-to-five city bore! You should never have given up your job there and got married and moved out. The bloody place owns you!'

He had slammed the door hard and the first pint was blissful and the second. And the third . . .

That night his thoughts had raced on home, while he staggered on as best as he could behind them.

He need not have hurried. She had already gone.

It took just one week of living alone to realize she wasn't coming back.

It took one more week of heavy drinking to lose his engineering job.

Now, Harry considered, his life had been saved by the friend who said, 'Stay here and you're done for.'

Then came the engineering job in South Africa.

And, now two years later, he was back in London.

He was on holiday. And it was the first week in July.

Playing happily with Brian, Anne did not see him – and he was shocked to find he could not go to her. A great fear that she would not want him, barred the short distance he would have to go to discover the bitter truth.

There might be another man, another dad for Brian. For him there was no other woman. Yet he could not just walk away.

Relief from the fierce pain of indecision came unexpectedly, but blessedly.

An elderly man just leaving the gardens said, 'Nice day, isn't it?' Harry mumbled yes. In a daze he found himself drawn into conversation: Old London was disappearing, the traffic was increasing all the time, the buildings got higher, and higher . . .

'Let me buy you a drink,' said the anonymous friend at last. Harry began to follow him away from the shouts of the son whom he did not know and from the sight of the woman – his wife.

'It's better this way, after so long,' he lied to himself.

As the two men walked away, Harry looked back, watching his family as he might have done if he had been on a train moving slowly, but with appalling certainty, out of a station, away from loved ones.

He almost said goodbye out loud and did not hear the old man describe how, every summer, he enjoyed haunting various places in the city in the sunshine. There was little better to do, he added, laughing, as if over some small tragedy that really didn't matter.

The old fellow then realized, with resignation, that he wasn't being listened to. His acquaintance was watching that woman and her child.

He thought deeply for a moment. Then, as the gardens disappeared from view, said, 'Funny that.'

'What?' asked Harry, now determined to forget what had happened.

'Well, I always come to these gardens in the summer – one of my regular haunts. Always someone to talk to. And, funny thing, some people seem to pop up year after year. Think I've seen you before. Never forget a face!

'And I'll swear that young lady with the kiddie was here same time last year – first week in July. In the gardens every single day that first week . . .'

Then the old man was saying, 'What's the matter? Wait! Don't go – I'm buying you a beer!'

But Harry was running back to the gardens shouting, 'Fool! Fool! Fool!' His coat flapped wildly as he disappeared through the gate to the gardens.

'You certainly meet some queer ones,' the old man was saying. 'He must have left something behind. Probably gone to fetch it.'

JOHN ASTON *won a prize for his short story 'That First Week'. At the time of its publication he worked as a journalist on a Kent newspaper. A haunting story that has in its necessarily short length, regret, remorse, nostalgia and a happy ending.*

Looking for Clancy

L.F. LAMPITT

E lwyn trudged up the hill.
His eyes were on the ground, his ugly face set in a determination not to stop until he reached the top of the long slope, wherever that might be.

But then he changed his mind and paused to sniff the light breeze that cooled his face and stirred the quiff of yellowish hair on the top of his too small and sadly misshapen head.

Elwyn's eyes were his best feature, though few people had ever bothered to look into them; an uncommon amber ringing misty pupils. But they weren't very good at seeing; dim, like the rest of Elwyn's make-up.

That is why he was within sight of the horizon for perhaps twenty minutes before he could see the grey-blue line which distinguished sluggish water from sultry sky. But the sea smell was now unmistakable.

It was essential to Elwyn's vague plan that he must reach the sea, but since he was now satisfied that it was still there and that he would find it again, he allowed himself a brief rest, collapsing clumsily on to the salt-crisp of the headland, his ragged old khaki-coloured coat hanging in folds.

To Elwyn the sea meant Clancy. He had never been with Clancy except on the sea or in port for more than five years – until that fateful night when, arms swinging and great shoulders heaving, Clancy went down . . .

. . . Went down fighting under a wave of dark blue serge which washed him, tumbling helmets in his wake into a Black Maria.

Elwyn, never a fighter, did his best, but a clout on the side of his head from a police truncheon knocked him cold in round one, and when he came to in the gutter, Clancy had gone.

The trouble with Clancy of course was that he was such a terrible drinker.

So far as drink was concerned, Elwyn could take it or leave it. If Clancy banged a pint down under his nose he would drink it, out of a vague sense of duty, but he never acquired a real taste for the stuff.

When Elwyn, his head oozing, his vision double, dragged himself away from the scene of the conflict, it was some time before his battered brain registered the desolating fact that he was alone.

Even when not dulled by a police truncheon, his mental powers were limited. He had relied on Clancy for as long as he could remember, Clancy was the one who made the decisions, made sure of their next meal, set the compass for their every move, picked a ship to sail in, or a casual shore job when the sea palled.

Elwyn spent two years looking for Clancy after that harsh parting. At first he hung about the coast, walking from port to port; then somehow he found his way inland.

Then he took up with a mousy, whiskery little old tramp, one Henry Juniper, who taught Elwyn how to nobble a hen without a cluck.

Elwyn and Henry lived well, if somewhat plainly, for a few months – until Henry's arthritis let him down and he was shut up in a barn by a furious farmer until the police arrived.

Elwyn, never a hero, skulked in a dark corner of the farmyard, quaking at the familiar sight of blue serge, until all was quiet again, when he crept away, vaguely ashamed of himself.

He missed Henry for a week or two, but his old pining for Clancy still nagged him. For a while he joined a circus, sharing a tent with a sea lion in a tank and two superannuated clowns.

The sea lion resented the scruffy stranger's presence and barked himself hoarse, but the clowns saw Elwyn as a natural.

They lodged a ridiculously small straw hat on the top of his head, supporting an enormous scarlet feather, swathed his backside in a pair of baggy check pants, cut down to fit Elwyn's stubby legs, painted white rings round his eyes, and launched him into the ring for a matinee try-out.

Elwyn cringed at his reception. The crowds, with all the cruelty of a crowd, sensed his embarrassment, his outraged dignity and laughed their heads off.

But before Elwyn could back out of the arena and run for it, the clowns were chasing him round the ring, heading him off the exit. The biggest roar came when Elwyn, in frantic flight, shed his baggy pants.

It took a lot of persuasion to get him back into the ring for the next performance, but he had to eat – and the circus people, always hungry themselves, were generous at mealtimes.

He stayed with the little circus until that day when a faint whiff of salt in the air told him that the sea was not far away and he slipped by night out of the moonlight huddle of tents and caravans to resume his search for Clancy.

And so Elwyn came to the sea again, but the sea is a big place.

For weeks he went from dock to dock and pub to pub. Sometimes he would come upon an old acquaintance who would greet him with, 'Hullo, Elwyn, old son, long time no see.'

It happened at last, at the Mermaid's Nook in Axport. The public bar was crowded and dark with shag-smoke, Elwyn went in as was his wont, as one who wished not to be observed, only to observe.

For a moment or two he scanned the company, could distinguish little in the haze and was about to turn back to the door when he stiffened and listened.

It was the voice – the unmistakable voice of Clancy. Elwyn moved towards it, his heart thumping.

Clancy looked up from his pint, saw Elwyn, split his face into a vast grin, and opened his arms.

'Well, look who's here, mates! If it isn't old Elwyn . . . Where you been, you scruffy old bastard?'

Elwyn launched himself blindly at his old friend, missed his footing and landed on the floor, tangled in a fallen stool, his ear in a pool of beer.

Clancy helped him to his feet and extended a hand. 'Shake, me old pal,' he said. Elwyn's misted amber eyes held Clancy's wild blue ones for a second.

Then obediently, Elwyn sat back and raised his right paw.

The Frigate

KENNETH HADLER

The heavy waves smashed against the side of the frigate and fell back again.

Lightning ripped across the sky to precede the rending sound of thunder.

It was as if the flashing sword of the ancient Nordic god was tearing through the very substance of heaven.

Silver and grey clouds fled from the celestial torment, twisting and writhing as they scurried to find oblivion in the black merger of distant sea and sombre night.

A watery crescent moon intermittently peeped down to watch the ship as it dipped and rolled and heaved.

But the little vessel seemed to realize that to succumb would mean death, and it struggled bravely on.

As often happens in those Southern waters, the storm abated during the night and as if to do penance for its violence the Weather Goddess held the ship steady and gently bathed her in a glow of golden sunlight.

The sails of the becalmed vessel hung in shreds from the yards. Several crew members jerkily moved across the deck, carrying out their unnecessary and pointless duties aboard the stationary ship.

The bo'sun turned, firstly to the apathetic shuffling of his crew and then, with lowered head, to look down at the grey-green sea.

Without delight, emotion or interest, he observed that it was flecked with dancing and shimmering yellow flashes.

Each little sparkle seemed to be alive and eager to take advantage of every ripple in the water, depending on it for its very existence, knowing that its life would last only as long as the ripple lasted.

Far away, one solitary albatross hung motionless in the sky; its massive wing span of thirteen feet taking every advantage of an invisible flow of warmer air which only it and God knew existed.

As is the way with the albatross, its eyes were flickering, first this way, and then that – searching. Always searching.

It was these eyes that had given the bird its aura of mysterious spirituality and had induced superstitious wonderment among ignorant seamen.

Far below it, just above the surface of the water, fluttering a little, was Wilson's petrel. With its small wing span it could not hope to soar like the albatross.

One of the crew members relieved the Captain at the wheel, and this latter silently glided across the deck to join the bo'sun. Together they watched the birds for a while. The bo'sun was the first to break the silence.

'Cap'n,' he said. His voice was sepulchral and tinged with an awe which familiarity and interminable time had in no way effaced. 'You always know the answers to the questions I ask. Such a gift is not given to everyone.'

The Captain did not move. It was an introductory speech which he had heard hundreds of times before. He knew what would follow: 'What is that little bird doing out there?'

After a second or two came the inevitable words.

'What is that little bird doing out there?'

A long pause ensued, which neither of the men seemed to find in any way strange.

'Bo'sun,' replied the Captain. 'It is the damned soul of a landsman. No earthly aid can ever be given to it. It is for that reason that it has to keep to the sea.

'Though its tired little wings could drop from its body through sheer fatigue, it must never seek the solace and rest that the land would bring.'

The bo'sun seemed satisfied with the reply.

'And what of the albatross far above him, Cap'n? Is it true that up there we are looking at a seaman's soul in a state of bliss? Is it really true, Cap'n?'

'There are things that are not given to men to know,' replied the Captain. 'You too have seen the eyes of an albatross. You too know its ways.

'Tell me, bo'sun, are those the eyes of a bird or are they of some poor mute seaman trying to tell us something across the gulf that can never be bridged?'

The bo'sun remained thoughtful for a few moments. ''Tis you who know the answers to the questions like these, sir,' he replied. 'There's none better than yourself who would know things like this.'

'Aye, but there are some things that are hidden even from me. That is,' he added, 'until the last day shall dawn for this poor mariner.'

The weather continued calm and on the following day the Captain and the bo'sun were once more at the side of the ship.

Nothing had altered save two clouds in the sky. The two birds were still there; the one hardly moving, serene in its ethereal home; the other giving to a minute area of the sea-surface an appearance of agitated bubbling.

The figure of the bo'sun turned slightly so that it was facing more directly the starboard bow.

There were yet more questions to be answered. Questions that had been asked in similar words a hundred times before.

'Cap'n, what is that in the water, over there?'

The other figure also turned, the two ancient uniforms making a faint rustling sound as they rubbed together. Years of sea-spray had hardened and bleached the materials to a light shade of grey.

'They are floats, supporting a fishing net,' came the reply. 'A gale snatched it all away, long years ago.'

Both figures watched for the rest of the day as the net, with its haul of decomposing fish, floated past so slowly that movement could hardly be discerned. Daylight faded and the moon once more commenced her lonely voyage across the sky.

'It was a good catch,' said the bo'sun.

'Not when the gale originally claimed it,' came the reply. 'That net and those floats are not such that we used to know them, my friend. They now make them like us. They too can never rot away. This lost fishing tackle is destined to catch the oceans' fish until the end of time.'

A slight breeze caused movement in the strips of hanging sails, and Captain Vanderdecken of *Der fliegende Holländer* wearily prepared to meet yet another storm.

The spectre-ship *The Flying Dutchman* continued its aimless voyage through the Southern Seas.

And so did the modern imperishable floats and fishing net.

Port of Rye

DAVID R. MURDUCK

With an economy of movement born of the sea and old age, Bill the Skipper trod the shingle.

He eyed the winch cable snaking over the beach and then, holding the oak lintel for support, he stepped into the winch house and started the single-cylinder diesel.

The twenty-year-old Kelvin settled into its rhythmic thump and the old man took his pipe and tobacco from its customary place behind the rear engine bearer.

There were tears in his grey eyes.

Outside, the slack cable tautened as it took the strain of the *RX 596*, affectionately known as the *Anne*.

Two hundred yards down the beach, twenty-two-year-old Jan Pavlik put the greased wooden slides in front of the oak keel as fifty tons of trawler commenced the long haul to high-water mark.

It was hard work moving slides, dragging each to the bow, and positioning it under the quick release shackle. Then back to the stern for another.

It was work which gave a trawler-hand time for thought, but the tall, dark-haired Pole had little to spare for such a leisurely occupation.

They had always said that the Master of the *Anne* was a hard man and in the three years since Pavlik had signed on, he had learned that it was true.

He hesitated and glanced up at the great elliptic stern, each timber steamed and cut and forced into that classic shape. It would be good to own a boat like the *Anne*, registered, paid for, and seaworthy.

It would be good too to own the twenty stone of best Channel plaice whose slime still tainted his salt-hardened palms.

Sometimes Pavlik could not resist thoughts of jealousy and of late (for the old Skipper had aged a lot these last few months) the Pole had found himself increasingly hating the older man. And there were still two more years of apprenticeship to run.

Again the sullen Pole trudged to the stern for another slide, and the trawler inexorably mounted the acute slope towards her bed.

Old Bill knocked out his pipe on the winch frame and carefully adjusted the throttle to slow the diesel.

The Skipper knew that it was hard work with the slides. He had learned that under his father.

He leaned over the door once again and watched. For three trawling seasons now Bill had taught Pavlik the sea – as much as any man could. And yes, it was true, he had been hard on the younger man.

But the sea would be harder when the lad had a boat of his own. The Skipper stared long at the *Anne*, his father's boat, and tears stung his hard cheeks at the thought of the parting which had to come.

He slowed the winch, nearly to stalling speed, and turning, he called out, his voice pitched above the thump of the engine.

'Charlie, heard the forecast?'

The upper half of the nearest beach chalet door swung open and the retired coastguard showed his weathered face.

'Aye, Sovereign force five. Sou'westerly. 'Bout a thousand and six. Fallin' though.'

The Skipper grunted.

'Left any out, Bill?'

'Aye, three fleets.'

'Should be okay till tomorrow. Anyway you've a good mate even if she does up it to force seven.' He paused and then added, 'I'll bring those papers down in a minute, Bill.'

The old man nodded and simultaneously at a wave from Pavlik

he cut the diesel and the trawler came to a rest squarely on her bed. The brooding Pole wedged chocks on either side of the hull and together the two men started to unload.

'She'll be a rough'un tomorrow, Jan.'

The Pole nodded and heaved another half-hundredweight box into the winch house.

Yes, tomorrow would be the same. Pick up a trawl, shoot, beat and pick up. It was endless.

And Simone at the cottage, expecting their second, now.

He eyed the slippery fish. A share of the profits would be good but vague promises were all that the Skipper ever gave.

Old Bill's waders scrunched into the shingle as he leaned heavily against the stern timbers and watched Jan with the last box.

'Good catch today, Jan. If she blows a bit we'll have a full fleet tomorrow.'

Again the Pole nodded curtly, containing his anger.

'Oh, Jan there's something else.'

But Jan Pavlik had had enough. Slowly he trod the dry shingle beside the *Anne*, the box of fish clenched firmly to his chest. Out of sight of the Skipper, he knelt at the bow; quickly scanned the horizon and slipped the shackle.

There was a noise not unlike the felling of a larch in the forests of his native country, there was also a scream. The boat heeled over and lurched to rest thirty yards seaward of her bed, her keel timbers deep in the shingle.

Pavlik, frightened now, ran towards the dying Skipper but his were not the only pair of waders which pounded down the beach. As he knelt a hand came to his shoulder and the startled voice of Charlie the old coastguard was in his ear.

'God. What d'yer do a thing like that for, Pavlik?' he said waving the ship's papers in front of the younger man. 'Old Bill, sent me into town this morning to get the *Anne* registered in your name. It only needed his signature – not his death.' The two men stared in silence at the dead Skipper.

The Day Macey's Time Was Up

JOHN W.R. UNSWORTH

Mrs Amelia Hopgood had been a thorn in Detective Sergeant Macey's hide for the past ten years.

'I'd have made Inspector except for her,' filtered through his nicotine moustache with monotonous regularity.

So much so, that his Super worried about him, even to the point of considering recommending him for early retirement.

'A copper should keep an open mind,' he maintained. 'The man's a fool.'

Which was precisely Amelia Hopgood's opinion as she invited Macey into her neat little sitting-room.

She sat in a chintz-covered armchair, a short, plump smiling woman with shrewd blue eyes.

'I suppose you've come about poor Bert,' she said, watching him as he prowled restlessly about the room.

Macey swung round, rugged face displaying a wary triumph.

'How d'you know we'd picked up Bert Conner?' he demanded.

Mrs Hopgood shrugged placid shoulders.

'Do I ever see you unless one of my lodgers has got himself into trouble?' she asked.

'And please sit down, Sergeant. You make my poor old head

spin when you stalk about like a caged tiger. What's the silly boy done?'

'Of course, you wouldn't know!' Macey growled, ignoring her invitation.

'No.'

'His usual racket, smash and grab. Bassetts the jewellers.'

'Ah, well,' she sighed, 'I suppose I'm not surprised. There's a wild streak in him, poor boy.'

'Like in all your lodgers,' Macey sneered. 'Funny how you always take in blokes who've got form. Aren't there any honest chaps looking for a place to live?'

'You're all the same,' Mrs Hopgood snapped. 'If a man's been inside, he's a marked man.'

'So?'

'Can't you see that they need to feel secure?' she asked. 'They've done wrong and they've paid for it. When they come out I think it's up to us all to try and give them a fresh start.'

'Which is just what you do, isn't it?' Macey suggested ambiguously.

'We shall only pass this way once, Sergeant,' Amelia rebuked him. 'If there is some little good we can do . . .'

'Spare us the sermon,' Macey growled. 'I suppose it never struck you as odd that Conner should go out in the early hours of the morning?'

'Lord bless you, no.' She giggled. 'Sometimes they don't even come home all night. But there, shut away from women . . .'

'Conner wasn't interested in birds.'

'No, Bert was a loner, I'm afraid.' She shook her head sadly.

Amelia sighed and rose, walking to the French windows.

'I'm going into the greenhouse,' she said over her shoulder. 'We can talk as easily in there, and my poor dears must be watered.'

'You've not only got sticky fingers, they're green as well, eh?'

She turned, her eyes glinting coldly.

'If we weren't alone, Sergeant, you wouldn't dare make a remark like that.'

'Too right, I wouldn't,' Macey gave a grin. 'As we are, where've you stashed the loot?'

'Why not search the house?' she suggested closing the greenhouse door. 'Don't bother getting a warrant – not that I think they'd give you one.'

'I'll not bother,' Macey scowled, running a finger round his collar, sweat trickling down his face. 'What in hell d'you grow in here – bananas?'

'I've got some rare tropical plants,' she replied. 'Did poor Bert get away with much?'

'As if you didn't know! For the record, fifty watches, value approximately five grand. And all you gave the silly clot was three Cs!'

'I beg your pardon?'

'Oh, come off it,' he said impatiently. 'We both know you're a fence and a damned miserly one at that.'

A gleam of triumph showed in Macey's eyes as he looked round the greenhouse.

'I thought you were supposed to have green fingers?'

'You said that, Sergeant,' she replied, looking up from her watering. 'Why don't you go and leave me alone? This sort of thing isn't doing your career any good, y'know.'

'Damn my career,' he barked. 'I thought in summer, fuchsias had to be well watered.'

'They do.'

'These,' he pointed to a dozen large pots, 'are as dry as tinder. They're dying. Now I wonder why – and you with the green fingers!'

He picked up one of the pots, upended it and banged it on the edge of a crate. A mass of solid earth, bound together by a mat of roots, came neatly away.

He grunted with disappointment, but not discouraged, repeated the process with the next pot.

Mrs Hopgood watched him and giggled.

'Oh, Sergeant, you are a one! You think I've hidden the watches under the plants! Really, you'll be the death of me, I do declare.'

'I'd like to be,' he snarled, as he emptied the last pot without success.

'Why won't you accept me for what I am?' she pleaded. 'Have

I ever done you any harm that you keep after me every time one of my boys proves weak . . . ?'

Sergeant Macey's face purpled and she watched him, half-amused, half-anxious.

'I'll give you this,' he said at last, 'you're smart. Oh you're real smart. But you'll make a mistake one of these days. One of your "boys" as you call 'em, will grass and then . . .'

He drew a finger slowly across his throat.

'But surely you wouldn't accept the word of an ex-convict against that of an honest, God-fearing woman?'

'I'd accept the word of the Devil himself,' Macey ground out. 'But don't fret. I'll get you one of these days.'

'Be sure to let me know when you do, Sergeant.'

'Go to hell!'

He left the sweltering heat of the greenhouse, slamming the door violently behind him.

Something crashed down on his head and as he sank to his knees, he had a wonderful vision of taking Amelia Hopgood in on a GBH charge.

Half-dazed, he knelt outside the greenhouse and saw the sloping length of guttering responsible for his plight.

Slowly, his eyes brightened and he muttered something that could have been a prayer, as fifty watches slid gently down the guttering to the ground beside him.

JOHN UNSWORTH *was a regular contributor of short stories. He settled, or was persuaded, to write as John Unsworth from first calling himself J. W. R., then John W. R. By whichever* nom de plume *he can be greatly enjoyed.*

Checkmate

JOHN W.R. UNSWORTH

Toby Moston punched the pillows and lit his first cigarette. He switched on the tea-maker and leaned over to dig his wife in the ribs.

'Wakey-wakey, darling, another morn, another mug!'

'Beast! Give me a ciggy.'

He handed her his own.

'Ready for tea?'

She nodded and for a few moments they smoked and drank in silence. As he handed her a second cup, Toby decided it was time to get down to business.

'How'd you get on at Heathrow, pet?'

She reached over to the bedside table for a file.

'Four good prospects,' she replied. 'Two in Kent, one from Dorset and another near Epping.'

'Will the first three keep, sweetheart?'

She nodded.

'The Kentish men are off to South Africa and the Dorset boy's gone to New York.'

'They all signed the petition, did they?'

'Men never refuse me anything,' she said smugly. She passed over four forms headed 'Save Our Soil'.

Toby flipped back the top pages and examined the carbon copies with satisfaction.

'You know, Elaine,' he said, 'this new carbon paper's worth a mint. You'd think these were originals. With the agree-to-pay declaration typed in above, it's perfect. What about the Essex chap?'

'He thought "SOS" was something to do with stopping France pinching our good English earth when we enter the Common Market. That's him! But he didn't really care. He was too busy trying to persuade me to go to Paris.'

'Dirty old man!' Toby grinned.

'He's not,' Elaine asserted with a smug smile. 'He's a sweetie, really. Lives with his mother, got pots of money. She lets him off the leash once a year for a week on his own.'

'What d'you think, gold or silver medal?'

She pursed her lips.

'Gold standard,' she replied slowly. 'Depends on his old lady. She sounds a bit of a battleaxe. Better play it by ear. Twenty-five quid's nice, but a tenner is better than a kick in the pants.'

'You have the bathroom first,' he invited. 'I'll prepare the certificate.'

It was shortly after noon when he drove his Jaguar up the drive of Oriole Lodge.

'Definitely gold standard,' he muttered, strolling casually to the rear of the house. He firmly believed in the unconventional approach as the best means for promoting confidence.

His eyes lit up when he saw an elderly woman working in the garden. Toby walked towards her, trying to see in this plump, untidy little person, the battleaxe her son had described. He decided the man was a fool.

'Mrs Heatherton?'

'Yes.' She gripped the back of a garden seat to help herself stand and Toby gallantly took her other arm.

'Come and sit down,' she said. 'And tell me what I can do for you.'

'You can be proud of your son, Mrs Heatherton,' Toby said with dignity. 'Do you realize that he ranks among the finest in the country?'

Mrs Heatherton did not even blink. She leaned over and patted Toby's hand encouragingly.

'That's nice,' she murmured. 'What has he done to earn this distinction?'

'He's a CAD, dear lady.' Toby smiled blandly. 'One of the country's best. Personally I would rank him the greatest CAD. It's his reactions, of course.'

'I suppose it must be,' she agreed, her eyes crinkling with gentle amusement. 'I hope "cad" has a different meaning these days to what it had when I was a girl, Mr . . .'

'Moston, Toby Moston,' he introduced himself. 'Indeed it has, Mrs Heatherton. Your son has just gained the Gold Medal of the World Federation of Class "A" Drivers. CAD for short.'

'Well, fancy that,' she said softly. 'And Ray never said.'

'He wanted it to be a surprise,' Toby said. 'For weeks he's been submitted to the most stringest tests, both practical and theoretical, any driver can face. And he achieved one of the highest set of marks, I can remember. Ninety-seven per cent.'

He took from his briefcase the certificate he had prepared earlier, together with a covering declaration apparently signed by Raymond Heatherton.

'Is Mr Heatherton in?' he asked.

'Well, no,' she replied. 'He's in France. You wanted to see him?'

Toby nodded and shifted uncomfortably.

'How I detest red tape,' he sighed.

'Is something wrong?'

'Well . . .' Toby hesitated and shrugged. 'You see, Mrs Heatherton, Ray agreed to pay £25 to cover the tests . . . only if he passed, of course . . . as soon as the results were available.' He handed her the declaration signed by her son. 'I'm not allowed to leave his medal or the certificate without the money. One of these silly things.'

She patted him on the arm.

'I quite understand, young man,' she said softly. She looked at him shyly. 'Would you do me a favour while I go and get my cheque book?'

'Dear Mrs Heatherton, but of course.' Toby opened his arms expansively. 'Anything.'

'Well . . .' She pointed to a heap of stones against the wall. 'I'm building a rockery and I need those rocks moved over by the summerhouse. Do you think . . . ?'

Toby swallowed hard and gave a brave smile.

'And you want me to move them.' He fortified himself with the thought of £25. 'Think nothing of it.'

Nearly half an hour later Toby tipped the last load and sat on the edge of the barrow, mopping his brow and wondering what was keeping her.

'Oh, you have worked hard!'

Toby gave her a sickly smile and looked at her companion curiously.

'Let me introduce you to my friend,' she twittered. 'Mr Moston . . . Detective Inspector Garthur.'

Toby rose slowly, eyes wary.

'He was as surprised and interested in my son's great achievement as I was,' Mrs Heatherton continued brightly.

'Indeed, I was,' Inspector Garthur agreed with a grim smile.

'You see,' she added, 'dear Ray can't even drive.'

Death Through a Glass
... Darkly

RIK ASHARD

'It'll be no worse than going to sleep,' she had said, 'believe me, Philip.

'She'll feel no pain – none at all. Just drift off into a long . . . eternal sleep.'

Philip had been confused, scarcely able to believe their conversation was real.

'And . . . and afterwards?' Laura's reply had been gentle but reassuring. 'Nothing. Nothing at all. It will be over – for all of us.'

Doubt still lingered. 'But . . . a post mortem? Surely it would be inevitable?'

'Trust me, darling. I'm a doctor. I know the procedure.'

She had cradled his hands in hers, as if to transmit some of her confidence. 'And I know how Dr Adam will react. He's been treating Elizabeth for, what – three years now?'

'He knows her medical history and he is as surprised as we are that she has lingered for so long – against all medical logic. When she does . . .'

It was Laura's turn to hesitate; to search for words that would help soften the harshness of reality. 'When her end does come, Dr Adam will see it as a blessing, natural inevitability. Nothing more would be necessary.'

Now that he was alone, Philip gazed at the small phial of colourless liquid she had given him and harboured fresh doubts.

Could it really be *this* easy? Half a glass of water ... this odourless liquid in it and ... and a twist of lemon to counteract the slight brackish taste.

For twenty-four years he had been married to Elizabeth and for twenty-three of them he had been faithful to her in body, if not in spirit. The marriage had been a mistake; both had soon realized as much.

Philip had been obsessed with his work as an architect and had drifted into the relationship without being fully committed. Elizabeth had hoped she could make him change. She had failed.

But she was a remarkable person, with love enough to sustain them both and although it had been a compromise, the marriage had survived.

She had given unselfishly – sacrificing a career of her own in order to strengthen his, so that now he ran a successful practice.

And then, nearly three years ago, Philip had discovered what his wife had characteristically contrived to keep from him – that she had a terminal illness.

What had once been a fleeting, almost imperceptible ache, had gradually become a raging torment of pain.

The warning had been ignored for too long; surgery had merely delayed the inevitable. 'It's just a matter of time, I'm afraid,' Dr Adam had told him. 'A year, maybe more, maybe less. One can never say.'

The weeks had passed and the months had lengthened to become years; the ever-present reminder of her mortality softened by the balm of drugs.

Yet, although now bedridden, Elizabeth had not succumbed to bitterness; she faced the future with a bright optimism – as if it held limitless happiness.

He had met Laura a year ago, in his capacity as a design consultant for a London hospital where she was a doctor. For a brief period they had been merely business acquaintances until, on one sudden and inexplicable moment, their eyes had met in a different way.

Nothing had been said but each knew that one day, somewhere, sometime, they would be lovers.

Time had now become their burden, too. To be in each other's presence was to suppress an intensity of emotions that were as exhilarating as they were exhausting.

When they finally made love the relief had been overwhelming. But a new frustration had entered their lives – the strains of deception and waiting – waiting for Elizabeth to die.

Philip walked from the kitchen, crossed the passage and entered the bedroom. Elizabeth was asleep. The smile with which she habitually concealed her pain was no longer on her lips. Now at forty-nine, she looked nearer seventy.

Philip felt a wave of compassion. Laura was right – it would be a mercy.

Gently, softly, he placed the glass on her bedside table, and retreated from the room with an emptied water jug. It was done. Finished.

He was in the kitchen, trembling with tension, when there came a knock on the front door. A greasy coldness seemed to envelop his skin and his heart pumped erratically. He stood still, rigid with fear; staring without seeing; his mind in a turmoil. Who . . . who could it be at this time of night?

'Philip?' It was Elizabeth calling. 'Darling, are you there? It's the front door.' He moistened his lips. 'It's all right, Liz. I'm . . . I'm just going.' The distance was a few yards but seemed immeasurable. He forced himself to relax then opened the door.

'Hullo, Philip,' said Dr Adam. He was a hearty man in his late thirties, built like a rugby full-back. He bustled in, smiling. 'Sorry if I disturbed you, but . . .' He lowered his voice, and gestured towards the bedroom. 'She awake?'

Philip nodded; unable to speak. 'Good,' said the doctor, and then, in an undertone, added, 'Thought I'd put her onto something a little stronger.'

Panic swept through Philip. . .he must get rid of the glass of 'water' at once. But Dr Adam had already passed and entered the bedroom.

'Hullo, Elizabeth,' he roared. 'How are you?' She smiled a

sleepy greeting – words between them nowadays were often unnecessary . . .

'Got something better for you to take tonight, my dear,' he said, squeezing her with a tenderness that belied his appearance. 'Help you get a good kip.'

Philip moved to edge past him, reaching for the glass. 'I'll er . . . I'll just get some fresh water,' he said. But Dr Adam brushed him aside. 'No. Not water for this lady tonight,' he explained, sitting down beside the bed and blocking Philip's view of the table.

'A nice cup of weak tea will go better with what I've got.' He looked at Elizabeth and grinned. 'I make you drink too much Adam's ale as it is, eh?' She smiled.

Philip was in despair, realizing it would look odd if he didn't do as he was asked. He backed out of the room but felt a lift of relief when the doctor said, 'To tell you the truth, Philip, I'd quite like a cuppa myself.'

As Philip waited for the kettle to boil he told himself that what he and Laura had planned was sheer madness; murder not mercy. They'd been given a second chance. They must wait.

The kettle was steaming when the door swung open and the doctor came in, coughing and laughing at the same time. 'That'll teach me, won't it!' he roared. 'Pinched one of her grapes and the bloody pips went down the wrong way.'

Philip stared in horror as the doctor, still coughing, strode to the sink to rinse a glass from which he had drunk nearly all the contents.

Big Dippers

JOHN DUNCAN

I've retired from the game now. Fingers get too stiff and, anyway, no one carries much money these days.

Mind you, in my day, I was King of the dips. 'Dennis the Dip' they called me.

I could lift a wallet from right under their noses and they wouldn't see or feel a thing.

No one could do it as well as I could. Well, maybe that chap at the theatre, The Great Sartoria.

I remember when he first came to town. He was a sensation.

'Here, Dennis,' Harry said to me. 'The chap at the Hippodrome. He's a dip. He does it for a living.'

'So do I, Harry boy,' I said and I felt a bit peeved that Harry could speak so admiringly about this theatrical bloke.

'Yes, but he does it up *on the stage*. Everyone is watching him and he challenges anyone to catch him at it.'

Well, I had got used to Harry being around, praising and admiring my efforts and I was having some difficulty hiding my jealousy.

'Probably some trick,' I told him. 'They've got all sorts of gadgets nowadays. And he could have people planted in the audience and doesn't dip them at all.'

'No, honest. Ask George Hawkins. He went up on the stage last night and this Sartoria dipped his wallet and his handkerchief and *then got his braces off him.*'

'There you are.' I replied, crushing like. 'Hawkins couldn't lift his elbow off the bar. He calls himself a dip and he has to take a night job at the Blue Boar to make ends meet.'

'But this chap, Sartoria, is good, Dennis. Really. Very, very good.'

'As good as me?' I looked at Harry straight in the eye.

'Well, I don't know Dennis . . .'

That did it! Harry was inferring that someone could out-dip me. On my own patch too. I had worked hard to build up a franchise in the area and nobody so far had dared to challenge it. Except this variety act, this Sartoria bloke.

'I think I had better go and see this geyser and find out if he's as good as you say, Harry.'

'Last night tonight,' Harry told me. 'You'd better get a ticket now, Dennis, in case they have a sell-out.'

'Tell you what, I'll treat you, Harry,' I told him. 'I'll treat you to a good seat and a pint when the show's over . . . and I'll show you who is still the best dip in town.'

It's all so many years ago now that I can't recall much more of what happened that day. I know that I went round to the Hippodrome and got a couple of tickets. I know that I put in a couple of hours' practice at the bus station and made quite a bit.

Came the evening I was so tired that I didn't really want to go to the Hippodrome. This Sartoria was an entertainer and after all he wasn't actually working my patch. He was some sort of conjurer – not really a challenge to me.

Harry called around early and said that if we hurried we could get a pint before the show started.

I told him that I had promised him a jar after the show, not before.

'But you may not have your wallet after the show.' Harry giggled and that made me really angry.

'We'll see,' I said, in my extra calm voice. Even Harry respected my extra calm voice. He knew that I meant business.

The seats weren't too bad, apart from a damn great spring sticking out of mine, and we settled down to watch.

We sang with the singers . . . made rude noises at the song and dance team and then came the big spot, the dip.

Sartoria came striding down the centre aisle of the theatre and shook hands with some of the audience as he passed. They were all clapping him. Nobody ever clapped me and I really can dip.

He shook my hand and his little assistant came wiggling along behind him – a real smasher.

Then he strutted up on to the stage and shouted through cupped hands, 'Can anybody tell me the time?'

What an uproar there was! 'Somebody's stole me watch!'

'Hey, my wallet's gone!'

About ten or twelve people were on their feet, all shouting.

Sartoria laughed and pulled their watches and wallets out of his pocket with a flourish.

'Come and get them ladies and gentlemen,' he cried.

I watched, tickled pink. This man *was* good. He wasn't a conjuror after all, he was a dip and a real good dip at that.

'Someone hasn't collected his watch,' he called out to the audience and I waited as a hush came over the crowd.

'It's mine,' I said standing up and noting how Harry's eyes nearly fell out of his head.

'Yours Dennis?' Harry couldn't believe it.

'I'll come and collect it,' I said walking slowly through the theatre, '*and I'll give you your watch back.*'

I drew Sartoria's watch from my pocket.

The audience loved it and Sartoria was a good sport too. He laughed his head off and invited me to go on the stage.

I gave him back his watch and he gave me back the one I had lifted off a chap on Paddington Station.

'We have a challenger tonight.' He put his arm round my shoulders, 'And he is worthy to be called a challenger.'

I could see Harry, sitting next to the empty seat, clapping his hands and cheering.

Then my trousers came down.

My moment of pride had turned to shame and I could imagine the disappointment on Harry's face.

The audience laughed at me as Sartoria handed me back my braces.

I gave him back his wallet amidst more cheers and he returned the handkerchief that he had nicked from my breast pocket.

Things were getting very serious.

I gave him his tie and then he turned nasty.

Amidst the thunderous applause he gave me my tie and my wallet and my watch and then he stole my bloody braces again!

I could just about see Harry beyond the footlights. He reckoned I was beaten.

Then I had the idea.

'That was a dirty trick, Dennis,' Harry said with a smile as we walked over to the pub afterwards.

'Desperate situations require desperate remedies,' I grinned opening the pub door for him.

'She was pretty though, wasn't she?' Harry smiled again.

'The audience loved it when you gave her back her bra.'

I treated Harry to about five whiskies and counted the money I had lifted out of Sartoria's wallet. He wouldn't dare shout about it. He had his reputation to think of, hadn't he?

Yes, I was the King of my patch again and to this day I often talk about it with my missus. Always know what you are after, I told my kids.

I knew what I was after. And I got it – Sartoria's pretty assistant – my missus, bless her.

You and I are About to Die

BILL BRYSON

When the lift broke down somewhere between the seventh and
eighth floors, the man beside me – the only other passenger
– said rather a strange thing. He said, 'I was afraid this might
happen.'

I looked at him in some amazement. 'You expected the lift to
break down?'

'Or worse,' he said enigmatically and lounged back against the
wall, watching without evident concern as I pushed the buttons
on the control panel, all without effect.

After a moment, I sighed. 'Nothing. Even the alarm bell doesn't
work.'

'I was afraid of that as well.'

I looked at him again. He seemed curiously resigned and wholly
unperturbed. 'Either you know something about this lift or you're
a remarkable pessimist,' I said.

He smiled and straightened up slightly. 'It's just that I've come
to expect these things. They happen to me all the time.'

'Indeed?'

He nodded grimly. 'You see, I'm the unluckiest man in the
world.' He gave me a moment to absorb this disarming confession,
then said, 'I have something I think I should tell you, something
rather important.' He paused significantly. 'Not to put too fine a
point on it, you and I are about to die.'

'I beg your pardon?'

'Yes, it's most unfortunate.' He glanced at his watch. 'We have just over five minutes. I think at the least you're entitled to an explanation.'

Clearly he was either joking or mad. I broke into a nervous smile and started to speak, but he silenced me.

'I assure you that in just over five minutes we will both be dead. Would you like to know how?'

There was nothing in his expression to show that he was joking; quite the contrary. Nor was there even the slightest indication that he might be mad. He was an affluent-looking man – self-made I would have guessed – with a well-cut suit and a leather-bound attaché case. Dubiously, I nodded.

'You see,' he said, 'nothing goes right for me any more.

'I have only to pick up a teacup and it falls to pieces or enter a lift and it breaks down.' He indicated our present circumstances.

'Until about three years ago the very opposite was the case. Once, for instance, a friend gave me a tip on the Derby. I misunderstood him, bet on the wrong horse and won £600. That was the story of my life – always lucky, always winning long shots, always finding fivers in the road.

'Even when things went wrong they turned out for the best; one time hurrying to catch a plane I had a puncture and missed my flight. The plane crashed. Eighty-one people were killed.' He looked at me. 'Do you get my point?'

Again I nodded.

'I had a wonderful wife, two splendid children, a half share in a small but prosperous factory. I inherited some money unexpectedly and invested it in stocks which climbed quietly and resolutely. My life was free of even the most minor setbacks.'

I was uncomfortably conscious of time slipping away. 'I'd like to know about the dying,' I said quietly.

He looked at me with the slightest hint of irritation. 'And then,' he went on, 'things very gradually started to go bad. I lost my car keys. Someone spilled a drink over me at the pub.

'I was bitten by a dog. None of this had ever happened to me before. My stocks began to decline and then to plummet. My car was stolen. It was found, returned and stolen again. My father died and my brother died. My house was burgled.

'I became obsessed with my misfortune. I was afraid to go out for fear I'd be hit by a bus. Finally, my partner came to see me and suggested I go away somewhere for a rest. It seemed a good idea, so I booked into a private clinic in Scotland. On my third night there it burned down.'

He looked at me searchingly.

'When I returned home I found out that my wife had moved in with my partner and that he was quietly easing me out of the business. That was three weeks ago and that, I'm afraid, was the final straw. I built this.'

He held up his leather-bound attaché case. 'There's a bomb in here,' he said simply.

I stared at him and felt my legs go weak. Without a word, I turned and began pushing the buttons on the control panel.

'I was on my way to see my partner just now,' the man went on. 'My life is finished. I thought at least I'd take him with me.'

I began pounding on the doors and bellowing for help.

'I'd keep my voice down if I were you,' said my companion. 'I'm afraid this thing is noise sensitive.' I stopped and looked at him. 'It will also go off if it's shaken or in any way tampered with.' He shrugged apologetically. 'I'm a munitions expert. I thought of everything.'

He seemed calmly resigned. He looked at his watch and said, 'We have just over thirty seconds. I'm sorry.'

I felt no panic, but instead a rage, a sense of incredible injustice that this should be happening to me. I pushed the control buttons fruitlessly. What else could I do? I was vaguely aware of the other man sitting himself down in the corner with the attaché case on his lap.

'Twenty seconds,' he said, his eyes fixed to his watch.

It is an amazing thing how slowly the seconds tick away when there are only a handful of them left to you. They say your life passes before your eyes, but mine didn't.

All I could think about was the next few hours, the confusion our deaths would create, the police tramping around, someone having to tell my wife, her inevitable bafflement. Would she ever know how I'd come to be blown to bits or would it remain a mystery to her for ever?

'Ten seconds,' said my companion and then began the long, monotonous countdown.

'Nine . . . eight . . . seven . . . six . . . five . . . four . . . three . . . two . . .'

I shut my eyes and wondered what it would feel like. There was an enormous and palpable silence.

Nothing happened.

I opened my eyes. I don't know how much time passed, but it was at least a minute, perhaps a good deal more. My companion was staring at his attaché case. He held it to his ear, shook it once and pushed it away in disgust.

'You see?' he said to me. 'You see? Nothing goes right any more.'

The Unadulterated

LOUIS ALLEGRI

His eyes stared feverishly around my small, bedsitter as he sat picking at an eruption on the arm of my favourite chair.

I sat in the other.

I admired Tom Matthews; we had both come up the hard way together – starting in the same orphanage – and seen the inside of prison.

But he had managed to overcome his disturbed beginnings and was now the manager of a large company, his past hidden.

I had become disentangled with the law more recently.

'They'll kill her, Steve, unless I do exactly what they say!' He looked like death and I had the chills.

My old friend doted on his young, angelic-looking wife, Isabel, who was as attractive as a Botticelli model.

'They want fifteen thousand,' he went on, 'and I'm giving them every penny to save Isabel's life . . . !'

During his confused blabbering that followed, I gathered the kidnappers would be telephoning him again to tell him where to leave the ransom.

I felt disturbed by the nagging thought that such men often murdered their victims. He humped a large briefcase onto the table.

'What's that?' I eyed it suspiciously.

'I'm responsible for the company safe,' he said. 'It's unlikely the money will be missed until next week – but I can't take any chances with Isabel's life! I . . . I want to leave it with you, Steve, until I've been told what to do.

'Then, if the money is missed too soon, I hope you will be able to carry out the kidnappers' instructions.'

I gulped down a Scotch. 'The police – '

'No! They said Isabel would then die immediately . . . !'

The familiar sound of iron grilles rang in my head, but, after an argument, I nodded.

He then gripped my arm gratefully and opened the briefcase. I swallowed hard at the sight of the fivers.

'I'll pick up the money as soon as I hear from those . . . those . . . God help my poor Isabel . . .'

And God help you as well, chum, I thought, as he stumbled down the narrow staircase. My old friend deserved a lot better.

I'd had nothing to fall back on when a speeding driver, warm with booze, killed my wife. I had survived, but I doubted whether Tom would be as resilient. Whatever happened to his wife, he was finished.

Pinching fifteen thousand from his firm – for whatever reason – wouldn't win him friends, unless it was the occasional happy prison warden.

Tom Matthews collected the briefcase the following evening. 'They let Isabel say a few words,' he said, as he hurried out, a muscle twitching violently around his mouth. 'She . . . sounded so frightened . . .'

'Don't hand over that dough until you've got Isabel back,' I said, as he left.

Late that night, he telephoned and asked me to go to his luxurious suburban house. His wife obviously wasn't around when he poured me a Scotch in his low-beamed drawing-room. It gave me a sinking feeling.

'Where is Isabel?'

'I left the money where they told me . . .'

'Where is she?' I raised my voice.

'They are going to call me Saturday evening to tell me where to find her. She's quite safe, Steve! Locked up somewhere with food and drink.'

'You bloody fool!' I stood up angrily. 'I told you not to . . . !'

'They wanted time to get away. It's understandable, isn't it?' he yelled.

I felt sicker than I'd ever felt as he went on.

'I've done everything they asked, Steve. The money won't be missed until next week. I'll give myself up as soon as Isabel is home.'

I did nothing useful during the next two days except profit the whisky distillers. Then on Saturday evening I returned to Matthews' place where we sat waiting for that telephone call . . .

The guilt stuck in my gullet as the evening wore on and no call. Matthews kept talking about his new life with Isabel when it was all over.

As the hours passed, Matthews slumped disturbingly in his chair. 'Whatever happens, old friend,' I eventually stammered, 'you've got to keep going in this life. It . . . it won't be the end of everything.'

'With Isabel gone! And . . . and my career finished – a lousy thief again . . . ! What is there left?' he croaked.

I decided then he had to be told what stuck in my craw – even if he killed me . . . 'I've still got the money, Tom . . .'

He looked blank.

'I managed to get some old counterfeit stuff – not perfect but . . . Anyway, when you collected your briefcase from my place, I'd switched your money for snide. I think they're amateurs, Tom! Anyway it's unlikely they would have spotted the difference right away.'

I could see his face, now heavily lined, turn red with rage as the words sunk in.

'I thought, Tom, that if . . . if they were going to release Isabel they would have done it during the exchange. Wanted to help you. Told you not to let go of the money until Isabel was safe! I didn't think you'd survive the loss of all you've worked for . . . !'

'You might as well have put a pistol to my wife's head,' he hissed. 'Murderer!' He suddenly lunged towards me, swinging blows, one of which sent me sprawling to the floor. I didn't move as he grasped a heavy, bronze figure and raised it above my head.

The front doorbell stopped him in his tracks, unable to comprehend for a few moments, then dropping the figure, he hurried into the hall.

I had wiped the blood from my face when he returned, accompanied by a stranger.

'Well, Inspector?' he said to the hefty man, and then, unable to contain himself, gripped the CID man's arm. 'Is it . . . Isabel, my wife? Answer me!'

'I'm sorry, sir,' the Inspector gently removed his hand.

'Oh, dear God,' Tom whispered, and I felt like blowing my brains out. 'She . . . she's . . . ?'

'In serious trouble, I'm afraid, sir. We caught her buying airline tickets with counterfeit money – together with a young man . . .'

LOUIS ALLEGRI *was another frequent contributor to the short story page. His was a concise, often clipped, no-nonsense style, getting on with the plot. For in an Allegri story the plot was strong.*

Father's Day of Reckoning

MARGARET WEBB

Henry rehearsed the scene several times in his mind between putting the car away in the garage and entering the house.

'Polly, I've got to talk you . . .'

'Look here, Polly, I've got to tell you . . .'

'Polly, I know this is going to be a shock to you . . .'

Oh hell, he groaned to himself, it all sounds like a third-rate TV melodrama. Husband deserts wife and child for blonde secretary . . .

Of course Pip would have to be told. That was almost worse than telling Polly. Pip didn't say much; you never quite knew what he was thinking. But sometimes you felt that those grey eyes of his didn't miss much. As if they were quietly taking notes of things and assessing them fairly and squarely in his seven-year-old mind.

A great kid Pip. What would his assessment of his father be, after today?

The phone was ringing as he entered the house. He went to answer it and at the same moment Polly appeared from the kitchen.

Neatly sidestepping him she picked up the receiver almost, it seemed to Henry, snatching it from his hand.

'Oh, it's for you,' she said, handing him the receiver, 'it's your secretary.' Her face was flushed and it appeared to Henry that she looked relieved.

It was Liz. Henry said hastily, 'I've asked you not to ring here, Liz. Yes, I'm telling her tonight. No, I won't dither. Just don't ring here.'

'Oh yes I shall, darling. I'll ring again in an hour, at seven o'clock, when you've told her. 'Bye darling.'

As Liz's cool voice faded into silence Henry gave himself a mental shake. Dithering was precisely what he was doing.

Liz was young, sophisticated and direct. When he was with her the shadow of middle-age looming just over the horizon seemed to disappear. 'You mustn't let yourself go, Henry,' she told him, 'you're in a rut. Life is for living!'

Straightening his shoulders, he went into the dining-room. Polly was reading a letter, but she stuffed it quickly into her pocket when he came in, and went on setting the table.

Henry opened his mouth to speak to her, and then closed it again.

The meal was rather a scratchy affair, not up to Polly's usual high standard. She seemed not quite herself.

When Pip arrived they glanced at each other and then quickly away again.

For the first time Henry sensed something in the air. Covertly he studied his wife. There was something almost . . . furtive about her . . . She was ill at ease. Concealing something!

That letter! And the phone call she was so obviously expecting and afraid of his answering. Could it be . . . could it possibly be another man?

No, of course it couldn't. Not Polly! Guileless, open-hearted Polly?

He found himself looking at her searchingly. Not very young, not quite as slim as she had been, but still a good-looker.

Not that he was jealous. Not at all. Couldn't have been more opportune, really. But Polly . . . !

'What's the matter, Dad?' Pip asked.

'Matter? Nothing. Why?'

'You just looked funny, that's all, Dad.'

Pip glanced at his mother. Again that look passed between them. Furtive. Conspiratorial.

It was too much, Pip as well, shutting him out of their cosy conspiracy. Had that fellow already supplanted him in Pip's affections?

The door bell rang. Polly was on her feet in an instant, but Pip was even quicker. 'I'll get it,' he said, closing the dining-room door after him. Polly began to chatter animatedly, but Henry was not listening. He heard the front door being opened, then a man's voice.

'Just thought I'd make sure . . . just in case . . . Call back later . . .'

'Who was that?' Henry demanded when Pip returned.

'Er . . . just a man,' Pip said.

The telephone rang. Polly jumped up.

'This is it,' she said to Pip.

She walked around the table to the door and on the way she laid her hand on Henry's shoulder. Just a little affectionate gesture, but it went to Henry's heart. As if she was saying, 'I'm sorry old boy!' A consoling pat to the loser.

She came back slowly. She was smiling. She looked at Pip and nodded.

'I knew!' Pip shouted, 'I knew when that man came. He's coming back later. He's a photographer!'

'Henry darling,' Polly said. 'We'll have to tell you all about it now. But first I want you to read this.'

She drew the letter from her pocket. Only it wasn't a letter. It was an essay written in Pip's square childish handwriting, very black and thick.

My Dad is all rite. My Mam likes him a lot and so do I. He can swim two miles and he mends my bike. When my Mam was ill in bed he cooked our dinners and we eat them nearly always.

He says you have to see the funny side. like when a lorry ran into our car and he flung himself across Mam to save her and his head was cut open, all bluddy. And when I said does it hurt he said. Only when I larff. My Dad is the best.

Polly said, 'That call was from the Editor of the *Courier*. Pip's won their competition – at least you and Pip between you.

'Congratulations, darling. You've been elected Dad of the Year!'

The clock struck seven. Right on cue the telephone rang. And rang. And rang.

He let it ring.

The Pick-Up

EDGAR WALLACE

I t was the day before Mr Vernon Strate went back to London –
where his presence was urgently required – that he proposed in
his quiet way to Margaret Brand. He did it so quietly, so
unemotionally that she did not, at first, realize what he was saying.

'I am, of course, your senior by ten or twelve years, and I realize
that in many ways I am not the kind of husband you would have
chosen.'

'I really don't know what to say, Mr Strate – I hardly know
you.'

Which was true. They had met in the train to Brightsea and his
courtesy and attention had been charming. She was now quite
sure that he had changed the luxury of the Marine Hotel for the
bare comforts of Acacia House just to be near her. He had
admitted as much.

'I am a fairly rich man,' he went on, 'and I have no ties and no
relations. I have to go to town tomorrow and I'd like you to give
this matter your earnest consideration while I'm away.

'On the day we marry, I'll settle £10,000 on you.'

In his absence, she found herself considering the offer seriously
for he was a kind and considerate man. And yet . . . Vernon Strate
was a 'pick-up' – a man who had come into her life without
introduction.

In the upper-class world in which Margaret had been born, you were warned about 'pick-ups'. You met them on the promenade, on the pier – sometimes on trains.

They remarked on the weather and gradually you came to know them and found yourself discussing quite intimate things like relations and appendicitis.

But Mr Strate clearly didn't belong to this dubious category – no man could have simulated such good manners, and courtesy.

Margaret was becoming quite fond of him and that was her frame of mind when a second, apparently more obvious 'pick-up' hove in sight.

He was not an inmate of Acacia House – where middle-aged ladies who knitted jumpers in London came to knit jumpers in Brightsea. Nor did he drop carelessly into a chair by her side on the front, nor stroll past her several times trying to catch her eye.

She was sitting on one of the hard bench seats, when he came swinging along the deserted pier. It was eight o'clock in the morning, and only energetic fishers were up and about.

A rather tall, brown-faced man he was, dressed in flannels and a dark blue blazer. He passed her without a glance, and she looked up from her book and watched him idly until he disappeared round the side of the pavilion.

She was still reading when he came back and was so engrossed in her story that she did not notice him at all till he tripped and fell sprawling at her feet.

'Damn!' he said calmly, as he picked himself up. 'Shoelace . . . Terribly sorry!'

He put one foot on the bench and jerked savagely at the long lace that had tripped him up.

She said nothing – turned her eyes to the book again, though she was no longer reading.

After a moment he said, 'I know what you're thinking. But if I were trying to make your acquaintance I should attempt something less painful.'

He was dabbing a scratched hand with a handkerchief.

'But I'm not. And I won't tell you that we've met before, because we haven't.' Without invitation he sat down.

His next words startled her. 'You're Margaret Brand. My sister went to school with you. My name is Denman – Ian Denman.'

In her schooldays at St Mary's when Margaret was senior prefect and Helen Denman was head girl, there arose the legend of the Awful Brother. He was Helen's brother and his awfulness lay in his total indiscipline.

Finally, in their last school year, the Awful Brother did something so awful that Helen – something of a prig, Margaret always thought – would not even tell her dearest friend what it was.

All she could recall was the Awful Brother had been guilty of an act of Supreme Awfulness. Did he marry a barmaid or seduce the Vicar's daughter? The secret, whatever it was, never revealed itself.

'You're not the . . . Awful Brother?'

He nodded unsmilingly.

'That's me,' he said calmly. 'I'm the Awful Brother. And I'm in an Awful Tangle right now. Father died last year, and I've been trying rather desperately to hide my past.

'You see, I'm now a Baronet, and that doesn't go with a certain . . . lifestyle I have. If the newspapers got hold of the story they'd really make things impossible for me.

'Actually, I'm turning over a new leaf next week . . . chucking everything. I'd like one last fling, though, before I clear out!'

He spoke rapidly, jerkily – and to her, incoherently. She hadn't the slightest idea what he was talking about. But bit by bit an Awful Suspicion was forming. The Awful Brother's Awful Secret was that he was a con man.

As suddenly as he had sat down, he rose again.

'I must go,' he said. 'Awfully glad to have met you. You won't give me away will you?'

To her surprise that afternoon when he 'accidentally' met her again, she didn't snub him. She even found herself agreeing to afternoon tea.

Unbelievably she later found herself at the theatre with him and next morning – incredible this – he was instructing her in the art of sea-fishing.

She thought it only fair at the end of the third day to tell him that she wasn't unattached.

'Engaged?' His rather good-looking face was suddenly blank. 'Really . . . I didn't know.'

'Well, not exactly engaged,' she explained quickly and told him as much as she thought necessary, about the very courteous Vernon Strate.

'Now what about you?' she asked. 'Have you had that last fling you were talking about?'

He shook his head. 'No – and I don't expect I shall.'

That afternoon Mr Strate returned from London, and she plucked up courage to tell him her decision.

'Can you come for a walk? I want to speak to you.'

He hesitated. 'The sun is rather strong for my eyes,' he began; but ten minutes later they were walking along the pier.

'Let's sit here.' She sat down, he at her side. 'Mr Strate, I want to tell you something. I don't think I can marry you. You see, I've just met . . .'

'But my dear . . .' he began.

And then there appeared in the distance the lank figure of the Awful Brother.

'Tell . . . your friend . . . I'm not well.'

But it was too late. Ian Denman had come up.

'This is Mr Strate,' Margaret said haltingly, 'the friend I spoke to you about.'

'This is a friend of mine,' she began.

To her amazement, Mr Strate jumped to his feet with an oath.

'I don't want to see anybody!' He almost shouted the words.

The Awful Brother was glaring down at them. His face was grim. 'My last fling, Margaret, and I can't take it – well, not without involving you.'

Then turning to Strate he said, 'You're in luck, Smith. Just beat it before I change my mind.'

To her horror, the placid Mr Strate rose and ran off at the double. She last saw him vanishing through the entrance of the pier.

'You've spoilt it my dear!' said the Awful Brother taking the seat so hastily vacated by Mr Strate. 'I wanted to go out of the force in a blaze of glory, and now I can't!'

'Who . . . who are you?'

He laughed.

'Didn't you know I disgraced my family by joining the police?

I'm now a Detective-Inspector and I've been looking for Smith alias Bosco, alias Strate – for months.

'He's a professional bigamist, and wanders round looking for lonely young ladies who have some money.

'Now let's forget the police, and Vernon what's-his-name. I have something really important to ask you.'

EDGAR WALLACE *was born on 1 April 1875. On the 100 years eve of the anniversary of that birth the* Evening News *published this short story found amongst his papers by his daughter Penelope.*

Two of a Kind

DOUGLAS BAKER

Dear Mum,
    I regret to inform you that another of me recent exercises in search of the bent nicker went awry.

It terminated in fact in a fog of frustration, leaving the joy of your life up to the eyeballs in debt to society again.

Me wretched attempt to make crime pay started when me and me mate Nutty Slack went to case the offices of a loan company in the hope of making an unofficial loan, like.

The loan company has got the top floor of this big office block, ain't it, and we marched into the foyer and the first thing I sees through the rubber plants is this geezer.

Well, I just stares, don't I? I mean, I'm looking at meself. You never seen nobody more identical in all your life than what this bloke is to me, mum. Its uncanny. Straight.

The geezer's the spitting facsimile of me, a biological replica. He's got the same classical nose, alert eyes, intellectual forehead, determined jaw and humorous mouth. We're two peas out of the same pod.

Then Nutty spots him and intones, 'Stone me! Clock that geezer, Spraggo. It's you all over again. Could be your twin. He's got the same flat nose, faded eyes, unintelligent forehead and weak jaw.'

Before I can shoot the Nut down with a burst of spontaneous wit, the geezer spots us and comes over, looking dead surprised.

'Good heavens!' he ejaculates. 'How terribly bizarre! How frightfully . . . Et cetera, et cetera.'

Well, he might be me physically, but orally and sartorially we ain't in the same league. He's obviously an educated toff and it's dead cert he's got one of them long names you have to break down with a hyphen.

When the bloke reaches his final exclamation mark, Nutty introduces us and we learn that my double's handle is Algernon Plunkington-Plodgett.

'Tell you what, Algy,' the Nut says, 'Albert and me are in a frightful hurry just now and can't stop to talk, but as this incredible physical similarity demands further discussion, may I suggest that we take you out to dinner this evening, when we can – '

At which point I interposes with unconcealed vehemence, 'Hang about, Nut! We can't afford to – '

But he interposes my interposition with a swift kick on me ankle, and I realizes that the Nut, who claims to have a brain that would make all of IBM's hardware redundant, is up to something bent nickerwise. So I shuts me trap and leaves him to his scheming.

Algy's handsome features have lit up and he enthuses, 'By jove, yes, I'd love to dine with you! How kind!'

'Not at all,' Nutty smiles. 'Now let me see if I can think of a place worthy of the occasion . . .'

'How about Sam's Kaff?' I suggests. 'His meat pie and chips blow you right out and . . .'

Nutty kicks me other ankle and says, 'The Granchester, I think. Excellent place. We shall be well looked after there.'

'Absolutely wonderful!' Algy beams.

'I suggest we meet in the bar,' Nutty suggests. 'At seven-forty-five, shall we say?'

'Yes, let's,' Algy responds, his white, even smile bisecting his mush.

So we shakes his mitt and bids him good day and exits. In the street, I says, 'Why are we buying the geezer a dinner and where are we getting the money from?'

'We ain't buying him no dinner,' the Nut tells me, 'and we're getting the money from old man Thompson's safe.'

'Come again,' I blinks.

'Don't you recognize the perfect alibi when you see it?' Nutty grins. 'We ain't been able to do Thompson's safe 'cos the law sussed us when we were casing it last month.

'If we'd pulled the job, they'd have known it was us. But now we've got an alibi they can't break.'

'Have we?' I says, still blinking.

'Look,' the Nut sighs, 'breaking it down into words of one syllable, when we knock over the safe at seven-forty-five, Algy will be seen by the barmen etc., in The Granchester, who will think it is you when they see you in the ID parade, on account of you both look alike.'

'Nutty,' I grins, 'you've got a brain in your head!'

'And just as soon as they are able to transplant them,' he smiles back, 'you'll have one, too.'

Well, mum, at seven-forty-five we jemmies the back door of Thompson's pawnshop (he don't live on the premises) and opens the safe with the key which the silly old faggort hides where anybody would think to look. There's only ten nicker inside, but it's better than nothing, I suppose, and burglars can't be choosers (comical pun).

Two hours later, I'm at home losing my half of the loot to Nutty at cards, when there comes the usual loud authoritative knock at the door.

This time we don't get that sinking feeling, on account of we've got an insurmountable alibi, ain't we?

Nutty lets the gendarmes in, including our 'friend' Detective Sergeant Cox, and asks them if there were some inquiries they wanted us to help them with.

Cox stabs me with a sharp eye and says, 'Where were you around eight o'clock?'

'In The Granchester,' I responds, consolidating my position with a bit of innocent blinking, like.

'I'm surprised you admit it,' he says.

Which remarks turn me cold, 'cos it shouldn't be in the script at all.

'One of our chaps, name Collins, was in The Granchester, too,' Cox continues. 'He was nearby when Legger Lamb walked up to you at the bar.'

I'm getting colder by the second. Legger, another member of the bent brigade, owed me for a fur caper we'd pulled weeks back.

'Collins says you put on a bit of an accent,' Cox goes on, 'and pretended at first you didn't know Lamb, probably for the benefit of eavesdroppers.

'But when he said he'd got five hundred quid for you for the furs he'd fenced, you changed your tune.

'You said, "Only joking mate – 'course I know you. Albert Spraggin don't forget his pals, do he?"

'Then you took the five hundred he gave you and scarpered so quick you lost Collins. But we always know where to pick you up, don't we?'

So there I am, mum, snookered. I could've told Cox about the pawnshop caper and maybe got orf lighter, but that meant involving Nutty. So I had to swallow it.

I'm surprised at Algy taking the money, he had such an honest face. Still, that's the way it goes.

As the gendarmes march me out Nutty does a bit of tutting and says, 'You are a silly lad, Spraggo. Why don't you give up crime like what I done?'

I sneers at him and he says he'll bring me some nuts on visiting day.

That's all for now, mum – and it's enough. Hope you're having fun down there in Holloway. All me love from your everloving son.

Yours faithfully
Albert Spraggin.

The Hairpiece

N.A. HILTON

The guardian angel sighed as she looked at Soul/Earth/19664/ MG.

She should be used to it by now but it still hurt. She raised her arm and the Disposal Cherub began to materialize in a rosy glow beside her . . .

Everything was quiet, as usual, in the convent high in the Italian hills, Sister Benedict prayed happily, absorbed as usual in her one-sided, but satisfying conversation with Our Lady.

The birds sang and the sun shone but the little Sister heard nothing of the world outside.

Reverend Mother had been right to rebuke her; her mind had wandered during evening meal yesterday, while Sister Mary was reading from the *Life of Saint Teresa*. However, penance had been done, and it would not happen again . . .

In her London flat, Julia sat and looked at herself in the dressing-table mirror. Not too bad, everything considered. Thank God it was all cut and dried now, all arrangements made.

She looked at her watch – 10.30. The taxi should be here in fifteen minutes. Time for the finishing touches. No crawling there looking like a wreck, she was going to march into that clinic with her head held high and looking her very best.

Why had she hesitated so long. She had written three times to

Alan, the first time a gay, chatty letter asking him about the tour, asking how the Americans liked the British orchestras, and how she missed him.

She wasn't really surprised to receive no reply to her letter. Travelling around from town to town on a concert tour would take a little time to catch up with him.

Next time she wrote she was sure about the baby, but said nothing, only how were things over there, and she missed him . . . missed him.

The third letter had been very hard to write. The version she finally sent said, 'Darling, guess what? We're going to have a baby, isn't it a mad thing to happen? No regrets darling, only write if you want to. Love Julia.'

She hadn't really expected a reply, and she didn't receive one.

Of course, she could not look after a baby alone so she made a phone call to Cynthia, she scribbled down a telephone number, collected her savings from the Post Office, and made an appointment for today at a discreet clinic. She looked at her watch; just half an hour.

Three days, all over, no baby, no Alan.

She looked again in the mirror, nearly ready, nails done, false eyelashes helping to hide the dark shadows under her eyes; hair brushed back, ready for the finishing touch.

She lifted the hairpiece out of its box, lovely long silky hair, pale gold, coiled into a neat twist, and pinned it carefully into place.

The thought struck her like a slap in the face, like icy fingers squeezing her very being. 'Can't do it . . . I can't . . . my baby, no they shall not.'

The face staring back at her in the mirror was deathly white, the black-circled eyes shrunken. Oh God, she thought, I look like a clown. She started to laugh quietly, then biting her lip and shaking, 'Stop it, stop it, you fool,' she said aloud.

No food, that was it, no breakfast.

She looked at her watch again, just time for coffee and toast. She made sure the varnish was dry on her nails, put the hairpiece carefully back in its box and went into the tiny kitchenette of the flat. She put the coffee on to perk, and felt better.

Of course she was doing the right thing, whatever had caused that absurd moment of doubt earlier, everything was quite clear now in her mind.

She drank the coffee, nibbled the toast and went back to finish getting ready. Now ... handbag ready, yes, suitcase for three days, yes, note for the milkman. She lifted the hairpiece from its box, pinned it into place, and heard the taxi draw up outside.

This time the clarity of the sudden realization of what she was going to do hit her mind with such force that it was all she could do not to fall off the chair.

She gripped the dressing table with both hands while great sobs wracked her body. There was a knock on the door, 'Taxi, madam.' No, no, go away. Shocked silence.

'Are you all right, madam?'

She pulled herself together and went to the door. 'Sorry, plans changed.' She thrust some money into his hand and shut the door, then sank down on the floor, sobbing quietly, almost happily.

We'll manage, she thought, my baby and I. We'll manage, somehow. She must have slept there on the floor till she woke with a bell ringing, urgently.

It took a few seconds to gather herself together and open the door. She stared stupidly at a small boy in a postman's uniform. 'Telegram, miss.'

She opened it and read, 'Coach in accident. Don't worry. All well, darling. Letters just reached me. Marry me next week. Look after yourself and our offspring. Love always, Alan.' Now she was really crying, but this time they were tears of pure joy ...

The Guardian Angel paused, a rare smile on her face. Gently, she lowered Soul/Earth/19664/MG back into the rosy cloudiness where he would stay for six more months, and before she turned away she put back the label on his incubator. Male/1st class/genius/music ...

In the Italian convent the birds had gone to roost, the candles flickered as little Sister Benedict rose stiffly from her knees. She was deeply ashamed of herself. It had happened again – her thoughts had strayed. It was unforgivable, to think about herself.

It was just personal vanity to wonder what had become of the long pale gold hair she had so willingly allowed them to cut off when she gave herself to God for ever. How could she think such dreadful thoughts when she was supposed to be praying for the souls of all unwanted children?

The Traveller

J.S. BRENNAN

The traveller was weary. He had covered many miles since dawn and was ready to put to rest.

He paused briefly to get his bearings, every muscle tensed against further action.

He looked back along his own trail. Once or twice he had thought he was being followed but there was no sign.

The sky was a dirty yellow and full of snow. The bitter wind was pushing the laden clouds swiftly towards the hills and peaks he would be traversing the following day. A few heavy flakes began to fall as he moved on.

He was unfamiliar with the terrain, but the very nature of it afforded cover to the experienced, and there were many places he could rest unseen.

It was important to remain undiscovered for as long as possible. That was why he and his race kept to the high lands. Years of travelling from place to place in that fashion had inured him to the hardships and dangers of such a life.

Luck was with him. He located a small cave where he would be unfortunate to be found even in good weather and the impending snowstorm ensured protection.

He was glad to get out of the vicious wind that howled among the peaks forming the brief flurries into drifts as it went. By morning the snow would be feet thick.

In the cave, shielded from the elements, he made himself as comfortable as he could. His thick coat was ample protection. He settled down and waited for sleep to steal over him, but it eluded him and he felt vaguely disturbed.

It sometimes happened when the mind was overactive. Suddenly he realized; he was in inhabited territory. Some sixth sense must have warned him but there was no need to worry. The falling snow would eliminate his tracks.

He might be found by a wild animal but this was the least of his worries. It was the smooth-skinned people from the valleys and plains he had learned to avoid. They tended to be much smaller than the people of his race, maybe because of the sedentary life they appeared to lead.

He had watched them from a safe place many times and once, when much younger, had tried to make contact with them although it had been expressly forbidden by the elders of his tribe.

He remembered being angry, not with them but with himself for not trying harder to communicate. They seemed such likeable people, but rules were rules and he was obliged not to try again.

The traveller yawned and stretched out on his back. The comparative warmth of the still air in the small cave was having its effect. He slept for a time and then suddenly awoke, every sense alert. Something had given warning. Then he realized with a sigh that the wind had dropped and the only sound was the light splat-splat as the fluffy snowflakes hit the mounting first layer.

It was imperative that he reach his destination before nightfall. The northern tribe would be waiting at the pass and if he were not there at the appointed time there would be great trouble.

In view of the snow he decided to go higher and keep to the sheltered side of the hills. Although more exposed to a possible sighting by the valley people, it would be quicker.

He got up and went to the opening. The sky was still full – the real fall had not yet begun. He smiled. That meant almost complete security. He had been trained never to take anything on trust but there were times when safety was obvious. He relaxed and stared out through the falling snow.

Dimly in the valley below he could see the scattered lights of a small township and way over to his left a small line of winking lights moved steadily up to the lower slopes. So he had been followed!

He judged the rate of the climb expertly. They could not possibly be in the area before morning and by that time he would be gone. The sound of dogs barking was borne on the wind and he smiled. He liked dogs.

He was amazed by the way the smooth-skinned people multiplied. There always seemed to be children running about among the huts in the valley.

It was sadly different with his own people. They were a pure race and their ancient laws forbade inter-breeding with the lowland peoples. At one time they had been numbered in thousands, according to the elders. Now they were counted in hundreds. Only after oft-repeated requests by the northern tribe had the council agreed to send him on his mission.

If he was successful and the gods smiled upon him there would be new mouths to feed in the springtime and the joyful gatherings, which always took place after a happy event, would last for days. He lay back happily and slept again.

In the morning greatly rested he made swift preparation for the final stage of his journey. There was enough food for two meals but he saved just a small amount for the later one. He broke off a piece of ice and sucked on it for refreshment.

Outside the snow was deep and ice crusted. He could hear the sounds of the search party he had seen the night before and they were very close.

It would be necessary to back-track and make a detour to avoid them. The dogs would make very heavy weather of it in the deep snow and he had no fear of being caught.

He pushed his large frame into the packed snow round the cave entrance and fought his way with terrifying power to higher ground to get round the back of the hill.

Once, he broke cover and moved into open space. Someone in the search party saw him immediately and shouted excitedly.

'Quick, there it goes, the Abominable Snowman! Shoot, shoot you fool!'

The traveller smiled to himself. They seemed an impetuous people. He wondered what the words meant. Probably some form of greeting, but he had no time to stop, and gaining speed with every stride made his way north to fulfil his mission.

Revenge of the Golden Lady

NIGEL POCKNELL

The whinny of the horse echoed down the mountainside.

The sun, beating down mercilessly from a metallic blue sky, made the sweat trickle down my forehead and splash on to the rim of my binoculars.

I ranged across the parched yellowing slopes of the mountain. Tussocks of grass bent in the light breeze whilst the lower slopes were beginning to purple with heather. Sheep plaintively bleated in the distance. Clusters of wild ponies dotted the landscape.

I looked at the far ridge and stiffened. A white horse stood on the shoulder of the mountain. It tossed its flowing mane and ambled purposefully away to my left.

I watched it pick its way through grass and bramble over the most impassable of slopes. I shivered, for not even a blade of grass seemed to stir beneath its feet.

Soon it reached a line of pines and sweet-smelling mountain ash huddled together on the slope.

I heaved up my knapsack and glanced at the map. Round the corner was Bryn Fawr Reservoir. I stuffed the map into my capacious pocket and slithered down the sheep track to the pot-holed road.

Ten minutes later I stood heaving and panting at the side of the dam. The drought had taken a pitiless toll. I could see where the water should have been, but now it lay in ever diminishing circles forty feet below its normal level. Three-quarters of the reservoir consisted of brown clay, cracked into pieces like an enormous jig-saw puzzle.

I lifted my binoculars again. In the middle of the reservoir stood the remains of a brick wall sticking out incongruously above the dry, cracked mud.

In front of the wall stood the white horse. It turned its head and seemed to look directly at me. Then I noticed something else. Near the wall in what must have been the front garden of the house, the mud had fallen away.

'A *human* skeleton?' echoed the landlord as he leaned against the counter of the Drunken Duck an hour or so later. The whole bar was suddenly silent.

'What did you say?' snapped a voice in the stillness. A tall, thin man with a kerchief round his neck rose to his feet.

'I said I saw a skeleton. In the reservoir. It was just under the mud. I wouldn't have noticed it if it hadn't been for the horse.'

The man yanked me up by the lapels of my coat and thrust his tanned face into mine.

Anger blazed in his eyes. 'Is this some sort of joke?' he hissed.

I roughly pushed him away and brushed myself down. 'Who the hell do you think you are?' I demanded.

'Hold on, hold on,' warned the landlord, putting up a restrain-ing hand.

'He's only a stranger passing through. He probably doesn't know about Mary.'

The man banged his glass onto the counter.

'Where are you going now?' demanded the landlord.

'Some people still have work to do even if others haven't,' the man growled. Next minute he was gone.

Before I could interrupt, the landlord nodded in the direction of the door.

'Arthur's wife disappeared five years ago. She went out riding on her mare and completely vanished. They found her horse wandering on the mountainside. It died a week later. Pined away, some say. But they never found Mary.'

'Yes, but . . .'

'You see, the police thought that Arthur had done her in and buried her somewhere.'

'More like she had a lover,' opined a farmer from the corner. 'By God, but she went round a few in her time. Nice-looking wench, mind. With that long, golden hair.'

'And I can remember that red scarf of hers. She always wore it round her neck. But flighty as they come she was. Went after anything in trousers.'

'You ought to know, Bill,' grunted a burly-looking man near the fireplace. He looked me up and down. 'Are you sure it was a skeleton you saw?' he asked.

I flushed angrily. 'I'm so certain I went to see the police constable to report it, but he was out.'

The landlord roared with laughter and slapped the burly man on the back. 'There you are, Evan, I told you your sins will find you out.'

He looked half-apologetically at me. 'Sorry, sir,' he said. 'This is Constable Davis.'

'You know,' went on the constable, "You must have been mistaken. It could have been a few sheep bones. We do get a lot of sheep falling into the reservoir and drowning.'

That got my back up. 'Look,' I said, 'I was going to push on to Llanserig for the night, but if you don't believe me, I'll take you back up there and prove it to you.'

And that was the reason why I was once again toiling along the slope with the policeman beside me. The sun had just set in an orange ball and dark shadows fingered their way up the opposite slopes.

In the greying light everything seemed eerie and silent . . .

I stepped on to the low bridge over the dam. It was hard to realize that a thriving village had once occupied the whole area of the reservoir. In the fading light I pointed out the wall standing in the middle and my trail of footprints going to and from it.

Constable Davis looked somehow pale and strained and as he stared at me, he smiled a crooked smile.

'If it wasn't for the drought nobody would ever have found out,' he said quietly. 'I really loved that girl, but it was just another sordid affair to her.'

Memory flashed into my mind. I remembered looking up at the wall behind the skeleton and seeing the small oval stone set between the bricks. The faded words had been hard to read on it but now they clicked into place in my mind – 'Local Constabulary'.

Instinctively, as he clenched his truncheon, I knew what he was going to do. Suddenly he froze, his eyes widened in terror. He stood transfixed, staring at the slope.

I turned and saw a figure slowly walking – a figure with golden hair and a red scarf.

A horse whinnied. From behind the wall in the reservoir stepped the white horse. Davis swung round, overbalanced, and his scream was still ringing in my ears long after he disappeared into the water below.

The figure straightened and dropped the pitchfork of straw it was carrying. As it ran towards me I recognized Arthur from the pub, with his red kerchief flapping round his neck.

In the meantime, as if satisfied, the horse turned and trotted steadily away up the reservoir and round the corner. To this day I swear it left not a single hoofprint.

The Gong

ANTHONY STEEL

I t had been several years since I was last there.

I had almost forgotten just how similar to the Scottish Highlands the landscape of this small part of Africa was.

I entered the once so familiar rest-house which was the focus of all social life for the senior officials of the area and felt overjoyed to meet up with my friends: Stephen Roko, Prefect of the province, and Colonel Alex Cook, once military adviser in the Republic, but now, he told me, a UN representative.

In the lounge, we found some free chairs by the window. Glancing round, I sensed the atmosphere to be far more subdued and tense than in my day.

I noticed that all the others in the room, expatriate and African, were talking quietly and earnestly in small groups, glancing out through the open veranda doors to the track that led to the boulder-strewn foothills of the dominating Koi mountain.

Nothing moved, yet the guests appeared to be waiting for something to happen.

Away to the west, the village of thatched, round huts seemed unusually still.

Stephen saw the expression on my face.

'Yes, there is something worrying us all,' he said. 'You remember the old Chief of the Koi?'

Alex interrupted. 'Oh, it's really all a piece of exaggerated nonsense.'

The Prefect continued. 'The old man is dying and everyone is worried about what comes next. He's been Chief for sixty years and his people can't remember any other leader. They're going to feel totally lost.

'For days all the elders from his villages have been trekking to the oracles and shrines to plead that the spirits don't take him away, but it looks as if they will.'

'It's 1971, not 1871, you know,' muttered Cook.

'Nevertheless, we are keeping the police at the ready,' Stephen was firm and very serious.

'And waiting for the gong,' I added.

'You know then,' he half-smiled.

'I know that at the moment death claims the Chief, the great gong will be struck. And that every Koi community in the mountains will hear the echo.'

'Anything else?' queried Stephen, in a schoolmasterly tone.

'Oh, for goodness sake,' said our friend, irritably.

I went on, 'In the old days, as the gong sounded, a tested and valiant warrior was always sacrificed so that his high spirit would escort the spirit of the Chief to the spirit land.'

Stephen nodded. 'That's what has always happened but we are hoping to prevent it this time. I'm going out to the Chief's compound this afternoon to size up the situation.'

'Do you know,' said Alex turning to me, 'my grandfather was the police commander who tried to stop the last sacrifice – when the present Chief's own father died in 1911?

'My family has had a long connection with this part of the world, but it's an amazing coincidence all the same.'

'What happened last time?' I asked.

'He was too late to prevent the sacrifice, but he caught the head priest and had him hanged as an example – notwithstanding the hundred and one curses he laid on my grandfather.'

The self-righteous tone must have stung Stephen, but he said nothing.

The sun grew higher and the village women returned from their farms in the bush. Brightly robed horsemen rode in from the dry northern scrubland with carvings and metalwork from desert forges.

Stephen rose to go. Alex begged him to let us accompany him. It would be a fascinating experience to be present in the very palace of a Great Chief as his people gathered to await the inevitable.

The Prefect yielded. At the adjoining stable five policemen were already waiting.

A groom soon had horses saddled for us and we set out on the ten-mile ride.

The journey took us through vistas of mountain peaks which rolled away into the distance, surpassing anything it was possible to imagine.

The main village of the Koi Chiefdom lay on the slopes of a slumbering volcano. No enemy in days gone by dared invade for fear of provoking the spirits that could sometimes be heard rumbling in the depths of their mountain home.

We found every member of the clan gathered outside the royal compound. Occasionally the drums beat, whilst a giant of a man covered in gold chains and bangles stood waiting by the gong.

Alex and I remained mounted. The others dismounted and entered the compound.

Young warriors lined the enclosure, most of them carrying weapons. Hundreds of women sat by the walls in attitudes of complete dejection.

An air of desolation enveloped the whole village. The Koi people were facing a great test as their herbalists and medicine men came and went.

After a bit Stephen and the policeman came out and started to remount. Just at that moment a despairing cry rose from the Chief's chamber. Instantly it was taken up by all the assembled villagers.

The wail grew louder and louder till it was deafening. When it was almost unbearable the giant by the gong turned to pick up a wooden striking pole.

As he did so, Alex shouted. I swung round and saw that one of the young men had gone down on his knees. Towering over him was one of the elders, slowly raising a huge sword.

Alex spurred his horse forward – I don't know whether to halt the descent of the executioner's sword or to stop the swing of the gong-beater.

Whatever his intention, the result was to halt the execution – but not the striking of the gong.

As the awesome sound rang out, all our horses reared. I just managed to stay in the saddle, but out of the corner of my eye, I saw Alex thrown violently. He crashed on his head, under his horse. He must have died instantly.

Lt-Colonel Alex Cook, late of the West Country Rifles and grandson of the man who had tried to stop the last Ceremony of the Gong was the sacrifice chosen to accompany the Great Chief to the spirit land.

ANTHONY STEEL, *an immensely popular film actor of the post-war period noted for his 'Officer-type' roles, was brought up in Kenya, and his love of Africa has stayed with him.*

Sold for a Farthing

EDWARD TURBERVILLE

There was nothing wrong with the small country town of Munstable.

Its only mistake was to have had founders, seven centuries ago, who were careless enough to site it in the path of the motorway planners due to come along a few hundred years later.

The promise of new playing fields on the other side of the town, with glossy pavilions and swimming pool, had been rejected by the ungrateful citizens.

Three of them had even stronger views. It was Joe Bywaters, English master at the local grammar school, who hatched out the tadpole of an idea that was to grow into a whale.

Joe held the view that Christopher Marlowe, poet, was the real author of the Shakespeare plays, and here was an opportunity to halt the motorway boys and redress history in one grand gesture.

In Reggie Andrews he had someone with an animus against authority and plenty of time on his hands, for Reggie had offended the Lords of the Admiralty by rubbing his submarine's bottom on the mud in Plymouth Sound.

Hugh Watson, pushing eighty years, was a stone-mason and loathed cars with the ferocity of an octogenarian.

The plan was simply that Christopher Marlowe should be found to have been buried in the churchyard of St Matthew's which adjoins the doomed playing fields.

As Joe explained to old Hugh, Marlowe was contemporary with Shakespeare and was really the author of the Stratford Bard's plays. It was an historical lie that Marlowe had been killed in a duel, at twenty-one years of age, and buried at Deptford.

When the three surveyed the rotted slab of stone, recovered by Reggie from a corner of the churchyard, and on which old Hugh had wrought his skill, it was difficult to disbelieve their own story. The barely discernible letters said:

HRIST PH R M LO E

H re Leith

God re t is Soul

1616

Moss was rubbed into the porous stone and the sight was awesome in its antiquity.

Lifting a paving stone from the path to the door of St Matthew's in the dark, and replacing it with the Marlowe stone, face down, was no problem. The accidental discovery of the bogus stone was, likewise, easy. It was the effect of the discovery that took them by surprise.

They had only intended to halt the motorway boys, not stop the world.

Scholars in places they had never heard of, in Ashanti, Peru and China, sprang like demons from the earth.

At home, the Shakespeare armies lined up and faced the cohorts of Marlowe. It looked like bloody civil war.

Amid the clamour, St Matthew's Church stood serene and eternal, quietly nudging all other news competitors from the TV screens in millions of homes.

Joe was appalled at the way coaches and cars choked Munstable, and Reggie prayed that all would be forgiven and that he would be recalled to service in the peaceful depths of the ocean. Nevertheless at eighty, old Hugh chuckled with glee.

The motorway planners dragged out dusty alternatives from the files. Rumours were about that a Royal Commission might be set up.

Miss Weatherly was not exactly a Trojan Horse, although her existence had much the same impact.

A recluse of eighty-two, she had been four months catching up on the story that had shot Munstable into literary orbit. It came to her in a newspaper wrapped around some lettuce. She swept into Munstable and up to the doors of St Matthew's vicarage.

'This is a lie,' she declared, thrusting out the crumpled newspaper, still wet from the lettuce. 'My father would never have used old stones when he laid the path to St Matthew's in 1907. He took pride in dressing new stones. Never an old one. Never.'

The Reverend Stopforth Nuneaton was not so much troubled by Miss Weatherly's anger. This was a presentiment that the glories that had come to St Matthew's might fade, after all, into nothingness. His voice was soothing.

'But this is no reflection on your dear, dead father, Miss Weatherly. I do not agree with the way the writer has put it when he says "1907 Paviour Re-Buries History", but craftsmen down the centuries have often used materials on hand, to complete their wonderful work. It is no reflection on your dear father. Not at all.'

'Never. Never,' repeated Miss Weatherly. 'I saw every stone laid. I was only a little girl at the time and I liked brushing off the loose mortar. And what's more, he got me to put a farthing under every stone he laid.

'Said the poor would walk to church on riches. He was a God-fearing man, was my father.'

'He what?' said the Vicar incredulously.

'Yes, under every stone,' asserted the old lady.

Just in case Miss Weatherly's memory was at fault. Mr Nuneaton decided to have some of the stones lifted, very discreetly. 'There it is,' she cried as the first one was dragged back. Each stone had its cache. The stone which had temporarily replaced the Marlowe slab had no coin. When Joe heard, he raced round to Reggie.

'Did you find a farthing under the stone you lifted?' he asked.

'Come to think of it, I did. I felt it in the dark with my hand when I was smoothing the ground underneath,' replied Reggie.

'What did you do with it?' Joe's voice was laden with disaster.

'I thought it had just been dropped there. It had the date 1907, so I gave it to young Nuneaton. He collects coins,' said Reggie.

Joe eyed Reggie with understanding. No wonder he had grounded his submarine. The miracle was that he hadn't sunk it with all aboard.

If you should stop off in Munstable, do not mention the motorway that cuts like a swathe right past the town. They will probably tell you, anyway, that it is a scandal, so near to the burial place of Christopher Marlowe.

Legends die hard.

The Tramp

DILLIBE ONYEAMA

Commander Harry Oakley's wife sat back in her rocking chair in her lavishly decorated sitting-room and wrestled with an impossible problem.

She was a thin, straight-backed woman of fifty and as she concentrated, her gaunt frame became more angular till she looked like nothing so much as a praying mantis clutching a letter.

Two years since her husband's death and now suddenly this letter; this astonishing, this utterly impossible letter. Who was this absurd Guy Lintott who wrote in illegible writing and expressed himself in barely literate sentences?

How could such a person be an old friend of Harry? Not just an acquaintance; not even just a friend, but a war-time comrade.

Mrs Oakley had never heard of Guy Lintott, though no doubt there were friends of her husband she had never heard of. But this man, this friend of her husband, was a common tramp!

She stopped rocking, straightened up and read the letter for the hundredth time.

Of course Harry I could come to your house old pal but I might embarris your wife and your respectible family. I'm afraid I don't look too respectible Harry seeing as I am still following my chosen way of life which as you know is a Gentleman of the Road.

The letter went on to hope that they could meet again soon and have a talk about the old days. Mrs Oakley noted the 'again' each time she read the letter and never ceased to shudder.

Finally, in a discreet but rather insistent way, the astonishing Mr Lintott intimated that the usual small payment in cash would not come amiss 'to somebody in my difficult situation.'

Mrs Oakley lived in a world in which tramps were allocated to a zoological order only marginally human. Her group loyalties rejected the genus tramp. But her attitude was also personal and individual; tramps frightened and disgusted her. The thought of one setting foot in her house made her shudder.

Yet a tramp, a real tramp, the writer of this letter had incomprehensibly but beyond all doubt been an intimate of her beloved Harry. And Harry, it seemed, had been in the habit of making money payments to Mr Lintott. In an inverted, lunatic way, she supposed this was understandable. Harry had always been a generous man.

In every way Harry had been an excellent husband and a wonderful father to their children – both now grown up.

She had never got over the loss of her husband and, in a perverse way, rather hoped she never would. She had been a dutiful wife and she could continue the relationship by being a dutiful widow.

Harry, clearly, would have expected her to pay this Lintott man, so pay him she would. She would have to write to the unshaven and no doubt unwashed Mr Lintott, explaining that Harry had been killed in a car crash two full years ago and was not therefore in a position to renew acquaintanceship with war-time friends however close (or, she would add in mental parentheses, peculiar).

Here she would conclude with a paragraph saying where Harry was buried and right at the end, as though an afterthought, she would mention the cheque enclosed.

It was at this point that duty and inclination got locked in stalemate. Every personal instinct rebelled at the thought of handing out money to the improvident and the unworthy. But even more she hated the thought of disloyalty to the Commander. From the mists of memory she seemed to recall Harry being tolerant of tramps, making excuses for them. 'Prepared to pay the 'price of freedom' echoed back to her in Harry's well-loved voice. Oh dear, it was all so confusing.

Her son and daughter were home for dinner the following evening and over the meal in the elegant large dining-room they discussed the amount it would be correct to send to the impecunious and improvident Mr Lintott.

'Correct' was the word Mrs Oakley used and somehow she contrived to pronounce it with a capital C. Her own tentative suggestion was fifteen pounds but the others protested that Father would certainly have sent more. Hadn't he been a close friend? A comrade in arms even? Weren't they moderately wealthy? Finally, an amendment to send the sum of fifty pounds was carried.

Mrs Oakley felt at the same moment resentful and relieved. The matter was distasteful but it had now been disposed of. The letter was addressed to Mr Guy Lintott *poste restante* at the village Mr Lintott had nominated. On his way to London next day the Oakley boy posted the letter. And that was that.

An observer in some fourth dimension whose attention was caught by the Oakley affair would at this point have swung his zoom lens away from Oakley Manor to a village post office in the next county.

There, observing one Guy Lintott, he would have concluded that Mr Lintott was no mean judge of human psychology. In the traditional garb of the tramp he strolled up to the post office he had nominated barely an hour after the arrival of the letter he was expecting.

Mr Lintott opened his letter and extracted the cheque. This he folded and inserted in the innermost of a series of nondescript garments which fitted him like Chinese boxes. Then, satisfied that the essentials had been taken care of, he sat down by the roadside to read his letter.

He sniffed from time to time in a most inelegant way and our observer, if he had been able (or willing) to get in really close, would have detected a smile under the grime and stubble which was the badge of Mr Lintott's tribe.

At the end of his reading, Mr Lintott delivered himself of only two words but they clearly summarized his views about the letter writer. 'Silly cow,' said Mr Lintott.

235

Our conjectured observer, if he had followed the footsteps of G. Lintott, Soldier of Fortune, in the week that followed, would have discovered no act or word to throw further light on the Oakley affair. If, however, our observer had persevered for one more day he would have witnessed an incident which, though simple and indeed touching in itself, nevertheless performed the function of locking the whole puzzle together into an instantly understandable whole.

Mr Lintott was strolling, with the leisurely gait that befitted his calling, through a neat little cemetery on the outskirts of a small town.

Mr Lintott had in his left hand an old writing pad and in his right a ballpoint pen.

Mr Lintott was reading the names of the dear and recently departed from the tombstones, estimating dates and locations and from time to time making a careful note.

Each time he did so the stubble on his face parted slightly and the smile which had ruffled the undergrowth was unmistakable.

Issey Walk-About

PETER KNIVETON

Abbie the thief stretched out his fleshy hand to the green baize table. He turned the card over, nine of diamonds, and a sigh went up round the Chemmy table. A Winner!

Alfie Goldmine looked across to Abbie. 'Good card,' he said.

Abbie nodded. 'A winner is always just right.'

Again the hand reached across the table, and as the diamond ring came within the circumference of light the ceiling flashed with a thousand reflectory segments.

Abbie counted the chips. 'That's funny,' he mused, 'One hundred and thirty-two pounds.'

'Good pot, Abbie.' Fair Ann stood behind him.

'Yeah, yeah,' said Abbie a little absently.

'Something wrong?'

'Oh no, just reminded me of a couple of years ago. It was Issey Walk-About.'

'Who?' laughed Fair Ann.

'Look, it's late,' said Abbie, 'do you want to play anymore?'

'No, let's have a drink and blow,' Alfie stood and made his way from the card room to the club bar.

A moment later six of them sat around a table. Alfie leaned over and lighted Abbie's cigar. 'Tell us what reminded you of Issey Walk-About?'

'What sort of name is that?' insisted Fair Ann.

Abbie grinned. 'Well, it's this way. Issey used to live on the Green, opposite this club in fact. He and his old woman, Sadie, had a flat in Poddy Buildings.

'Issey was a gambler. Mind, he was good to Sadie, but if he had any money on him at all, he could never keep still, always looking for a game to get into.

'So they called him "Issey Walk-About". Well this particular time, Issey had been having a bad spell. He'd been cleaned out a couple of times, and was having the sort of luck we all get from game to game.

'You know, friends that would normally stake you realize the luck is bad and will look the other way, until you can raise, and win a pot to break the luck.

'So this night I'm talking about, Issey came in here, with two pals, Manchester Freddie and Sleepy Sam. Those two played, and Issey walked around the room, until Manchester Freddie just couldn't stand it any longer.

'"Here Issey," he says, and gives him a pony.

'So down sits Issey with the twenty-five. Blind Liza has the bank. They called her "blind" 'cos of the dark bins she wore.

'Anyway it happened. Issey struck, and as the game went, he cleaned out Blind Liza to the tune of a hundred and thirty-two pounds, same as tonight.

'Well as you can imagine, after a couple of weeks with no games and a month or more of rank bad luck, Issey was on top of the world.

'"I just got to tell Sadie," he yells. "I'll just nip over." Remember he lived opposite. So over he goes, and tells me later what happens.

'"Sadie," he shouts, "I've broken it, look." He shows her the wedge, a hundred and thirty-two quid he's got. Now what Issey Walk-About is not prepared for, is what happens next. Sadie takes one look at the wedge, snatches it, counts it.

'"That's mine," she says, "now go to bed Issey. You are not going out again tonight. This money we will spend in the West End tomorrow; I need clothes."

'She locks the door, takes the key out, and pushes Issey into the bedroom.

'Now I should tell you that Issey stood five-foot small in his elevators, Sadie was nearly six foot, and double Issey's weight.

'Issey could do nothing, but get to bed. Sadie hid the key, and slips the loot under her pillow. Issey lay there. Imagine how he felt. Weeks of bad luck. He just breaks it, he's got a stake but he can't play.

'He's in bed but he can't sleep. He tosses and turns, and through the window, on the dressing table mirror, shines the reflection of this club's neon sign.

'It's more than flesh and blood can stand, and Issey can't. He looks over, Sadie's fast a-kip, a smile on her face like the cat's got cream. Issey slips out of bed, gets dressed, slowly eases the lolly from under Sadie's pillow, opens the window and climbs out.

'Issey Walk-About does just that. Into the club as large as life he goes. I'm in there so I see it all. Manchester Freddie is there, Sleepy Sam has gone with a bird. So down sits Issey. Chemmy's the game and Pop-it-on-Patsie has the shoe. Now that should have warned Issey, but no, he's away, and an hour and a half later, he's cleaned out.

'Poor Issey was dumbstruck, couldn't believe it. Then it hit him. Sadie, what on earth can he tell her? "Abbie," he says to me, "what'll I do? She'll kill me." Well what can I say?

'Manchester Freddie tells him, "Go and tell her now and get it over with." And then Issey tells us how he got out.

'"*Well*," says me. "Tell her she dreamed the whole thing."

'"No, it would never work," said Issey.

'"It's the only way," says me. So that's what Issey decides to do. Over he goes, does a creep on his own gaff, gets into bed and Sadie don't move.

'So he tells me of the morning. It takes him a long time to get to sleep, consequently he is half-doped in the morning. He's woken up to a roaring and a screaming, he's being pummelled by Rocky Marciano, then he comes to.

'He hears Sadie yelling things at him like, "You no good lay-about, pint-sized creep, idiot schmuck", and Issey is so pooped, he can't think straight.

'"What's the matter woman?" he squeaks.

' "Don't you woman me, you mug," Sadie yells. "Where's the hundred and thirty-two quid you won at Chemmy?"

'"What hundred and thirty-two quid?" shouts Issey.

'"The hundred and thirty-two quid you won in the club, you crumb!"

'"I never won any hundred and thirty-two quid in any club, you know I haven't played for weeks. You must have dreamt it, you great mountain. Make some tea now you're up." Issey pulled up the sheets, and fearfully lay there.

'What seemed ages later, he looked up, Sadie was sitting on the edge of the bed, with wonder in her eyes. "Issey," she says, "I'm sorry, but you know it was so real, all of it, a hundred and thirty-two pounds it was, I can feel the notes now. You were so excited at breaking your luck, and we were going up to the West End to buy clothes. It was so real, Issey, I never never had a dream so real before."

'Issey knew he was out of it. "Never mind, lover," he says, "the next win I have, I'll treat you to a complete outfit, just you see."

'And he did, the very next pot he won, he did Sadie proud. And for years Sadie told everyone about this fabulous dream. Yes, he was a boy was Issey Walk-About.'

Abbie the thief stood up. 'So who wants a lift to Finchley?'

Hassan the Sweet Puts the Bite on Us Suckers

BOB MONKHOUSE

Let's face it, age hasn't improved me a bit. I'm seventy-four and difficult with it.

My narrow waist and broad mind changed places a long time ago. So I never thought I'd hear myself giggling like a schoolboy and saying, 'Dig that rock'.

Looking back over my forty-two years in the confectionery business, at the millions of boiled sweets, peppermint whirls and whipped cream bon-bons I've turned out to give infinite delight to countless children, only one word occurs to me. The word is 'Humbug', for I hated every minute of it.

Oh yes, I did well in the game. Began as a delivery-boy-cum-factotum in Fotheringay's Holiday Toffee Co., Beacham-by-Sea, when I was sixteen.

I became Managing Director when I was thirty-four, owner when I was forty-five, and by the time I retired six years ago, I'd built that little tin-shed of a factory into the biggest independently owned manufacturer of cakes, soft drinks and sweets in the whole of South Kent.

Then my son Elliott took over. I've never liked him either.

When Elliott took over Holiday Confections Ltd on my sixty-eighth birthday, he knew as much about selling sweets as I know about Sanskrit.

I supported that boy through years of academic failure at Redbrick, five failed businesses and a wrecked marriage. Frankly, I needed him in my business like that Kojak character needs a shampoo. But could he see that? Not that conceited little swine.

'Look, pops,' Elliott grinned like a piranha fish lurking in a public swimming bath. 'You're too old to go on working and, frankly, your business is rheumatic.

'I can inject modern business and marketing methods into your creaky old company and double the turnover in a year! And that's being modest.'

Since his mother, God rest her, first put that boy in long trousers, he's been carrying on one of the world's greatest love affairs – unassisted.

He hired Hassan quite by accident in his second year of lording it in my office. Hassan had been sent along by the Labour Exchange to work as a mixer and blender which was, looking back, a difficult job for an Asian in the conservative little town of Beacham-by-Sea. Mixing and blending, I mean.

Though, as my old works manager told me over a pint at the Lighthouse, he made friends very quickly with the staff.

'Brilliant lad that Hassan is,' confided Ernie. 'Waiting for his degree in Chemistry or something. Works hard and got a lovely sense of humour. Your son . . .'

Ernie stopped and tried to blush through a complexion so ruddy from years of boiling sugar it looked like the rear end of a London bus. I said, 'Don't be daft, old lad.'

'Well, Mr Elliott's our new boss and we all respect him like, being as how he's a chip off the old block.

'But he's got this posh briefcase, see, with his name and the words "Market Research" in gold on the leather.

'Hassan calls it his "fruit and nut case".' Here Ernie gurgled into his bitter. 'It don't sound so funny in the telling but it's the way Hassan says things. He's given us all new names. Old Mrs Thorpe is "Candy", Harry in the stockroom is "Sugarfoot", Fred the cashier is "Mint Imperial" and 'cause he's sort of dark-skinned he calls hisself "Liquorice Allsort" . . .'

'Are you raving mad, boy?' I stormed at Elliott next day, 'turning over all our production to seaside rock?'

'Pops, take it easy,' he smarmed. 'My business sense tells me that we must major on a market leader. All the big boys make chocolates, candies, bars, toffees ... but the coming thing is nostalgia. People longing for the old values, old brands, old traditions – and Original Seaside Rock is our national winner!'

I fumed and swore but Elliott wasn't slow to point out that I was no longer the boss. Furthermore, by switching everything to producing rock, Elliott could fire half the old staff.

'I'm putting a young discovery of mine on to all those jobs,' he said airily. 'Eager little wallah named Hassan.'

Well, what would have happened to Elliott's lunatic scheme to flood the coast with sticks of rock if it hadn't been for Hassan, I just can't imagine. The Asian lad *was* brilliant, just as Ernie claimed. He concocted a tangy flavouring for the rock that really tasted marvellous.

'He's all right,' Elliott conceded, condescendingly, 'for eighteen quid a week and all found.'

'*How* much? That's slave labour, for God's sake. ... If the unions had representation in our works ...'

'But, pops, they haven't,' purred my offspring. And annoyingly enough, his policy was proving successful. With half the man-power, plus the gifted Hassan, Holiday Original Seaside Rock was being churned out by my little factory in Beacham-by-Sea by the jumbo jet load.

Everywhere from Dover to Deal, Brighton to Bognor, the South Coast was buying – and sucking – like the kiddies of the 1930s only ten times faster. It was a terrific hit.

It could have gone national with a takeover bid from a major company. But Elliott, you'll remember, had a built-in failure factor. It's called greed.

It seems young Hassan finally got his Bachelor of Science degree – by post or Open University or something. At any rate, he asked Elliott to accept all his innovations as a gift and to wish him well on his return to Asia to fulfil his ambitions as an industrial chemist. The answer he got was, 'No chance!'

The snag was a service contract Elliott had tricked Hassan into signing. Smoothly my bonny son told him, 'Try to quit and I'll wrap you up in so many law and patent suits you'll never leave the country. Get back to work.'

No raise, no holiday. Not for Hassan, that is. Elliott took a month in Barbados. But when I next saw him, about a week ago, he was dead white under his tan.

'That creepy little Indian! He's gone!' he sobbed. 'Worked out his month's notice while I was away and then some swine must have lent him the air-fare to the East.'

I hoped my expression didn't look too swinish.

'You're still in business,' I ventured.

'I'm ruined! Four weeks' production written off! That damned fellow and his sense of humour. What am I going to do with two million sticks of rock with "TOOTH DECAY" printed all the way through?'

I told him. Bury it. If one stick gets loose, he's had it with the Press. That's why I took a spade round to Elliott's maisonette last night. And that's why I giggled like a schoolboy as I murmured, 'Dig that rock!'

BOB MONKHOUSE *has been a writer all his life, an entertainer with the gift of providing the right sort of material at the right time.*

As a writer of radio and theatre sketches, plays, TV shows, he has provided material for most of the great comedians of our time as well as himself.

A man who gives much value for money in his business of entertaining, Bob Monkhouse also is always prepared to give his time for show-business charities.

The Birthday Book

LESLIE THOMAS

When Uncle Henry died he left me a considerable slice of his fortune and the green book with the golden bird on the cover.

'But why only one book?' everyone said. 'Uncle Henry had thousands.'

But this is a very special book. I recall the day he told me about the book with the golden bird on its cover.

'I suppose,' he said, lying back in the deep chair, 'I'm a very wealthy man. But if it had not been for this book I should never have amounted to a thing. Yes, it's a wonderful book . . . I really must read it sometime.'

It was a copy of *Pilgrim's Progress* and inside was a faded inscription saying it was given to Uncle Henry on his tenth birthday by the Governors of the Compassion Orphanage, in the hope that he would 'read, mark and learn' it.

'They always gave you a book like this when you were ten,' he explained. 'Always the same green cover and the golden bird; always *Pilgrim's Progress*, too.

'I had nothing then,' he said. 'Nothing and nobody. And I thought it was meant to be that way, and would always be that way.

'Compassion's was a great pile of a building, all yellow bricks. That was my world. The brown jerseys, the wooden forms and tables.

'I wasn't ashamed of it, frightened, or even very unhappy. It was my world and I didn't know of any other. It was when I went into someone else's world that the trouble started.

'That happened because I fell down a flight of stairs and knocked myself out cold. I came to on the way to the doctor's in the town, sitting in the dog cart with my head in a bandage like a turban.

'When the doctor had patched me up, a lady and a gentleman who were in the waiting room came over and spoke to me and insisted on taking me back to the home in their carriage.

'The next day they called to see how I was, and not long after that the Gaffer sent for me, and Mr and Mrs Trenchall – that was their name – were in his office.

'He told me to shake hands with Mr and Mrs Trenchall and I did. Mrs Trenchall had small hands with lots of rings on her fingers and I felt them when I shook her hand. Then Mr Trenchall, who was a bulky, smiling man, about twice the Gaffer's size, held out a huge hand and I shook that too.

'They asked about my head, and then the Gaffer, who never was one for anyone gentle or kind, and who was getting impatient, told me that I was going to stay with them for a week.

'I did not grasp it for a moment. Then I did, and my heart gave a jump and seemed to turn over like a mole turning over in its tunnel.

'They came for me the following Saturday. I was waiting, scrubbed and stiff in my church suit, and trembling with the wonderfulness of it all. Mr Trenchall lifted me up, and I sat there on the carriage, high above the ground, as we jogged down to the iron gates. They opened and I looked back and saw all the boys hanging over the walls and out of the windows as we drove away. I was never so happy in my life.

'Down through the crowded town we went, then across the humped bridge and down under the trees by the river. Mrs Trenchall told me that their son Roger had a real pony and a hide-out in the elm at the back of their house, and was waiting to show them to me.

'She was still chatting gaily as we turned a bend and came suddenly to the house. There never was such a house. It was white in the sun and it had steps right down to the river's edge. There was a little landing stage and a boat tied up and a wide lawn and three big stretching trees.

'All the shutters of the house were bright green and a big lantern hung over the front door. There were flowers in neat beds and bright boxes, and somewhere a woman was singing.

'She was still singing when she opened the door. A bulging happy woman, who overpowered me with a frightening hug. They all laughed and we went in. My feet sank into the carpet in the hall and on the walls were shining brasses. It was all so amazing. I just stood there and stupidly stared. And they just stared at me. The curtains hung in thick, rich folds. I could have got lost in the chairs, and above was a chandelier like a jewelled crown.

'Roger, who was about my age, came in before tea and we sat down drinking from cups as thin as eggshells, with me so terrified in case I should drop mine. But I didn't and afterwards Roger took me to see his pony.

'We saw the pony. I fell off it the first time. Then we climbed to the tree house in the elm, and then down again, went across the garden, through a secret hole in the hedge and across some fields to a stream where, Roger said, the fish lay in shoals in the afternoons. We played in the boat by the landing stage, and the summer evening seemed to go in a moment.

'Suddenly it was dark and they were calling us from the house. We jumped from the boat, and ran up shouting towards the lighted windows.

'While we drank our milk Roger's father said he would take us in the boat next day. The room was warm, and I watched the lights bringing the rings to life on Mrs Trenchall's fingers.

'Then the bulging woman came in and hustled us off to bed. I had a huge bed with soft, unfamiliar sheets around my tired body. The bulging woman came in and planted a heavy, motherly kiss on my cheek. Then she put out the light.

'All at once I was alone. I lay on my back, small in the middle of the wide bed. A moon came from nowhere and shone through the leaded windows splaying a pattern on the ceiling.

'I thought of the moon flooding through the bare windows of the dormitory at Compassion's and lying across the rows of beds.

'Then all the happiness of that day seemed to ebb from me. I knew that next week I would be back and all this would not be real. Roger would ride his pony and play in the boat and the Trenchalls would live in their white house, and the bulging woman would sing, and I would still be a Compassion's Boy. That would always be. Even when I was grown up I would still be a Compassion's Boy and the Trenchalls would be the Trenchalls and live in their house.

'For a long time I lay thinking of these things and the pattern on the ceiling seemed to blur. I heard Mr and Mrs Trenchall come up the stairs and my door opened softly. I breathed deeply and she said, "He's asleep, John."

'I lay there for hours. Then, for no special reason, I climbed from the bed, went to the window and looked out across the moonlit garden and the smooth, pale river.

'Then I saw the book. It was lying on top of some others on the window ledge. A green book with a golden bird on the cover.

'I knew it was a Compassion's Birthday Book before I had even touched it or saw that it was *Pilgrim's Progress*.

'I opened it. The inscription was dated about twenty-five years previously – presented, on his tenth birthday, to a boy called John Trenchall.'

Scoring off Jeeves

P.G. WODEHOUSE

*B*ertie Wooster is in a mess. His friend Bingo Little – always in love
with the most unsuitable girls – has fallen for Honoria Glossop, 'a
large, brainy, strenuous, dynamic girl', who's been to Cambridge.

Bingo is tutor to Honoria's brother Oswald, a small boy whom Bertie
describes as 'pestilential to a degree'. Bertie's Aunt Agatha has decided that
Bertie should get married . . . and orders him to get engaged – to Honoria
Glossop!

Arriving reluctantly at the Glossop home in Ditteredge, Bertie has his
brainstorm. He sees a way of getting himself off the matrimonial hook, and
giving Bingo his 'tender Goddess'.

His plan is to hide Bingo in the bushes and take Honoria and her pimply
brother for a walk. At a planned moment he will push Oswald into the
millpond.

Bingo will rush from the bushes to the rescue and Honoria will embrace
Bingo as her hero.

In one fell swoop Bertie will have sorted out the whole mess – and prove
his independence from the redoubtable Jeeves.

Walking with Honoria, they approach the moment of truth . . .

'I do wish Oswald wouldn't sit on the bridge like that,' she said,
'I'm sure it isn't safe – he might easily fall in.'

'I'll go and tell him,' I said.

I suppose the distance between the kid and me at this juncture was about five yards, but I got the impression it was nearer a hundred.

And, as I started to toddle across the intervening space, I had a rummy feeling that I'd done this very thing before.

Then I remembered. Years ago, at a country house party, I had been roped in to play the part of a butler in some amateur theatricals in aid of some ghastly charity or other.

And I had had to open the proceedings by walking across the empty stage from left upper entrance and shoving a tray on a table down right.

They had impressed it on me at rehearsals that I mustn't take the course at a quick heel-and-toe, like a chappie finishing strongly in a walking-race.

And the result was that I kept the brakes on to such an extent that it seemed to me as if I was never going to get to the bally table at all.

The stage seemed to stretch out in front of me like a trackless desert, and there was a kind of breathless hush as if all nature had paused to concentrate its attention on me personally.

Well, I felt just like that now.

I had a kind of dry gulping in my throat, and the more I walked the farther away the kid seemed to get till suddenly I found myself standing just behind him without quite knowing how I'd got there.

'Hallo!' I said, with a sickly sort of grin – wasted on the kid, because he didn't bother to turn round and look at me.

He merely wiggled his left ear in a rather peevish manner. I don't know when I've met anybody in whose life I appeared to mean so little.

'Hallo!' I said. 'Fishing?'

I laid my hand in a sort of elder-brotherly way on his shoulder.

'Here, look out!' said the kid, wobbling on his foundations.

It was one of those things that want doing quickly or not at all. I shut my eyes and pushed.

Something seemed to give. There was a scrambling sound, a kind of yelp, a scream in the offing, and a splash. And so the long day wore on, so to speak.

I opened my eyes. The kid was just coming to the surface.

'Help!' I shouted, cocking an eye on the bush from which young Bingo was scheduled to emerge.

Nothing happened. Young Bingo didn't emerge to the slightest extent whatever.

'I say! Help!' I shouted again.

I don't want to bore you with reminiscences of my theatrical career, but I must just touch once more on that appearance of mine as the butler.

The scheme on that occasion had been that when I put the tray on the table the heroine would come on and say a few words to get me off.

Well, on the night the misguided female forgot to stand by, and it was a full minute before the search-party located her and shot her on to the stage.

And all that time I had to stand there waiting. A rotten sensation, believe me.

This was just the same, only worse. I understood what these writers mean when they talk about time standing still.

Meanwhile, the kid Oswald was presumably being cut off in his prime, and it began to seem to me that some sort of steps ought to be taken about it.

What I had seen of the lad hadn't particularly endeared him to me, but it was undoubtedly a bit thick to let him pass away.

I don't know when I have seen anything more grubby and unpleasant than the lake as viewed from the bridge; but the thing apparently had to be done.

I chucked off my coat and vaulted over.

It seems rummy that water should be so much wetter when you go into it with your clothes on than when you're just bathing, but take it from me that it does.

I was only under about three seconds, I suppose, but I came up feeling like the bodies you read of in the paper which 'had evidently been in the water several days'.

I felt clammy and bloated.

At this point the scenario struck another snag. I had assumed that directly I came to the surface I should get hold of the kid and steer him courageously to shore.

But he hadn't waited to be steered. When I had finished getting

251

the water out of my eyes and had time to take a look round, I saw him about ten yards away, going strongly and using, I think, the Australian crawl.

The spectacle took all the heart out of me.

I mean to say, the whole essence of a rescue, if you know what I mean, is that the party of the second part shall keep fairly still and in one spot. If he starts swimming off on his own account and can obviously give you at least forty yards in the hundred, where are you?

The whole thing falls through. It didn't seem to me that there was much to be done except get ashore, so I got ashore. By the time I had landed, the kid was half-way to the house.

Look at it from whatever angle you like, the thing was a wash-out.

I was interrupted in my meditations by a noise like the Scottish express going under a bridge. It was Honoria Glossop laughing. She was standing at my elbow, looking at me in a rummy manner.

'Oh, Bertie, you are funny!' she said. And even in that moment there seemed to me something sinister in the words. She had never called me anything except 'Mr Wooster' before. 'How wet you are!'

'Yes, I am wet.'

'You had better hurry into the house and change.'

I wrung a gallon or two of water out of my clothes.

'You *are* funny!' she said again. 'First proposing in that extraordinary roundabout way, then pushing poor little Oswald into the lake so as to impress me by saving him.'

I managed to get the water out of my throat sufficiently to try to correct this fearful impression.

'No, no!'

'He said you pushed him in, and I saw you do it. Oh, I'm not angry, Bertie, I think it was too sweet of you. But I'm quite sure it's time that I took you in hand. You certainly want someone to look after you.

'You've been seeing too many moving pictures. I suppose the next thing you would have done would have been to set the house on fire so as to rescue me.'

She looked at me in a proprietary sort of way.

'I think,' she said, 'I shall be able to make something of you, Bertie, it is true yours has been a wasted life up to the present, but you are still young, and there is a lot of good in you.'

'No, really there isn't.'

'Oh, yes, there is. It simply wants bringing out. Now you run straight up to the house and change your wet clothes or you will catch cold.'

And, if you know what I mean, there was a sort of motherly note in her voice which seemed to tell me, even more than her actual words, that I was for it.

As I was coming downstairs after changing, I ran into young Bingo, looking festive to a degree.

'Bertie!' he said. 'Just the man I wanted to see. Bertie, a wonderful thing has happened.'

'You blighter!' I cried. 'What became of you? Do you know . . .?'

'Oh, you mean about being in those bushes? I hadn't time to tell you about that. It's all off.'

'All off?'

'Bertie, I was actually starting to hide in those bushes when the most extraordinary thing happened. Walking across the lawn I saw the most radiant, the most beautiful girl in the world. There is none like her, none.

'Bertie, do you believe in love at first sight? You do believe in love at first sight, don't you, Bertie, old man?

'Directly I saw her, she seemed to draw me like a magnet. I seemed to forget everything. We two were alone in a world of music and sunshine.

'I joined her. I got into conversation. She was a Miss Braythwayt, Bertie, Daphne Braythwayt.

'Directly our eyes met I realized that what I had imagined to be my love for Honoria Glossop had been a mere passing whim.

'Bertie, you do believe in love at first sight, don't you? She is so wonderful, so sympathetic. Like a tender goddess . . .'

At this point I left the blighter.

Two days later I got a letter from Jeeves.

'. . . The weather', it ended, 'continues fine. I have had one exceedingly enjoyable bathe.'

I gave one of those hollow, mirthless laughs and went downstairs to join Honoria. I had an appointment with her in the drawing-room.

She was going to read to me.

PELHAM GRENVILLE WODEHOUSE, *knighted in 1975, wrote more than eighty books and three hundred short stories.*

His characters – the impeccable butler Jeeves, his master Bertie Wooster, Aunt Dahlia, Stiffy Byng, Barmy Fotheringay-Phipps and the appalling Gussie Fink-Nottle – weave a web of escapism that no living writer can match.

The Gift of the Magi

O. HENRY

One dollar and eighty-seven cents. That was all. And sixty cents of it was in pennies. Pennies saved one and two at a time by bulldozing the grocer and the vegetable man and the butcher until one's cheek burned with the silent imputation of parsimony that such close dealing implied. Three times Della counted it. One dollar and eighty-seven cents. And the next day would be Christmas.

There was clearly nothing left to do but flop down on the shabby little couch and howl. So Della did it. Which instigates the moral reflection that life is made up of sobs, sniffles, and smiles, with sniffles predominating.

While the mistress of the home is gradually subsiding from the first stage to the second, take a look at the home. A furnished flat at eight dollars per week.

It did not exactly beggar description, but it certainly had the word on the look-out for the mendicancy squad.

In the vestibule below was a letter-box into which no letter would go and an electric button from which no mortal finger could coax a ring. Also appertaining thereunto was a card bearing the name 'Mr James Dillingham Young.'

The 'Dillingham' had been flung to the breeze during a former period of prosperity when its possessor was being paid thirty dollars per week.

Now, when the income was shrunk to twenty dollars the letters of 'Dillingham' looked blurred, as though they were thinking seriously of contracting to a modest and unassuming D.

But whenever Mr James Dillingham Young came home and reached his flat above he was called 'Jim' and greatly hugged by Mrs James Dillingham Young, already introduced to you as Della. Which is all very good.

Della finished her cry and attended to her cheeks with the powder rag. She stood by the window and looked out dully at a grey cat walking a grey fence in a grey backyard.

Tomorrow would be Christmas Day, and she had only one dollar and eighty-seven cents with which to buy Jim a present. She had been saving every penny she could for months, with this result.

Twenty dollars a week doesn't go far. Expenses had been greater than she had calculated. They always are. Only one dollar eighty-seven cents to buy a present for Jim. Her Jim. Many a happy hour she had spent planning for something nice for him.

Something fine and rare and sterling – something just a little bit near to being worthy of the honour of being owned by Jim.

There was a pier-glass between the windows of the room. Perhaps you have seen a pier-glass in an eight-dollar flat.

A very thin and very agile person may, by observing his reflection in a rapid sequence of longitudinal strips, obtain a fairly accurate conception of his looks. Della, being slender, had mastered the art.

Suddenly she whirled from the window and stood before the glass. Her eyes were shining brilliantly, but her face had lost its colour within twenty seconds.

Rapidly she pulled down her hair and let it fall to its full length.

Now, there were two possessions of the James Dillingham Youngs in which they both took a mighty pride. One was Jim's gold watch that had been his father's and his grandfather's.

The other was Della's hair.

Had the Queen of Sheba lived in the flat across the airshaft, Della would have let her hair hang out the window some day to dry just to depreciate Her Majesty's jewels and gifts.

So now Della's beautiful hair fell about her, rippling and shining like a cascade of brown waters.

It reached below her knee and made itself almost a garment for her. And then she did it up again nervously and quickly. Once she faltered for a minute and stood still while a tear or two splashed on the worn red carpet.

On went her old brown jacket; on went her old brown hat. With a whirl of skirts and with the brilliant sparkle in her eyes, she fluttered out of the door and down the stairs to the street.

Where she stopped the sign read: 'Mme Sofronie. Hair Goods of All Kinds.' One flight up Della ran, and collected herself, panting.

Madame, large, too white, chilly, hardly looked the 'Sofronie'.

'Will you buy my hair?' asked Della.

Down rippled the brown cascade.

'Twenty dollars,' said Madame, lifting the mass with a practised hand.

'Give it to me quick,' said Della.

Oh, and the next two hours tripped by on rosy wings. Forget the hashed metaphor. She was ransacking the stores for Jim's present.

She found it at last. It surely had been made for Jim and no one else.

It was a platinum fob chain simple and chaste in design, properly proclaiming its value by substance alone and not by meretricious ornamentation – as all good things should do. It was even worthy of The Watch.

Twenty-one dollars they took from her for it, and she hurried home with the eighty-seven cents.

With that chain on his watch Jim might be properly anxious about the time in any company. Grand as the watch was, he sometimes looked at it on the sly on account of the old leather strap that he used in place of chain.

When Della reached home her intoxication gave way a little to prudence and reason. She got out her curling tongs and lighted the gas and went to work repairing the ravages made by generosity added to love.

Which is always a tremendous task, dear friends – a mammoth task.

Within forty minutes her head was covered with tiny, close-lying curls that made her look wonderfully like a truant schoolboy.

'If Jim doesn't kill me,' she said to herself, 'before he takes a second look at me, he'll say I look like a Coney Island chorus girl.'

'But what could I do – oh! What could I do with a dollar and eighty-seven cents?'

At seven o'clock the coffee was made and the frying pan was on the back of the stove, hot and ready to cook the chops.

Jim was never late. Della doubled the fob chain in her hand and sat on the corner of the table near the door that he always entered.

Then she heard his step on the stair away down on the first flight, and she turned white for just a moment.

She had a habit of saying little silent prayers about the simplest everyday things and now she whispered, 'Please God, make him think I am still pretty.'

Jim stepped inside the door, as immovable as a setter at the scent of quail. His eyes were fixed upon Della, and there was an expression in them that she could not read, and it terrified her.

It was not anger, nor surprise, nor disapproval, nor horror, nor any of the sentiments that she had been prepared for.

He simply stared at her fixedly with that peculiar expression on his face.

Della wriggled off the table and went for him.

'Jim, darling,' she cried, 'don't look at me that way. I had my hair cut off and sold it because I couldn't have lived through Christmas without giving you a present.

'It'll grow out again – you won't mind, will you? I just had to do it. My hair grows awfully fast. Say "Merry Christmas!" Jim, and let's be happy.

'You don't know what a nice . . . what a beautiful, nice gift I've got for you.'

'You've cut off your hair?' asked Jim laboriously, as if he had not arrived at that patent fact yet even after the hardest mental labour.

'Cut it off and sold it,' said Della. 'Don't you like me just as well, anyhow? I'm me without my hair, ain't I?'

258

Out of the trance Jim seemed quickly to wake. He enfolded his Della. For ten seconds let us regard with discreet scrutiny some inconsequential object in the other direction.

Eight dollars a week or a million a year – what is the difference? A mathematician or a wit would give you the wrong answer.

The magi brought valuable gifts, but that was not among them. This dark assertion will be illuminated later on.

Jim drew a package from his overcoat pocket and threw it upon the table.

'Don't make any mistake, Della,' he said, 'about me. I don't think there's anything in the way of a haircut or a shave or a shampoo that could make me like my girl any less. But if you'll unwrap that package you may see why you had me going awhile at first.'

White fingers and nimble tore at the string and paper.

And then an ecstatic scream of joy; and then, alas! a quick feminine change to hysterical tears and wails, necessitating the immediate employment of all the comforting powers of the lord of the flat.

For there lay The Combs – the set of combs, side and back, that Della had worshipped for long in a Broadway window.

Beautiful combs, pure tortoiseshell, with jewelled rims – just that shade to wear in the beautiful vanished hair.

And now they were hers, but the tresses that should have adorned the coveted adornments were gone.

But she hugged them to her bosom, and at length she was able to look up with dim eyes and a smile and say, 'My hair grows so fast, Jim!'

And then Della leaped up like a little singed cat and cried, 'Oh, oh!'

Jim had not yet seen his beautiful present. She held it out to him eagerly upon her open palm. The dull precious metal seemed to flash with a reflection of her bright and ardent spirit.

'Isn't it a dandy, Jim? I hunted all over town to find it. You'll have to look at the time a hundred times a day now. Give me your watch. I want to see how it looks on it.'

Instead of obeying, Jim tumbled down on the couch and put his hands under the back of his head and smiled.

'Dell,' said he, 'let's put our Christmas presents away and keep 'em awhile. They're too nice to use just at present.

'I sold the watch to get the money to buy your combs. And now suppose you put the chops on.'

The magi, as you know, were wise men – wonderfully wise men – who brought gifts to the Babe in the manger. They invented the art of giving Christmas presents.

And here I have lamely related to you the uneventful chronicle of two foolish children in a flat who most unwisely sacrificed for each other the greatest treasures of their house.

But in a last word to the wise of these days, let it be said that of all who give gifts, these two were the wisest.

Of all who give and receive gifts, such as they are wisest. Everywhere they are wisest.

They are the Magi.

O. HENRY, *perhaps the most famous of all short story writers, was really William Sydney Porter, a doctor's son born in Greensboro, North Carolina, in 1862.*

His stories – they made twelve volumes when he died at the age of forty-eight – have become international folklore. They are simple stories, 'the stories people tell one another', but redeemed by O. Henry's genius that would expose in a few deft words the ultimate irony of human life.

It was an irony he knew well. A tragic and lonely man most of his life, he was finally, on his own admission, drinking two quarts of whisky per day. He died as resignedly – and as jauntily – as a character in one of his stories.

'Pull up the shades, nurse,' he said, 'I don't want to go home in the dark.'

A Child's Christmas

DYLAN THOMAS

One Christmas was so much like another in those years around the sea-town corner now and out of all sound – except the distant speaking of the voices I sometimes hear a moment before sleep – that I can never remember whether it snowed for six days and six nights when I was twelve or whether it snowed twelve days and twelve nights when I was six.

All the Christmases roll down toward the two-tongued sea, like a cold and headlong moon bundling down the sky that was our street; and they stop at the rim of the ice-edged, fish-freezing waves, and I plunge my hands in the snow and bring out whatever I can find.

In goes my hand into that wool-white bell-tongued ball of holidays resting at the rim of the carol-singing sea, and out come Mrs Prothero and the firemen.

It was on the afternoon of the day of Christmas Eve, and I was in Mrs Prothero's garden, waiting for cats, with her son Jim.

It was snowing. It was always snowing at Christmas. December in my memory, is white as Lapland, though there were no reindeer.

But there were cats. Patient, cold and callous, our hands wrapped in socks, we waited to snowball the cats.

Sleek and long as jaguars and horrible-whiskered, spitting and snarling, they would slink and sidle over the white back-garden walls, and the lynx-eyed hunters, Jim and I, fur-capped and moccasined trappers from Hudson Bay, off Mumbles Road, would hurl our deadly snowballs at the green of their eyes.

The wise cats never appeared. We were so still, Eskimo-footed arctic marksmen in the muffling silence of the eternal snows – eternal, ever since Wednesday – that we never heard Mrs Prothero's first cry from her igloo at the bottom of the garden.

Or, if we heard it at all, it was, to us, like the far-off challenge of our enemy and prey, the neighbour's polar cat. But soon the voice grew louder. 'Fire!' cried Mrs Prothero, and she beat the dinner-gong.

And we ran down the garden, with the snowballs in our arms, toward the house; and smoke, indeed, was pouring out of the dining-room, and the gong was bombilating, and Mrs Prothero was announcing ruin like a town crier in Pompeii.

This was better than all the cats in Wales standing on the wall in a row. We bounded into the house, laden with snowballs, and stopped at the open door of the smoke-filled room.

Something was burning all right; perhaps it was Mr Prothero, who always slept there after midday dinner with a newspaper over his face.

But he was standing in the middle of the room, saying, 'A fine Christmas!' and smacking at the smoke with a slipper. 'Call the fire brigade,' cried Mrs Prothero as she beat the gong.

'They won't be there,' said Mr Prothero, 'it's Christmas.'

There was no fire to be seen, only clouds of smoke and Mr Prothero standing in the middle of it, waving his slipper as though he were conducting.

'Do something,' he said.

And we threw all our snowballs into the smoke – I think we missed Mr Prothero – and ran out of the house to the telephone box.

'Let's call the police as well,' Jim said.

'And the ambulance.'

'And Ernie Jenkins, he likes fires.'

But we only called the fire brigade, and soon the fire engine came and three tall men in helmets brought a hose into the house and Mr Prothero got out just in time before they turned it on. Nobody could have had a noisier Christmas Eve.

And when the firemen turned off the hose and were standing in the wet, smoky room, Jim's aunt, Miss Prothero, came downstairs and peered in at them.

Jim and I waited, very quietly, to hear what she would say to them. She said the right thing, always.

She looked at the three tall firemen in their shining helmets, standing among the smoke and cinders and dissolving snowballs, and she said, 'Would you like anything to read?'

Years and years and years ago, when I was a boy, when there were wolves in Wales, and birds the colour of red-flannel petticoats whisked past the harp-shaped hills, when we sang and wallowed all night and day in caves that smelt like Sunday afternoons in damp front farmhouse parlours and we chased, with the jawbones of deacons, the English and the bears, before the motor car, before the wheel, before the duchess-faced horse, when we rode the daft and happy hills bareback, it snowed and it snowed.

But here a small boy says, 'It snowed last year, too. I made a snowman and my brother knocked it down and I knocked my brother down and then we had tea.'

'But that was not the same snow,' I say. 'Our snow was not only shaken from whitewash buckets down the sky, it came shawling out of the ground and swam and drifted out of the arms and hands and bodies of the trees; snow grew overnight on the roofs of the houses like a pure and grandfather moss, minutely white-ivied the walls and settled on the postman, opening the gate, like a dumb, numb thunderstorm of white, torn Christmas cards.'

'Were there postmen then, too?'

'With sprinkling eyes and wind-cherried noses, on spread, frozen feet they crunched up to the doors and mittened on them manfully. But all that the children could hear was a ringing of bells.'

'You mean the postman went rat-a-tat-tat and the doors rang?'

'I mean the bells the children could hear were inside them.'

'I only hear thunder sometimes, never bells.'

'There were church bells, too.'

'Inside them?'

'No, no, no, in the bat-black, snow-white belfries, tugged by bishops and storks. And they rang their tidings over the frozen foam of the powder and ice-cream hills, over the crackling sea. It seemed all the churches boomed for joy under my window; and the weathercocks grew for Christmas, on our fence.'

'And then they stood.'

'Get back to the postmen.'

'They were just ordinary postmen, fond of walking and dogs and Christmas and the snow. They knocked on the doors with blue knuckles . . .'

'Ours has got a black knocker . . .'

'On the white Welcome mat in the little, drifted porches and huffed and puffed, makings ghosts with their breath, and jogged from foot to foot like small boys wanting to go out.'

'And then the presents.'

'And then the presents, after the Christmas box. And the cold postman, with a rose on his button-nose, tingled down the tea-tray-slithered run of the chilly glinting hill. He went in his ice-bound boots like a man on fishmonger's slabs. He wagged his bag like a frozen camel's hump, dizzily turned the corner on one foot, and, by God, he was gone.'

'Get back to the presents.'

'There were the Useful Presents: engulfing mufflers of the old coach days, and mittens made for giant sloths; zebra scarfs of a substance like silky gum that could be tug-o'warred down to the galoshes, blinding tam-o'-shanters like patchwork tea cosies and bunnysuited busbies and balaclavas for victims of head-shrinking tribes; from aunts who always wore wool next to the skin there were moustached and rasping vests that made you wonder why the aunts had any skin left at all; and once I had a little crocheted nose bag from an aunt now, alas, no longer whinnying with us.

'And priceless books in which small boys, though warned with quotations not to, *would* skate on Farmer Giles' pond and did and drowned; and books that told me everything about the wasp, except why.'

'Go on to the Useless Presents.'

'Bags of moist and many-coloured jelly babies and a folded flag and a false nose and a tram-conductor's cap and a machine that punched tickets and rang a bell; never a catapult; once, by mistake that no one could explain, a little hatchet; and a celluloid duck that made, when you pressed it, a most unduck-like sound, a mewing moo that an ambitious cat might make who wished to be a cow; and a painting book in which I could make the grass, the trees, the sea and the animals any colour I pleased, and still the dazzling sky-blue sheep are grazing in the red field under the rain-billed and pea-green birds.

'Hard-boiled, toffee, fudge and allsorts, crunches, cracknels, humbugs, glaciers, marzipan, and butterwelsh for the Welsh. And troops of bright tin soldiers who, if they could not fight, could always run. And snakes-and-Families and Happy Ladders. And easy Hobbigames for Little Engineers, complete with instructions.

'Oh, easy for Leonardo! And a whistle to make the dogs bark to wake up the old man next door to make him beat on the wall with his stick to shake our picture off the wall.

'And a packet of cigarettes; you put one in your mouth and you stood at the corner of the street and you waited for hours, in vain, for an old lady to scold you for smoking a cigarette and then with a smirk you ate it. And then it was breakfast under the balloons.'

'Were there uncles like in our house?'

'There are always Uncles at Christmas. The same Uncles. And on Christmas mornings, with dog-disturbing whistle and sugar fags, I would scour the swatched town for the news of the little world, and find always a dead bird by the white Post Office or by the deserted swings; perhaps a robin, all but one of his fires out. Men and women wading or scooping back from chapel, with taproom noses and wind-bussed cheeks, all albinos, huddled their stiff black jarring feathers against the irreligious snow.

'Mistletoe hung from the gas brackets in all the front parlours; there was sherry and walnuts and bottled beer and crackers by the dessert spoons; and cats in their fur-abouts watched the fires; and all high-heaped fire spat, all and the mulling pokers.

'Some few large men sat in the front parlours, without their collars, uncles almost certainly, trying their new cigars, holding them out judiciously at arm's length, returning them to their mouths, coughing, then holding them out again as though waiting for the explosion; and some few small aunts, not wanted in the kitchen, nor anywhere else for that matter, sat on the very edges of their chairs, posed and brittle, afraid to break, like faded cups and saucers.'

Not many those mornings trod the piling streets: an old man always, fawn-bowlered, yellow-gloved and, at this time of year, with spats of snow, would take his constitutional to the white bowling green and back, as he would take it wet or fine on Christmas Day or Doomsday: sometimes two hale young men, with big pipes blazing, no overcoats and wind-blown scarves, would trudge, unspeaking, down to the forlorn sea, to work up an appetite, to blow away the fumes, who knows, to walk into the waves until nothing of them was left but the two curling smoke clouds of their inextinguishable briars.

Then I would be slap-dashing home, the gravy smell of the dinners of others, the bird smell, the brandy, the pudding and mince, coiling up to my nostrils, when out of a snow-clogged side lane would come a boy the spit of myself, with a pink-tipped cigarette and the violet past of a black-eye, cocky as a bullfinch, leering to himself.

I hated him on sight and sound, and would be about to put my dog whistle to my lips and blow him off the face of Christmas when suddenly he, with a violent wink, put *his* whistle to *his* lips and blew so stridently, so high, so exquisitely loud, that gobbling faces, their cheeks bulged with goose, would press against their tinselled windows, the whole length of the white echoing street.

For dinner we had turkey and blazing pudding, and after dinner the uncles sat in front of the fire, loosened all buttons, put their large moist hands over their watch-chains, groaned a little and slept.

Mothers, aunts and sisters scuttled to-and-fro, bearing tureens. Auntie Bessie, who had already been frightened twice by a clockwork mouse, whimpered at the sideboard and had some elderberry wine.

The dog was sick, Auntie Dosie had to have three aspirins, but Auntie Hannah, who liked port, stood in the middle of the snowbound back yard, singing like a big-bosomed thrush.

I would blow up balloons to see how big they would blow up to; and when they burst, which they all did, the uncles jumped and rumbled.

In the rich and heavy afternoon, the uncles breathing like dolphins and the snow descending, I would sit among festoons and Chinese lanterns and nibble dates and try to make a model man-o'-war, following the instructions for Little Engineers, and produce what might be mistaken for a sea-going tramcar.

Or I would go out, my bright new boots squeaking, into the white world, on to the seaward hill, to call on Jim and Dan and Jack and to pad through the still streets, leaving huge deep footprints on the hidden pavements.

'I bet people will think there's been hippos.'

'What would you do if you saw a hippo coming down our street?'

'I'd go like this, bang! I'd throw him over the railings and roll him down the hill and then I'd tickle him under the ear and he'd wag his tail.'

'What would you do if you saw *two* hippos?'

Iron-flanked and bellowing he-hippos clanked and battered through the scudding snow towards us as we passed Mr Daniel's house.

'Let's post Mr Daniel a snowball through his letter-box.'

'Let's write "Mr Daniel looks like a spaniel" all over his lawn.'

Or we walked on the white shore.

'Can the fishes see it's snowing?'

The silent one-clouded heavens drifted on to the sea. Now we were snowblind travellers lost on the north hills, and vast dew-lapped dogs, with flasks round their necks, ambled and shambled up to us, baying 'Excelsior'.

We returned home through the poor streets where only a few children fumbled with bare red fingers in the wheel-rutted snow and cat-called after us, their voices fading away, as we trudged uphill, into the cries of the dock birds and the hooting of ships out in the whirling bay.

And then, at tea the recovered uncles would be jolly; and the iced cake loomed in the centre of the table like a marbled grave. Auntie Hannah laced her tea with rum, because it was only once a year.

Bring out the tall tales now that we told by the fire as the gaslight bubbled like a diver. Ghosts wooed like owls in the long nights when I dared not look over my shoulder; animals lurked in the cubbyhole under the stairs where the gas meter ticked.

And I remember that we went singing carols once, when there wasn't the shaving of a moon to light the flying streets.

At the end of a long road was a drive that led to a large house, and we stumbled up the darkness of the drive that night, each one of us afraid, each one holding a stone in his hand in case, and all of us too brave to say a word.

The wind through the trees made noises as of old and unpleasant and maybe web-footed men wheezing in caves. We reached the black bulk of the house.

'What shall we give them? "Hark the Herald"?'

'No,' Jack said, ' "Good King Wenceslas". I'll count three.'

One, two, three, and we began to sing, our voices high and seemingly distant in the snow-felted darkness round the house that was occupied by nobody we knew. We stood close together, near the dark door.

> Good King Wenceslas looked out.
> On the Feast of Stephen . . .

And then a small, dry voice, like the voice of someone who has not spoken for a long time, joining our singing: a small, dry, eggshell voice from the other side of the door: a small dry voice, through the keyhole.

And when we stopped running we were outside *our* house; the front room was lovely; balloons floated under the hot-water-bottle-gulping gas; everything was good again and shone over the town.

'Perhaps it was a ghost,' Jim said.

'Perhaps it was trolls,' Dan said, who was always reading.

'Let's go in and see if there's any jelly left,' Jack said. And we did that.

Always on Christmas night there was music. An uncle played the fiddle, a cousin sang "Cherry Ripe", and another uncle sang "Drake's Drum". It was very warm in the little house.

Auntie Hannah, who had got on to the parsnip wine, sang a song about Bleeding Hearts and Death, and then another in which she said her heart was like a Bird's Nest; and then everybody laughed again; and I went to bed.

Looking through my bedroom window, out into the moonlight

and the unending smoke-coloured snow, I could see the lights in the windows of all the other houses on our hill and hear the music rising from them up the long, steady falling night.

I turned the gas down, I got into bed, I said some words to the close and holy darkness, and then I slept.